Curva Peligrosa

A novel by Lily Iona MacKenzie

Regal House Publishing

For Michael,
always my best reader

Jorge Luis Borges' visionary fiction set out a radical vision of time and literature that implied that time is an endless repetition, fact and fiction were easily confused, and that the text one was reading was no more or less real than the life the reader was living.

—D. P. Gallagher

The imagination is the power that disimprisons the soul of fact.

—Samuel Taylor Coleridge

One

Bone Song

The dead

don't have
cell phones.
They drift
from dream
to dream,
not waiting
for our calls
or permission
to visit. But
they eat,
appetites
voracious
and they want
news
of the living.

Bones Will Be Bones

They didn't think much about it when the wind picked up without warning late one summer afternoon and a dark cloud hurtled towards them over the prairies. Alberta residents are used to nature's unpredictability: snowstorms in summer; spring thaws during severe cold snaps; hail or thunderstorms appearing out of nowhere on a perfect summer day. At times, hot dry winds roar through like Satan's breath, churning up the soil and sucking it into the air, turning the sky dark as ink. Months later, some people are still digging out from under the spewed dirt.

But this wasn't just a windstorm. A tornado aimed directly at the town of Weed, it whipped itself into a frenzy. To the Weedites, it sounded like a freight train bearing down on them, giving off a high-pitched shriek the closer it got, like a stuck whistle. The noise drowned out everything else. Right before the tornado hit, a wall of silence descended, as if the cyclone and every living thing in the area had been struck dumb.

And then a completely intact purple outhouse dropped into the center of town, a crescent-shaped moon carved into its door. It landed right next to the Odd Fellows Hall and behind the schoolhouse. Most people thought the privy had been spared because its owner—Curva Peligrosa, a mystery since her arrival two years earlier—had been using it at the time.

Meanwhile, the tornado's racket resumed, and Curva sat inside the outhouse, peering through a slit in the door at the village dismantling around her. The funnel sucked up whole buildings and expelled them, turning most of Weed upside down and inside out. Unhinged from houses,

6

doors and roofs flew past, along with walls freed from their foundations. The loosening of so many buildings' restraints released something inside Curva. Never had she been so aroused. It was more exhilarating than riding the horse she'd bartered for recently, a wild gelding. The horse excited her, especially when she imagined herself riding its huge organ. In the midst of the noise and clatter, just as the tornado reached its climax, Curva had hers.

A heavy rain followed, some of it seeping into Curva's sanctuary and dampening the walls as well as her night-dress. So much rain pelted the town it created a flood that overran the main street. Protected from the worst of the storm, Curva drowsed and dreamt that she fell through the hole in the seat, landing on the ground with a soft thud next to a pile of bones, each about ten inches long, worn smooth from the elements. She grabbed one and—still aroused—used it, waking to the melting feeling of another orgasm and the sound of rain pelting the roof.

Aftermath

The Weedites clung to splintered roofs and walls so they wouldn't be swept away by heavy winds and the downpour, a prelude to hail the size of baseballs that battered the already beaten-up village and its inhabitants. Some were reminded of the Biblical Flood; they thought God was punishing them. Others believed Curva was responsible. If she could ride the whirlwind safely, perhaps she could also make nature attack them.

After the tempest, this idea was clearly on their minds as they poked through what was left, their intimate lives tossed about for all to see. They cast dark glances in Curva's direction and muttered among themselves, wondering what role she had played in their upheaval. Family photos and underwear and other personal belongings intermingled in the collective wreckage.

Despite the physical destruction of houses and homesteads, the tornado didn't kill anyone. Some received scratches, bruises, and a few broken bones. Old Man Hawkins had a mild heart attack, but he'd been having those for as long as anyone could remember. It wouldn't have been an occasion if he hadn't keeled over and clutched his chest.

When the tornado had first hit, the doctor was examining Olga Matoule, a pregnant patient. Her feet in the examining table's stirrups, she wore a dress decorated with blue forget-me-nots that hugged her belly. The doc had an eye for the ladies, and he enjoyed probing them: if he got the urge and the patient seemed willing, well, nature took its course. Neither pregnancy, nor illness, nor much of anything else restrained him. Married or single, he didn't care. He loved them all. And the patients didn't mind, not those, at least, who encouraged his explorations. He offered a distraction to women whose lives were confined to tending chickens and baking bread.

Still, Mrs. Hawkins managed to find the doctor in all that rubble, not always easy under the best of circumstances since he didn't keep regular hours. She said, My husband's dying. We need you *now!*

The doctor left Olga on the examining table. Fully exposed to the world outside, her feet still in the stirrups, she witnessed the wind ripping the walls from their foundations and carrying off part of the roof. The shock brought on labor. Olga's screams jolted awake her husband Henry, who'd been snoozing in the waiting room, its enclosure still partially intact. Olga, who knew Curva had some experience as a midwife, yelled, Get Curva, for Chrissake. This bloody baby wants out!

Frantic, Henry waded down the main street, asking if anyone had seen her. Nathan Smart, owner of Smart's General Store, pointed at the jauntily tilting outhouse, one of the few remaining undamaged structures. Reluctantly, Henry banged on its door. With all the speculation floating around about Curva, he didn't know what to think about her. But desperate to find someone to help his wife give birth, he couldn't be choosy.

Half awake and half asleep, it took a few minutes for Curva to orient herself. A beatific expression on her face, a bone dangling from her right hand, and wearing only a flimsy silk nightdress, she opened the door slightly.

Henry tried to ignore Curva's abundant body, clearly visible beneath the damp fabric. He cleared his throat: Could you help me out? The baby's ready to come and the doctor has his hands full.

Not yet fully conscious, Curva didn't respond immediately, so Henry repeated his request, his voice shrill and fretful.

Now fully present, Curva noted that Henry's eyes resembled those of a frightened horse. She had delivered enough babies to know that the child's father needed as much reassurance as the mother. She patted his arm, her touch settling him down, nodded, and followed him through the wreckage.

Up to her hips in water, unseen matter bumped against her legs. Curva ignored what she couldn't see, intent now on helping Henry. Rain, coming in fits and starts, pelted the two of them. Curva's long dark hair meandered about her face and bare shoulders like water snakes.

The two of them arrived at what was left of the doctor's office just as the baby's head, covered with a bloody sac, appeared between Olga's spread legs. The sight of this new life entering the world filled Curva with awe, reminding her of why she had become a midwife. To witness the moment of birth, an act repeated endlessly through the ages, gave her hope. She believed childbirth conquered death and would continue to do so after she had left this world.

Curva sent Henry off to search through the ruins for dry cloths and a bucket of clean water. Between contractions, Olga panted and gasped for breath, clutching and pushing at her stomach. She let out one last scream, and in a final spasm, the baby thrust himself into the world, landing in Curva's arms. A witness all these months to his mother's affair with the doctor, he recognized early he would need to fend for himself and had bit through the umbilical cord, exposing a mouth filled with fully formed teeth.

By now, the rain had stopped, and Henry had returned from his errand with the needed supplies. The sun flooded everything with light and warmth. Though relieved the ordeal was over, Olga looked at the newborn and crumpled in a puddle of tears, not up to motherhood—to the sacrifice and commitment involved. Curva held the boy by his feet, head down, so the mucous could drain. After, she gave a curt whack to his round, pink bottom, and his lungs started working, too. He's a loud one, Curva said. Olga just snorted and turned her face to what once had been a wall. The boy screamed, and Curva handed the baby to Henry, who was so nervous he almost dropped his first-born.

Through all of this commotion, Olga sniffled away. She still was glorying in the bathing suit contest she'd won when

10

she was five months' pregnant and didn't want this child chewing on her pert, brown nipples. The thought of her breasts hanging around her waist in a few years from bearing and breastfeeding too many babies also upset her. Surely her good looks entitled her to more of a future than changing soiled diapers and caring for a family she didn't want. These thoughts had grown in Olga since Curva's arrival in Weed. Having visited her new neighbor's place, Olga envied her unfettered liberty: Curva answered to no one but herself.

It didn't surprise the townsfolk when, a few weeks later, the doctor decided it was time to head south, seeking a healthier climate. Driving his old Mercury, he almost ran over Olga standing near the curb, a suitcase parked on either side of her, thumb stuck out in the direction he was going. He stuffed her bags into the trunk, and the two of them headed off into the sunset together.

Curva and the Prairies

Curva, originally from Mexico, had ridden a pinto into Weed. A second horse pulled a travois, and a mangy dog limped behind a younger one that led the way. Dressed gaucho style, she had turned up at dusk, a black, flat-brimmed, flat-topped hat tilted low over her eyes, a parrot on each shoulder. Sitting high in the saddle, she looked queenly, waving graciously at the townspeople, smiling. One gold tooth glowed when she opened her mouth, and her big breasts and shapely buttocks aroused the men.

Curva had stopped near the sidewalk on the main street and brushed off her black pants, turquoise rings flashing on every finger, trousers tucked inside scuffed riding boots. Spurs clinked against the metal stirrups, and she wore a wide, ornately tooled silver buckle. A beige serape hung casually from one shoulder.

Everyone had paused—elbowing one another, mouths hanging open—and stared at this tawny-skinned woman whose striking features reminded them of Katy Jurado, the alluring Mexican actress they'd recently seen in *High Noon* at a Calgary cinema. Curva had the same lush lips and brooding, heavy-lidded eyes. At over six feet, she was also the tallest woman many had ever seen. Her size gave them pause: clearly all woman, yet with the strength and authority of a man, she didn't appear to be a clingy, garden-variety female. She wasn't even a non-clingy type. She didn't fit into any category most were used to.

Curva surveyed the onlookers and laughed heartily at their ogling. Her response tickled their funny bones, and they joined in, eventually applauding her and her entourage as they moved past. Most thought she was heading for the Calgary Stampede to compete for title of Queen. But the rifle slung across the saddle and the two six-guns tucked into holsters riding low on her hips signaled something different.

On the move for over twenty years, Curva had ended up in Weed by chance. For much of that time, she had followed the legendary Old North Trail, a passageway that extends from the Canadian Arctic down to the deserts of Mexico and beyond. It runs along the base of the Rocky Mountains and the Continental Divide, following a kind of shoreline between the mountains and the plains for over three thousand miles. The Blackfoot call the trail "The Backbone of the World."

Though Weed hadn't been Curva's original destination, her twin brother Xavier's early death had caused her to pursue a substance that would cure all ills and prolong life indefinitely. She had thought studying nature on the trail might give her some answers. Over the years, she had tried many mixtures, thinking she was near her goal, only to be disappointed. The elixir eluded her, but not the desire to create it.

Curva wondered if the dandelion wine she made might be such a tincture. From helping her father make *vino* when she was a girl, she had picked up some tricks. Over the years, she had experimented with various flowers, fruits, and vegetables, learning to measure and balance ingredients like an alchemist until she had captured their essence in liquid form by soaking them in water and other fluids. The metamorphosis of earthly produce into liquor made her think she was onto something. The *vino* she had perfected over the years seemed miraculous, causing taciturn Canadian farmers to become talkative and animated.

If the Weedites had been aware of Curva's interest in alchemy and transformation, they might not have been so welcoming. Such notions didn't exist in their world. And while prairie people are usually wary of strangers, especially foreigners with a different skin color, Curva seemed oddly familiar, though for many she was the first Mexican they'd seen.

An enigma, Curva's belly laugh rang across the prairies, producing a series of vibrations that titillated everyone, bringing a smile to their faces. The sound reminded them of something they couldn't quite identify, teasing the edges of an ancient memory that didn't fully form. Curva's exuberance and natural warmth created a fire they wanted to huddle close to. But others had seen her communing with plants and animals as if she spoke their unfathomable language and they hers. The wheat growing in the fields bowed to her as she passed, and the cows nodded their heads up and down whenever she came near. These responses made her prim neighbors wonder if Curva used unnatural powers, things beyond their command or knowledge, and that made her a bit of a loose cannon as well. They feared she could alter their lives in ways they didn't understand and use her powers against them. Though they welcomed her into their midst, in truth, the Weedites didn't quite know what to make of the woman.

It also had seemed odd when Curva rode out of the wilderness that July day in 1953, looking for a farm to buy. Even more curious, she had the cash to pay for it, ending up with a ramshackle place a few miles outside of town. The owner had just died, and he didn't have any next of kin. It was auctioned off to Curva, the highest bidder, though some guy named Shirley, an *americano* from Sweetgrass, Montana, challenged her almost to a draw.

Curva won.

The *americano* bowed and said, The little lady can have it.

Curva bristled at being called a little lady and glared at the *hombre*. But, excited about winning the bid, she didn't pay much attention to the rude *gringo*. As soon as the auctioneer and other bidders had left, she surveyed her property. It included a vegetable garden, a small greenhouse, a few chickens, a rooster, cows, pigs, sheep, a broken-down horse or two, and a battered 1945 Chevy pickup. The barn wasn't much more than an overgrown shed, the house had two small bedrooms, and the kitchen and living room were one big space. Yet to Curva, it was *paraíso*.

A summer shower baptized Curva's new home and left a rainbow in its wake that arched across the blue sky. Golden wheat swallowed it at both ends, so it appeared to meet underground. Certain the rainbow contained a portent of some kind, Curva stepped outside and stared at it. The rainbow's appearance convinced her she had chosen the right place to settle.

Curva's horses looked ready for a home as well, and she stabled them in the barn. Then she hauled inside her travois' contents, chased away the mice that had taken over, unpacked, and looked over her *casa*. Relieved to finally put down roots, she never wanted to pack up again. She'd been running for too long from her past.

Hands on hips, she prowled the rooms, pausing and nodding her head now and then in appreciation of what she saw. After sleeping on the hard ground, or living in run-down rooming houses and hotels for years, it seemed like a *castillo*. Thrilled, she grabbed her shotgun, ran outside, aimed at the sky, and pulled the trigger, letting out a howl to express her pleasure. A passing duck took a pellet or two and landed with a thud nearby. Even when she didn't aim, Curva was a wicked shot. Soon, she had plucked the duck's feathers, gutted it, removed the buckshot, and popped the bird into the oven for a celebratory dinner.

It didn't take long for Curva to install herself, and she quickly put her mark on the place, transforming the house's exterior to match the Mexican flag's colors: red, green, and white—along with a yellow chimney. She painted the barn and the outhouse purple. The living room and kitchen walls ended up turquoise and yellow. She chose orange and red for the bedrooms. Curva even painted the fences surrounding her property in alternating shades of fuchsia and orange, the colors reminding her of a *piñata*. Alberta's abundant sunlight combined with these vivid colors and chased away

15

any dark thoughts that occasionally preoccupied her.

The house had electricity and a gas stove, lacking only an in-door *servicio*. Enjoying her new domesticity, Curva baked and sewed, planted and canned, reminded of her youth in Berumba, Honduras, when she had worked in her employer Ernesto Valenzuela Pacheco's kitchen. Curing her own meat or growing herbs and other things she now sold was familiar to her. And her prized, homemade dandelion wine provided additional income from a readily available source: dandelions grew everywhere in Alberta. She caught those bright yellow faces in their prime and parlayed them into something potent and flavorful.

But a woman making *vino?* And drinking it? No self-respecting Weed female would drink spirits, at least not publically, so Curva's loose behavior shocked some of the more conservative westerners, though not Weed's doctor. Before he left the area, he had worn a path to Curva's door in no time, causing tongues to wag; yet her charms seduced not only the doctor but the other townspeople as well. Curva's fractured English, spoken with a Spanish accent, attracted them, as did the husky quality of her voice. The sound of her vocalizations reminded everyone of rocks tumbled by the river's current, and they loved listening to her talk and sing. She would strum Xavier's old guitar for accompaniment and sing "Besame Mucho," closing her eyes and feeling the music deep inside her bones.

But it wasn't just Curva's voice and music that cast a spell on her neighbors. They also discovered her healing skills, many of them feeling better in her presence. Some even insisted that chronic backaches and limps disappeared after visiting her. Before long, the Weedites were calling on Curva to cure their ailments when the doctor was in his cups—a frequent occurrence. They thought she was better at diagnosing their problems than he was. She patted their aching bellies, clucked her tongue, and offered drinks that contained *especial* herbs she grew in her garden. She also gave the town folk other *medicinas* she had concocted, ones that mimicked the mixtures Ernesto Valenzuela Pacheco had made in his Berumba pharmacy. He had created remedies for diarrhea and stomachaches and hangovers, and she remembered their ingredients.

Nor was it unusual for townspeople to appear on her doorstep in the middle of the night, calling Curva, Curva, the baby's almost here! Despite severe snowstorms, she jumped out of bed, threw on some clothes, and grabbed her bag of tricks, a large multi-colored patchwork satchel she'd sewn together from samples she'd picked up at church rummage sales. The bag contained clean sheets, towels, a hot water bottle, alcohol, a thermometer, scissors, needles, thread, and a jug of her dandelion wine. Then she revved up the Chevy pickup and roared out of the driveway.

An expert midwife, a skill she had learned in the Pacheco household and had practiced at times on her travels, she never turned down these requests. Assisting a mother to give birth soothed Curva. The cries of squalling babies brought her solace, reminding Curva that new life could occur even during painful periods. It also amazed her to view this passageway that gave women and men so much pleasure. Life's origins seemed even more mysterious and wondrous when she participated in this ritual of bringing new life into the world. During these deliveries, Curva felt close to the miraculous genesis of all life.

Since many Weedites thought Curva had divine connections, they later brought their babies to her kitchen for her blessing, hoping to protect them from ill fortune. Of course, they did this secretly, after the local pastor had baptized them. Curva sprinkled a little *vino* on the parents' and babies' lips, giving them a taste for the fruits of the earth, and crooned a song to the child in Spanish that her mother had sung to Curva and to her brother Xavier:

De colores,
de colores se visten los campos
en la primavera.
De colores,
de colores son los pajaritos
que vienen de afuera.
De colores,
De colores,
vemos lucir.[1]

The parents thought she was chanting an ancient benediction and smiled appreciatively, believing their child was now doubly protected from harm.

It wasn't just Curva's healing arts or delicious *vino* that people sought. Her chickens produced eggs with double and triple yolks that were the talk of Weed. Her neighbors couldn't get enough of them, believing these hens had unusual abilities, too, though they couldn't have identified what these talents were. But the women also used the word magic to describe Curva's gift for reading their palms and tea leaves and cards. Gathered in her kitchen, they waited in line for her to study their teacups, poking and rearranging the leaves, trying to create interesting shapes. Or they stared at the lines in

---

1 Painted in colors, the fields are dressed in colors in spring. Painted in colors, painted in colors are the little birds which come from the outside. Painted with colors, painted with colors is the rainbow that we see shining brilliantly above.

their hands, wondering how these faint indentations could provide a map for Curva to interpret. Curva squinted her eyes and studied all of these things closely, whistling under her breath and exclaiming in Spanish at a line's curve or an image that turned up in the leaves or the cards.

The women *oohed* and *aahed* about the comments she made. Often, she saw or said things that took their breath away. Catherine Hawkins, Old Man Hawkins's child bride, nearly fainted when Curva told her there was another *hombre* in her future. A young one. The idea took on its own life in Catherine's mind; she couldn't look at a man without wondering if he was the one. The thought constantly kept her off balance.

And Edna MacGregor, the old maid schoolteacher, blushed when Curva said she had a very large Mount of Venus in her palm, a sure sign of someone with a highly sexual nature. Manuel and Pedro, Curva's two parrots, gifts from the Pachecos, mimicked their owner: "Sex, sex, sex," they cawed, making everyone laugh and dispelling the women's discomfort at discussing it so openly.

But thereafter Edna often found herself staring at her own palm, even while teaching. The sight of it sparked lurid fantasies about her young students, male and female. She watched them interacting so naturally, expressing interest in one another's bodies, their raging hormones causing Edna's to similarly ignite. She could barely contain herself till she got home and closed the door to her bedroom. There she expelled some of her built-up arousal and gave full expression to her lust, either with her fingers or with the help of a carrot from her garden. Curva's observations had now made it difficult for Edna to observe her strict Presbyterian upbringing.

In no time, Curva felt like a fixture in the Weedite's lives, her visitors paying what they could for her services, leaving fresh vegetables or canned jam if they didn't have any spare cash. Curva bowed and smiled, flashing her gold tooth. *Gracias, Gracias*, she said.

Curva was also known for her excellent brownies. After munching on one of them, her visitors found themselves giddy and lighthearted, more able to face the inexhaustible demands of farm life, their appetite stimulated not just for food but also for living. Stopping by her place was like taking a mini-vacation.

But mostly they dropped in out of curiosity and for the uplift it gave them. The women especially were intrigued to have someone in their midst who ignored convention and wasn't bound by the same rules as they were. Curva did pretty much as she pleased. No one else used bright colors to paint their houses and outbuildings. It took some getting used to, these gaudy blooms on the bland prairies, but the unusual tones grew on her neighbors, giving them a boost whenever they passed by and expanding their own palettes. Soon, other buildings showed signs of Curva's influence. Catherine Hawkins tried an intense orange trim around her windows; Sophie Smart painted her front door turquoise; Inez Wilson brightened her chicken house with yellow.

When these women stopped by Curva's place, they sipped a little *vino* or chomped on a brownie, watching their hostess bounce around the kitchen, her large breasts unconstrained by a brassiere. A blur of activity, she stirred, sifted, shook, and chopped, whipping up a medley of dishes, the odor of sizzling onions and stewing beef filling the house. While working, she chattered in a mixture of English and Spanish or sang Latin American songs. Manuel and Pedro perched on her shoulders, singing along with her.

Another attraction? Curva's guns added to her authority. They rested on the kitchen counter within easy reach should someone break in unexpectedly. The domestic surroundings made them seem almost innocent and incapable of inflicting harm. Female visitors glanced longingly at them. A few reached out and touched their smooth surface, soft as baby's skin. As for the men, when they stopped by Curva's place, they avoided the firearms altogether, ignoring their presence, unwilling to acknowledge that a woman might have the upper hand with such things.

When her visitors left, they carried Curva with them, her unintelligible words still echoing in their ears. The Latin rhythms possessed their bodies and feet (the *vino* and brownies also contributed), so they had trouble walking a straight line. Arms swinging to the music, they circled and swayed, finding it difficult to move forward. For the women, visions of swarthy, dark-haired, hot-blooded men made them dissatisfied with their lighter-skinned husbands. The men shared similar fantasies, only theirs were of females like Curva.

The men also wondered what she was up to with the farm. The property included an extra half-section of land, much of it in summer fallow. Curva didn't waste any time leasing out most of it to a local farmer because she liked his last name—Paris. He gave her a percentage of the crop. The men also wanted to know just how friendly she was. Everyone hoped that by getting a glimpse inside her house, they might figure out her game, so they dropped in to buy eggs or whatever else she had for sale.

They sniffed and gawked, checking the walls and built-in shelves and mantle for pictures or letters that would tell a story, but except for the vibrant colors, the place was pretty standard—and pretty bare, other than the hens wandering in and out, pecking on bits of ground cornmeal Curva had dropped on the kitchen floor. The main room contained scarred wooden chairs and a table the previous owner had made; a flowered yellow oilcloth that curled around the edges covered the top. Propped against a wall stood a sagging chesterfield in a faded blue slipcover; a rocking chair faced it. And in the center was a wood-burning stove.

A few pictures of unfamiliar settings and what looked like an Indian medicine bag hung on the walls. Yet what really caught their attention were several blue ribbons. Some of the visitors assumed she had earned them for baking, but they were wrong. Curva had followed the rodeo circuit for years, proving herself in the ring as a champion bronco-buster and bull rider. The purses she won had bankrolled the farm. Curva also was an expert sharpshooter and could nail a fly from thirty feet—a skill that also had put a few dollars in her pocket.

The many green plants contributed to the distinctiveness of her home, varieties the townspeople had never seen before. No one else kept plants inside the house. But Curva wasn't much of a housekeeper and didn't waste time chasing dust balls or dirt. Yet she always had a saucepan full of something stewing on the stove, the exotic smells unlike the usual pot roast or stuffed cabbage leaves that most women cooked. Curva's food flooded the house with odors of her homegrown *hierbas* and *especias*. They transformed even the most banal ingredients, turning them into a gourmand's delight: chicken mole, chayote corn soup, cumin-crusted pork, dishes she'd learned to make while working for the Pachecos. Curva shared her skills with the women hanging out in her kitchen, her deft hands shaping tortillas and creating succulent sauces.

When Curva merged meats and vegetables and various *especias*, they produced something unique and flavorful. Similarly, when she sowed seeds or seedlings, they took root and went through many transitions, growing from tiny seeds into fully grown plants, different at every stage, no two the same. So did various insects, but especially butterflies. As a child in Mexico, she'd watched the Monarchs return each year from Canada and had wondered about the source of their fertility and stamina. Now she could finally investigate them within her greenhouse, a laboratory where she explored their transformations.

The Greenhouse

Curva enlarged the glass-enclosed shed that came with her property, doing most of the construction herself. Bigger than her living quarters, the greenhouse was crammed with Curva's collection of flora that threatened to overflow the space. Colorful blossoms and green leaves pressed against the glass, their tendrils seeking cracks and crevices from which to extend themselves.

Morning and night, she sang her favorite songs while puttering with the plants, her vocalizations attracting numerous songbirds (prairie larks, wood thrushes, finches, yellow warblers), all drawn to her sanctuary and taking up residence there. Like bees around a hive, they hovered above her as she flitted around, often in the nude—watering, fertilizing, feeding. She liked the freedom of being naked, especially with her plants and animals. They didn't wear anything. Why should she? Her waist-length hair fell over her breasts and sensuously stroked them each time she moved.

Her skin felt as if it had feelers, the tiny hairs picking up on the slightest breeze and making her shiver with delight. It reminded her of traveling on the trail. In warm weather, she sometimes went for days without wearing any clothes. She also loved it when the sun penetrated her body like a lover. Clothing created artificial boundaries, and to be free of them for a time was liberating.

One day, Catherine Hawkins stopped by the greenhouse and found Curva flitting about in her birthday suit. Of course, after her visit, Catherine stopped at Smart's store and whispered in Sophie Smart's ear that Curva had been working naked in her hothouse. Both women sniggered. Before long, everyone in Weed was talking about Curva the nudist. The story took on its own life, flourishing like the lush plants in her greenhouse, with each person adding embellishments until no one knew quite what to believe. Some of the Weedites wondered if she should be charged with indecent exposure. But no one had the courage to alert the authorities, and, after all, Curva was on her own property. Besides, no one wanted to be responsible for having her arrested: she had become too valuable to the Weedites and they had developed a taste for her dandelion wine and other ministrations.

Though Catherine Hawkins was shocked at her new neighbor's boldness, it didn't stop her from secretly housecleaning in the buff. Having her breasts and genitals so exposed while she swept the floor and washed the dishes increased Catherine's sexual fantasies, and her ardor surprised her husband at the end of the day. And Sophie Smart? She tried weeding nude in her garden, hoping to get the hang of what Curva was doing. But the mosquitoes ganged up on her, and so did the black flies, leaving her feeling like a pincushion.

As a result, a flood of Weedites, men and women, dropped by Curva's whenever they could to observe her, pressing their faces against the greenhouse glass and steaming it up with their heated breath. Since she wasn't concerned if someone saw her naked, word soon spread about her splendid curves and unconventional attitude. Everyone also talked about her green thumb and her birds. In their minds, Curva's ability to make things grow in a hostile climate somehow got mixed up with having second sight and other powers.

No one realized that Curva's *madre* had been known as the curer of multiple maladies. She had taught her daughter about growing plants, passing on tricks for making medicines from them. Curva's *madre* could bring the scraggliest, dried-out stick back to life. Look at what she had done for Curva, who'd been a scrawny, waif-like kid. All bones. Scared of her shadow. But her *madre* soon took care of that. She fattened up the girl and drove away her fears with potions and chanting. Curva's *madre* had also awakened her daughter's interest in the healing arts. Curva's curiosity about immortality came later. With the right clues, Curva hoped her greenhouse and its inhabitants would reveal their secrets, deepening her understanding of life's mysteries.

In the winter, the prairies resembled the moon's surface. The land looked different covered with layers of snow, all vegetation lifeless and wearing pale shrouds. It seemed as if only browns and blacks and grays had ever existed. When snowplows swept through, they created hills and dales that didn't exist in the summer. Daily these shapes shifted. The main source of vitality during these wintry months was

Curva's greenhouse. It exploded in all seasons with tropical warmth, sounds, and color, its vibrations felt as far away as Berumba, where Suelita Flores lived.

Suelita—prostitute and fortuneteller—had taught Curva the arts of divination. Now, lured by the greenhouse, Suelita began to dream of this far-off place to the north and of her former apprentice. The dreams became so strong that they interfered with her bedding of the local men, sending her off into reveries. Some of them complained: Suelita, they said, I'm not spending my money to have sex with your shadow. Wake up! But by then she was too involved with her former pupil to pay attention.

Curva's world tugged on Suelita so much that she couldn't help stalking Curva, whispering in her ear, urging her towards this man or that one, and, in a sense, living vicariously through her former pupil. Like everyone in Weed and beyond, Suelita was especially drawn to the hothouse. Lit throughout the night by a generator and in the winter heated by propane, to some, the structure seemed to float above the land as if it were a temporary visitor, not quite of this world.

In the daytime, the sun bounced off its windows, the reflected light almost blinding passersby. At night, it could be seen glowing for miles, summer or winter, challenging even the moon's intensity. As alive as the organisms existing within its boundaries, the greenhouse appeared to breathe in and out, expanding and contracting. There were times when viewers swore it had grown overnight. The feeling it conveyed reminded Berumba residents of when their own town felt like the center of the world, everything blooming and abundant, caught in a time warp where nothing changed.

But the Weedites were most affected by it, a beacon that

could orient them during the darkest night or the worst blizzard. A miniature geyser burst out of the earth at its center, a fountain that mysteriously appeared one morning and gushed day and night, even in winter. The sound of water ceaselessly burbling, stronger than a babbling brook, made the dry, dusty prairies seem less arid.

Some thought Curva had tapped into the former inland sea that had dominated the area millions of years earlier. In their minds, the endlessly flowing *agua* connected her to that earlier time, giving the woman some primal influence. Sporadically, streams inexplicably appeared and disappeared like phantoms in her vicinity. Sinkholes also turned up, creating craters that were there one day, gone the next. The earth was like putty around her, responding to her presence, as unpredictable and uncontrollable as she was.

Even in sleep, the villagers felt the greenhouse's presence. Its contents grew in their hearts, causing them to dream again—and in color—of exotic lands, monkeys swinging boisterously through leafy jungles, bearded men zipping by on Persian carpets, and parrots squawking in a musical language. Suelita entered their visions, too, fornicating night and day, her heavy breathing exciting them. And they could hear their own farm animals, rutting in the barns.

Men and women turned to each other in sleep and groped under their nightclothes, touching and being touched, arousing and being aroused. Those who didn't have partners, like Edna MacGregor and her brother Ian, fondled themselves. An ecstatic howl rose over the town before dawn, almost in unison.

Though none had visited the southern hemisphere, they longed for the moist humidity of the tropics and its balmy days and nights. These sensual images kept them going through the long, cold winters and the driest summers. Curva offered them visions of a different way of life, so their previous existence no longer satisfied them.

While the rest of the area clung to winter, a few bare sticks poking out of the ground, inside Curva's nursery, flowers that looked like magenta butterflies caught on thin stems fluttered as did a whole chorus of dancers wearing yellow ball gowns. The villagers learned later that the trapped butterflies and female dancers were really orchids. Tulips, zinnias, mums, and many other flowers bloomed there, too. Some plants had strange names they'd never heard of before: blessed thistle, burdock root, chamomile, comfrey, savory, golden seal—*Cannabis sativa*.

Curva had brought many bulbs with her, picked up in her travels on and off the Old North Trail, and had spent hours coaxing them to sprout. Totally immersed, she dug and fertilized and transplanted, hovering over her tiny seedlings, talking to them (*vamonos mis bebes*), urging, coaxing, trying to give them the best possible conditions for growth. They responded to her attention by spawning abundantly.

In the dead of winter, she produced the reddest, ripest tomatoes and the greenest, plumpest avocados. While her neighbors grew tomatoes themselves during the short summer season, they had never seen an avocado and were eager to taste its flesh, uplifted by a squeeze of lemon.

The constant demands of the greenhouse, animals, and farm work absorbed Curva, not leaving her much time to spend in town. She visited only to pick up the necessities. Yet her door was always open, and she never knew who might appear. Sometimes a villager stopped by. At other times, it might be another voyager from the south, compelled to follow Curva's trail north. She'd dropped seeds along the way that, overnight, grew into lush foliage. The heady scent offered a reward for those determined enough to follow it. And, of course, her visitors weren't limited to the living. She had a following among the dead as well, whose taste for life was reawakened in her presence.

The only one she wasn't eager to see was Xavier.

Curva on the Old North Trail

Hola, mi estimado Xavier,

The compass I bought works, *mi hermano,* and I found the trail this time without too many *problemas.* If we'd had one to begin with, you might still be alive. And knowing the year is 1938 acts as another kind of compass. I can keep track of how long I've been traveling and that will help me figure out where I am. So will the passing seasons.

It's spring right now, and plants bursting with new life surround me. Wildflowers I've never seen before bloom everywhere, making me even more aware of losing you. How can nature be bursting with all this energy when you are *muerto?* There, I've said it. I hate that word.

I hope you aren't too angry with me, *mi hermano,* for continuing on the trail and for having a life you no longer can share. We started this adventure together. We should end it together as well. And that's why I'm writing you these letters, so you can be part of the experience. It also makes me feel closer to you.

The Pachecos gave me enough money to keep me going for a while. But it's hard to be so alone now, though I'm not alone exactly. Every bug you can think of is here. Animals too. And they all want to have a look at me. Some want more than a look. It's too bad none of them speak.

You know what a chatterbox I can be, especially with you. At least the Indians who traveled this trail before me had smoke signals to look forward to now and then. I just have clouds. I pretend they're signals from the gods.

I'm grateful for the compass, but I'm still afraid I might get lost again. I don't always trust these tools. What if I mix up the readings? It comforts me to think you're watching over me like those clouds in the sky. Still, I'm not sure I can trust you to help me out when I need it. Maybe you're too angry. I'm also afraid of what's ahead. I don't know what I'll run into on this path I've taken. Will it disappear and I'll die in the wilderness with no one to cry over my bones? I try not to think of the future too much because it scares me even more.

And there are *muchos problemas*. The trail isn't well marked—you know that!—and it hasn't been used a lot recently. Sometimes I have to *chop chop chop* at the undergrowth with your old machete. You took it from the *hombre* that tried to steal our supplies when we started out, remember? But I'm determined to fulfill our dream of following this trail to the end.

You'll laugh when you hear I've been wearing your coveralls and long-sleeve shirts so I don't get scratched when I have to bushwhack. It's hard to find clothes for tall women; I have to make my own or buy them in men's stores. Your things fit pretty well. I haven't washed them because they still smell like you, and I can fool myself you're still alive.

At night on the trail, I'm convinced you're one of those brilliant lights above me and you're better off in the heavens. And maybe you are. Life on this earth can be *muy difícile*. But all that activity in the sky makes me lonely—the shooting stars and comets grab my attention and then disappear. It's like seeing whole cities lit up, only they're too far away for me to touch. That's when I long for human contact.

The rest of the time, I daydream a lot. You remember Suelita Flores? It's her fault I don't want to be a woman who buries herself in raising *los niños* and caring for a *casa*. I never mentioned this before, but Suelita told me about some people who don't believe in wedding vows or the usual women's roles. They choose and change lovers whenever they want to. They even have children with many men and raise them in female-headed households.

After Suelita told me such things, I went around for weeks thinking and thinking. The idea I didn't need to marry if I didn't want to amazed me! You won't want to hear this, either, but I also realized I don't have to stick with just one man.

So now I'm really confused. I know, I know, you're saying, *But Curva you've always been confused.* It's true I'm *sometimes* confused about certain things, like reading a compass, and it's true I don't want to be the usual female. But I'm not *always* confused. Yet some day I would like to put down roots—just as plants do. Roots growing out of my feet and traveling underground all the way to Mexico.

I like that idea and wish you could settle down with me. My poor *hermano*. Every day I pray for your soul, though I don't put much stock in such things. Still, it doesn't hurt. I just hope you haven't ended up in that other place, the one priests talked about when we went to church as kids.

Sometimes when I look in a mirror I see your features, not my own. We have the same high cheekbones and firm jaw. And I resemble you even more since you died. Maybe you live inside me now. It's better than you being under the hard ground.

I have my gun and a rifle in case I run into *bandidos* or who knows what else. During my spare time on the trail, I practice shooting. I'm now an expert with a gun, but I only kill when I need some meat.

Remember when we served with that revolutionary group in Berumba? I saw men go down during the fighting and never get back up. That convinced me I never wanted one of my bullets to kill anyone.

If you were here, you would say, Okay, Curva, so why do you like guns so much?

And I would say, I love how smooth they are. I also like how *fuerte* I feel when I hold them. With one in my hand, I believe I could blast death to smithereens. I'm also not so afraid to be on my own as a woman. I can go anywhere and do anything I want. It might seem strange to you that these guns have opened up the world and made me believe I can face life head-on.

Oh, Xavier, I miss you terribly and sense you're guiding me. I can hear you saying, No, Curva, don't take that path, and No, Curva, those berries will poison you.

But the nights are dark like the inside of a bone, like the inside of my mind. I write these letters by firelight on scraps of paper I've sewn together. A nice little book for me to talk to. My life a necklace of words.

The fire snaps and cracks. Sparks fly into the air—tiny burning kites.

Sometimes I put words on paper and hide them outside the tent. I pretend I'm on a treasure hunt and the messages I find are from you. They make me laugh. My own words follow me around like lost creatures.

Hola, I say. *¿Cómo esta usted?*

Muy bien, I answer.

So polite this woman who is visiting me. She has my hair color. My eyes. My smile. Everything. But I don't recognize her. How can I live with this woman after what she's done? The firelight skitters across the surface of her eyes like a frightened animal.

I've been trying not to remember. Not to remember. That's what I repeat over and over. Do not remember. *No recuerde.*

What is it I'm trying not to remember?

Better not to ask. Better to pretend it didn't happen.

The Bones

Following the tornado, a deluge complicated the cleanup work in Weed and presented the town with a new problem. When the water subsided, the land was littered not only with household effects and splintered wood, but also with an abundance of bones. The rain and subsequent flood uncovered mounds in the earth that resembled newly dug graves, though clearly no one had been buried there recently. From them, yellowed human bones protruded. Household objects got caught in the skulls' mouths, eyes, and ear openings. Catherine Hawkins found a wedding photo of her grandparents, their faces framed by a skeleton's eye sockets. Mr. Hawkins saw another skull wearing a blue hand-crocheted baby bonnet that his wife had made for their last child. It almost set off another heart attack. Many such sightings were reported and commented on, the subject of conversation for months, the reports enlarged and embellished with each telling.

One man was certain he had stumbled upon remains from another planet that would come to life once the bones came in contact with earthlings. He warned his neighbors to stay clear of the area for fear they would be attacked. Another person, hearing this rendition, claimed the tornado heralded a sign from God of the apocalypse. Still others thought a world located at the Earth's center was now surfacing.

Meanwhile, Edna MacGregor, concerned about the bones' origins, invited authorities in Edmonton, Alberta's capital, to inspect the site. A close examination revealed that the whole village had been hiding something. An ancient Blackfoot Indian burial ground existed beneath part of the town. The Weedites had heard of people hiding skeletons in their closets, but this took the idea too far.

The more watchful among them noticed that overnight the bones rearranged themselves in unexpected positions. Several skeletons appeared to be lounging and others crouching. Some were fornicating. These suggestive postures only reinforced the locals' stereotype of Indians as lazy heathens, doing nothing all day but copulating. To those who witnessed these movements, it reinforced some of the stories floating around about the bones' unusual origins.

Inez Wilson and Sophie Smart, eager to see the bones for themselves, joined the other townspeople crowded around this scene. Inez whispered to Sophie, Jesus Christ, we've been living all these years among the dead—and they're not our folk. Sophie nodded, her eyes glazing over. Like many, she felt her firm foundations threatened. *They* were trespassers on this Blackfoot burial site. *They* were the outsiders, surrounded by an unknown number of skeletons. Something froze in Catherine Hawkins's belly to see the baby bonnet she'd knitted for her own child clamped on a skull's head—an Indian's, no less. She shuddered thinking of it.

The bones' appearance fueled much speculation, but other things also demanded the Weedites' immediate attention. Not only did they need to clean up the mess and rebuild some of the structures, but in the storm's wake came a flurry of monarch butterflies, lost, it seemed, blown off course. They already had laid eggs among a flurry of milkweed that sprung from the graves. Some speculated that the Blackfoot had buried the milkweed seeds with the dead. When the cocoons hatched, a cascade of color exploded above the land, butterflies hovering over the fields like poppies bobbing on long, invisible stems.

And then they were gone, as suddenly as they had appeared, heading south, some deep instinct luring them to Mexico. Curva was intrigued by the stages butterflies went through in order to reach their end state. The whole phenomenon almost made her believe in the church's ideas about resurrection. She had watched the whole process in her greenhouse, laughing at how roly-poly the caterpillars became from gorging on the milkweed leaves. After they metamorphosed, she closely studied the butterfly chrysalises, examining them from all angles, hoping they would teach her how humans might get wings. It made her wonder if angels gestated that way and folded up their wings in sleep.

Feeling some kinship with the monarchs—Mexico had fostered both Curva and these magical creatures—she wished to understand how such fragile insects could fly great distances and survive. But though she longed to spend more time examining these colorful *mariposas,* she had other demands on her time, including Henry's infant son.

When Curva heard that Olga had fled with the doctor, she stopped by Henry's place one afternoon to see how father and son were doing, bringing fresh bread she had just baked and vegetables from her garden. Henry answered the door, holding the squalling child in one arm, a diaper in the other, gripping two huge safety pins between his teeth. He looked like a wild man, his hair flying in different directions, shirttails hanging out of his pants, and his fly unzipped. Curva sized up things quickly. She grabbed the naked baby and diaper and strode over to the kitchen table. Pushing aside dirty dishes, she found a spot for the child. In a flash, she had diapered him, warmed a bottle in a pot on the stove, and cradled the boy in her arms, imitating his sucking motions and singing a Spanish lullaby:

Cierras ya tus ojitos.
Duermete sin temor.
Sueña con angelitos
parecidos a ti.
Y te agarrare tu mano.
Duermete sin temor.
Cuando tu despiertes,
yo estare aqui.[2]

Soon Victor was asleep, and Henry gave a huge sigh of relief. You've got the magic touch, he said.

Curva just smiled and nodded her head. *Sí, señor.* Wild things like me. This son of yours, he's very wild, too.

Henry just stood there, looking bewildered, not sure what to do with this woman who casually leaned against the table, unperturbed by the mess on its surface. But he soon learned. That day marked the beginning of Curva and Henry's relationship. She let both father and son suck on her large nipples, sometimes unable to tell the difference between one and the other, the boy's teeth as sharp as his father's. She

---

2 Close your eyes little one and sleep. And dream while the angels watch over you. I will hold your hand.

couldn't produce milk, but her breasts were better than a pacifier for the child and had a similar effect on the father.

In the midst of helping Henry care for Victor, Curva was also building a new outhouse. She planted it in concrete, determined not to have this one fly away.

As for the bones that turned up in town, the strange happenings didn't bother her. She'd seen more frightening things than skeletons in her life. Her travels on the Old North Trail had exposed her to scorching heat that sucked all the water holes dry and bitterly cold blizzards that concealed dangerous precipices. She also had run into *bandidos* avoiding the law, bears, wild cats, wolves, snakes, and plenty of dead adventurers who had lost their way or been attacked by wild animals.

Bones also had other connotations for Curva. They reminded her of those she had dreamt of in the outhouse, especially the one that gave her so much pleasure. Even Suelita Flores—laughing and grabbing for that bone, wanting to try it herself—acknowledged its size was unusual.

Curva on the Old North Trail

Hola, mi estimado Xavier,

While I was sleeping, something loud roared next to my ear and woke me in the middle of the night. I had been dreaming of you. I thought you were alive and playing a trick on me. You used to do this a lot at night, remember? Pretend you were an animal, growling and waking me up. Then you would laugh and hold me tight. Oh *mi hermana,* you would say. I scared you. But this roar wasn't you, unless you've come back as a mountain lion and want to attack me. Yes, a mountain lion.

I roared back. The animal snarled in response. Dios

37

barked loudly and ran around the inside of the tent growling and sniffing. Manuel and Pedro, my parrots, tried to imitate the roar. It came out a shriek.

I grabbed my gun, checked to be sure it was loaded, and then opened the tent flap a little. My flashlight pierced the dark and lit up a pair of eyes that glowed like Halloween lanterns. The beam frightened our visitor and it took off into the trees, tail between its legs. A close one. Maybe you helped scare it away. *Muchas gracias, mi hermano.*

These letters make me feel closer to you, though I am not utterly alone. I have my animals to talk with. They cock their ears and listen to me. Nod their heads at the right moments. The parrots speak a little. Remember the horses we bought when we sold the *casa?* I call them Melosa and Alanzo. They are good listeners.

I found the *perrito* digging in a garbage dump before I left Berumba. He looked lost like me and we both needed a friend. I named him Dios. If there is a god, he must feel very lost and lonely with no one to talk to. Dios looks like a jumble of different dogs (or gods). Some German shepherd. Maybe a little husky. A Scottish terrier. Who knows what else?

The animals are good company, but I still miss being with you. I can't believe you are gone and I won't see you again. The thought that I might run into you on this trail keeps me going, though I worry you might be consumed by hatred for me. Even so, I expect you to appear at any moment around a bend in the path. You have too much life in you, Xavier, to just disappear forever.

Do you remember when I hid in Ernesto Valenzuela Pacheco's workshop? I was afraid he wouldn't allow a *mujer* to view his experiments, so I took cover behind a curtain and watched him sift some strange-looking liquids and solids of dazzling colors from one beaker to another. He mixed them together and they changed into new combinations.

He burst out laughing and said, I know you're there, Curva. I hear you breathing. He threw aside the drape and exposed me. Show yourself, *señorita*. You're too big to hide.

I started to laugh, too, and joined him. After that he let me help him mix chemicals when I had some free time, but he never explained what he was doing. He worked silently, grunting now and then when something pleased him. Or he threw his arms up in the air in frustration and shook his head when an experiment didn't go well.

He helped me to discover a passion for transformations. But, *mi hermano*, I don't think these changes just take place in a laboratory. They are happening all around us in nature. I don't need special glass tubes and chemicals to know that. Everything witnesses it. One day I hope to find a magical potion that will prolong life indefinitely. Or definitely. Making death disappear would be the best transformation of all.

But for now I'm busy just staying alive and not joining you in the grave. Sometimes I think that might be a better place to be, especially when I feel loneliness and despair of ever reaching the end of this trail. At least if I died then we would be together again. I tell these thoughts to *vete*. This life has too much to offer. I'd be a fool to abandon it.

Recently, I found another wilderness, Xavier. I don't know how to tell you this. It sounds like I've really gone *loca*. Being alone for weeks at a time in this wild place makes me sensitive to every sound I hear. And I don't just hear the usual noises the birds and the beasts and the weather make.

A tiny voice inside my head says *Curva, Curva, listen.*

It isn't your voice I'm hearing. It isn't someone else on the trail. At first I could hardly make it out. Just a little meow, like a kitten wanting to be fed. Then it got stronger. More like a mountain lion demanding to be heard. *Curva*, it said, *Let's be friends.*

I looked at Dios, at the parrots, fearing they were playing tricks on me. But no. They were sleeping. So I said, Why?

A reasonable answer, no? Why would this voice want to befriend me and why would I want to befriend it? The idea of some stranger trying to make contact gave me the creeps.

Then I thought Don Quixote might be trying to connect with me.

Si, I know. You're wondering about this Don Quixote. I can feel you getting jealous. Don't! He's just an old man I found in a book I borrowed from the Pachecos' library before I left. It's in English and Spanish. I use it to teach myself this new language I'll need to speak in gringoland when I get there one day. Don Quixote thinks some bad *hombre* turned the windmills into giants and he tries to attack them. He's lucky they didn't hit him back, but they weren't really giants. They were just windmills. He seems *loca* at times but he's really not.

Don Quixote's a good instructor and *muy divertido*. He makes me laugh a lot with the crazy things he does, and I need that right now.

But the voice wasn't from Don Quixote. It didn't have a name. It wasn't even really a voice. There were just these words appearing in my brain, as airy and delicate as butterfly wings. I wouldn't have noticed them if I were surrounded by city sounds. It was more like a light pressure inside my head that I gave shape to when I wrote.

Hola, I said.

Hola, was the response.

What do you want from me?

The soundless voice said, *Look. Open your eyes.*

These words insulted me. I always look at my surroundings and I said so.

No, Curva. You only see what you want to see. You don't really see what's there.

Angry, I was ready to draw my gun and start shooting. What right did this bodiless voice have to criticize me? Who was watching me so closely?

I glanced around the tent again. My supplies filled most of the space. My bedding, Dios, and the parrots took up the rest. What was I not seeing? Dios was curled up next to me. His ears twitched, as if he heard something I didn't, but his eyes were closed. His grey and black coat shimmered in the lantern's glow. His nose looked damp and he drew in deep breaths. Before he descended again into the well of sleep, his eyes flickered open briefly.

Dios is my guide along this puzzling and overgrown trail. There rarely is a clear path. I have to look for signs along the way that confirm I'm actually on or near the Old North Trail. No one has put up markers that say WELCOME CURVA. THIS IS THE OLD NORTH TRAIL.

I know, such big words you must be saying, but this Don Quixote is teaching me *mucho*. And so is Dios.

Is this what the voice wants me to see? How dependent I am? I already know that. Dependent and very small like an ant on this *grande* earth. But I won't let that idea stop me. Even ants make progress and don't easily give up.

Billie One Eye Takes Charge

Though eager to rebuild Weed, the townspeople couldn't ignore the Blackfoot burial ground or the Blackfoot themselves—their reservation just a few miles from Weed. Nor could they disregard what had surfaced among the Indian remains. When the Edmonton authorities had completed their inspection, dinosaur bones had turned up, too.

Chief Billie One Eye investigated the situation, claiming the bones—all of them—and the land they were on for his people, insisting it was a sacred area that homesteaders had stolen from the tribe. When the locals resisted, claiming the town couldn't be subdivided to accommodate the Blackfoot, Billie temporarily set up a tent trailer next to the burial ground so he could watch over his ancestors' remains. Billie was a bit of an oddity in his black eye-patch, baggy blue trousers, green-checkered shirt, and long red hair tied back in a ponytail. Cross-legged, he planted himself in front of the tent day and night, nodding off periodically, waiting for his assistant, Joe Laughing Creek, to return from the Office of Indian Affairs in Edmonton where he'd gone for help.

The government officials supported the Weedites, insisting that the Blackfoot had no right to the land. Billie asked Adam Stillwater, his long-time friend, to take over his post at the burial ground. Then Billie took off for Edmonton and camped out at the Indian Affairs' Office for several weeks, refusing to eat until someone reviewed his case. *The Edmonton Journal* learned of his demands and published several articles about Billie and the tribe's quest. The stories captured the attention of Edmonton's more liberal residents, and they joined Billie in pressing for control of what they thought was rightly Blackfoot land.

Overwhelmed with these vocal protesters, the Indian Affairs' Office finally conceded, proclaiming that the townspeople must accommodate the Blackfoot, and the rebuilding of Weed should take into account their land. The resurrected Weed would embrace a cemetery and much more, a potential archeological dig—except no one was digging. A judge determined that since the relics were part of the hallowed Blackfoot burial ground, archeologists could not collect the dinosaur remains. They stayed under the tribe's domain and only the Blackfoot had a right to unearth the ancient relics.

Curva didn't pay much attention to this new wrinkle, though she did hear her neighbors complaining about it when she went into town or when they visited her. Giving the Indians so much power didn't sit well with Weed's elders, who weren't eager to submit to the tribe's authority. Nor did the Weedites want the Blackfoot in their midst; they preferred them to remain culturally and physically isolated on the reservation—mostly out of sight. Catherine Hawkins complained that the residents of Weed were no longer in charge of their own affairs. Edna and Ian Mac-Gregor thought the bones were unsanitary and could cause an outbreak of some dreadful disease.

Curva just shrugged her shoulders and said, *Cuál será, será*, though the remains intrigued her—the artful way they arranged and rearranged themselves stimulating her curiosity about the dead. Billie also interested her. While keeping watch over their bones, he made drawings of his imagined ancestors. It amazed her that he could bring them back to life in this way, in his art. Here was a transformation she hadn't anticipated, another way to resurrect the dead.

But the townspeople wanted to be rid of the bones. Period. Indian or prehistoric. They gathered in Smart's General Store and chewed over the curve the tornado had thrown at them. Nathan leaned on the counter, resting his elbows on its surface, clearing his throat before speaking: Why should we make room for these outsiders just because some remains have appeared on our doorstep?

The others nodded, glancing nervously outside from time to time, not wanting to break any laws.

Ian said, Bones are bones. Who can take them seriously?

Billie for one. He believed his ancestors and the dinosaurs had turned up for a purpose. He just didn't know yet what it was. Meanwhile, nothing could destroy the petrified fossils. They'd taken on a new life in his mind, something permanent, a kind of immortality because of their age. He wanted to be part of it and refused to let professional diggers make off with them. The dinosaurs as well as his ancestors deserved a proper resting place. Billie hoped to provide it. He envisioned a museum, a center for educating Indians and whites alike about Blackfoot culture and the prehistoric times that preceded them.

He imagined a kind of massive teepee near the burial site, appearing to hover, its profile visible for miles around. While living with the West Coast tribe, the Squamish Nation, he had learned about totem poles; he wanted them attached to the structure to guard the periphery. The hollow centers would contain some of the ancestors' remains, and the dinosaur bones could be displayed inside the building. The money from the exhibition would create employment opportunities for the youth in his tribe, making them proud of their origins.

And this unusual venture would help Billie carry out his plans as chief.

More Bones

At night a great deal of howling and yelping flooded Weed and the surrounding area. Packs of coyotes and wolves circled the perimeter, prowling, sniffing, sensing the town's vulnerability and something else—bones. Not just ones from the Blackfoot burial ground but the massive bones that had appeared with them.

Dinosaur bones.

Calling to wolves.

Waiting to be dug up.

Curva felt drawn to the bones as well. She wasn't sure why. Perhaps Suelita Flores, who was fascinated with any kind of bone, had put the idea in her head. Whatever the reason, in the middle of the night, Curva found herself atop her *caballo*, galloping over the plains to town. Once there, she picked her way through the disturbed graves, shining her flashlight on the remains and shooing away the occasional curious dog or coyote. She wondered why the dead couldn't replicate themselves as seeds did when placed in fertile soil.

Or maybe they did. She remembered her mother mixing animal remains with her potting soil. This may have been the secret to her lush garden: it contained fruits and vegetables of miraculous proportions.

So many bones! And the fossils hadn't lost their power to frighten, in spite of being disjointed and only partly recognizable. Massive claws gripped clumps of earth, and teeth the size of an elephant's tusk protruded from gigantic heads, dwarfing the human remains. Some of the ancient fossils resembled black rocks, preserved in dark sediment, making them difficult to see. It was like discovering another world among the living. The human skeletons had been covered with flesh once, eating and fornicating, working and dreaming. Another village had thrived in this spot, the women raising both babies and vegetables. The men had hunted game and hung out in packs, not much different from the animals they sought. How could they just disappear?

The full moon cast an eerie light on this scene, adding another layer of mystery to it and illuminating the area around her. Curva prodded the earth with her toe, striking a fossil. An electrical charge ran up her leg, as if she had uncovered the former current of life that once animated these creatures.

A small bone called to her. She picked it up, holding it in the palm of her hand. It seemed to thrum, pulsing as if it were still alive. She could be communing with something that had lived millions of years earlier. What would a dinosaur think of a human? Of a woman? Maybe it would be more frightened of Curva than she of it. Or did it even know fear? It probably would open that huge mouth and swallow her in one gulp.

Xavier's guitar hung from her saddle—never far from her fingers. Something riffled its strings, causing them to vibrate. She jumped. Her hand went to her hip, groping for her .38, but she hadn't brought it with her.

Then she realized the wind had caused the sound. Relieved, she strode to her *caballo*, grabbed the guitar, and strapped it over her body, plucking the strings with her fingernails and slapping the wood shell, allowing a song to emerge. At these moments, she always thought of her brother, her fingers becoming his, strumming, finding their own life.

A melancholy tune in a minor key rose around her; she hummed along with it. The coyotes and wolves joined in, and the skeletons rose slowly from the earth, twitching and extending their limbs in a stately, elegiac dance, assembling and disassembling, their movements speeding up as the music did. Even the fossils got caught up in the rhythms, tossing and turning in the dirt, sounding like muffled castanets.

Not to be left out were Berumba's residents—Suelita, Ana Cristina Hernandez, Ernesto Valenzuela Pacheco, and many more. They emerged from the shadows, looking just as Curva remembered them, but when she stopped playing for a moment and reached out her hand to touch Ana Cristina, Curva's fingers passed through the woman's body. Curva plucked the guitar strings again, excited by the sound's intensity. Everyone moved faster, the rhythms constantly changing. They snaked through the gathering, showing their approval with shouts of *Olé*.

Curva's feet also got caught up in the sounds. She bobbed and whirled among the bones and wove in and out of the Pachecos and their neighbors, the music whirring into a frenzy of movement that gradually came to a stop when Curva's fingers tired and she quit playing. The Pachecos roamed the area until Ana Cristina beckoned them to follow her back home.

But for Curva, the magical effect lasted beyond the dying musical notes. Tropical plants and trees fluttered under a passing breeze at the edge of a gigantic inland sea that once existed there. Strange creatures littered the landscape, silhouetted against the cloudless moonlit sky. She saw the first people sitting around campfires, huddled together for warmth. The smoke burned her nostrils, and she could smell charred flesh from animals they were roasting. So immersed in her vision of what this area had once been like, Curva didn't notice everyone leaving.

She shivered, suddenly aware of being cold. The skeleton parts had settled back into the earth, and seeing them again so inert made her feel even colder. And lonely. She needed contact with the living and climbed on her *caballo*, heading towards Henry's place. Once there, she slipped into his bed, seeking the one bone that gave her so much pleasure.

Weed

The Weedites never blamed Curva for the tornado, at least not to her face. The truth is, she overwhelmed her neighbors, at times a tornado herself, whirling through their midst. But, periodically, she also had a peculiar effect on time that gave them pause. Some days, when Curva showed up, time seemed to stop. The minute hands on clocks froze. Even the sand in their hourglasses didn't move. It made them wonder what other powers she possessed. They'd seen her perform at sharpshooters' competitions, and her skill with guns seemed extraordinary. Curva could pluck a target out of the air faster than they could track it, once hitting five cans in five rapid-fire hits. Those who witnessed it just shook their heads in astonishment.

When she first had arrived in the area, they'd also seen her breaking horses at the Calgary Stampede and later at smaller, local rodeos. She flew through the air on the back of a bucking bronco, its head lowered, spine arched, back legs thrown out behind. Gripping the rope, one hand held high, she leaned into its ear, crooning something. Before long, the horse settled down and stopped vaulting, allowing Curva to ride it around the ring. She smiled and waved, the crowd cheering.

The townspeople respected her skills, but they did think

it strange that during the tornado—except for the out-house being transplanted—her other buildings, including the greenhouse, remained intact. Yet so much else in the area lay in ruins. Wherever they gathered, in Nathan Smart's General Store or on the street, they muttered to each other in low tones, casting glances in the direction of her place.

It seemed clear they'd experienced a sign the day the tornado ripped through Weed. Not only had they been punished for their transgressions, and were now free to commit more, but the resurrected community grew up around Curva's throne—the outhouse. The structure later received an official gold plaque, commemorating the great tornado, the first of such intensity that had occurred in their generation.

Until Curva appeared, the Weedites' lives had been relatively uneventful, except when they were hit by a particularly severe winter, attacked by locusts, or forced to bury a family member or neighbor. But even before the tornado had struck, she had started shaking things up.

Not long after arriving—and prior to the doctor vamoosing—Curva appeared at a Saturday night barn dance on his arm. They made a dashing couple, he in his store-bought grey suit, black string tie, burgundy shirt, and black Stetson, she in a patchwork skirt that swirled around her long legs and a white peasant blouse. Deeply scooped at the neck, it revealed the 'V' between her breasts, the cleavage attracting many eyes. The couple swooped into the room, bowing and nodding, patting shoulders and shaking hands. Curva said over and over, *Buenas noches.* No one understood the words, but it didn't matter. They got the meaning.

Taller than her partner by at least six inches, Curva held

herself like a queen, smiling and flashing her gold tooth at everyone. She and the doctor joined in the square dances, *do-sí-doing* with the others, except they changed the rules of the game: instead of two dancers approaching each other, circling back to back, and then returning to their original positions, Curva and the doctor grabbed different partners and whirled them around, mixing up the whole square, whooping and clapping. The move caught on, until the whole room was a chaotic mass of bodies, zipping in and out, people landing in squares other than their own—and with new partners.

Then Curva hollered *vayamos!* and led them in a torrid tango. She and the doctor demonstrated the moves, their pelvises pressed together, the two of them shifting and slithering across the floor. The women giggled nervously, trying to imitate Curva's movements. She also showed them the rumba, snapping her fingers in the air and clapping her hands together to accentuate the rhythms, her hips rotating suggestively as she slowly revolved. Everyone formed a line behind her, trying to imitate her hip motion, though the movements eluded them. Her joints seemed elastic, her body swaying, her feet tapping out the bouncy beats.

Homemade beer and Curva's dandelion wine fueled them. If a few ended up in the hayloft, no one paid much notice. By Sunday, most forgot whose man or woman they had wandered off with. There had been a lot of hot breathing and plenty of wet kisses passed around behind the barn and elsewhere.

Luckily, their memories were as short as the winters are long. The dandelion wine they imbibed turned everything into a nice blur and induced a pleasant forgetfulness of their sexual escapades. When the next Saturday rolled around, they once again tried to follow Curva's lead, incorporating these new moves, the square dances taking on a Latin beat.

The weekly gathering resembled a kind of *Carnivale* without Lent at the end. Everything was up for grabs. Sex was doing what comes naturally. The long, bitter winters compelled them to find some entertainment, and it wasn't ducking for apples.

Curva on the Old North Trail

Hola, mi estimado Xavier,

I haven't written you for a long while because I've been too busy. I know, I know, it shouldn't be an excuse. But it's hard work traveling through all kinds of weather. Setting up camp each night and packing up in the morning. At the end of the day, I'm too tired to do anything but feed the animals and myself—and sleep.

Can you believe it's been a couple of years since I started out? I can't. I ended up in Tlaxiaco after I left Honduras and found some *charreadas* nearby to compete in.

You're thinking only men can be *charros*. It's true. So I pretend I'm you. Even use your name. Wear your chaps and boots (you used to laugh because my feet were as big as yours). I also use padding to hide my breasts and protect myself when I get bucked off. Then I tie back my long hair the way you did, and I don't wash for a few days. That makes my skin rougher looking. Of course, my sombrero partly hides my face. Also, I'm taller than some of the men. The height makes a difference. And while I'm a *charro*, I feel closer to you. I can fool myself that you still live on in me. Then I don't feel so guilty.

I learned a lot from you when we were younger about becoming a *charro*. That was your dream. Remember? I imitated the rope tricks you did as well as the bull riding and bronco busting and steer roping. We practiced for hours on any stray animals we found in the fields. The *rancheros* were always chasing us away.

You never admitted this but I was as good as you were—better even. We fought about it all the time. You stuck your stinking sock in my mouth once to stop me from saying I was best. It didn't work. I spit it out and bit your hand until it bled. Then I made a *bandera grande* and wrote my name on it in *cartas grandes*—CURVA PELIGROSA ES EL MEJOR CHARRO—and hung it over our front door so everyone could see it.

You were so mad you didn't talk to me for weeks.

I hated the way other girls spent all their time worrying about their hair and their clothes and their dolls. I didn't want to grow up and be one of those dainty women in frilly dresses that only think about such things. I guess I shouldn't have worried. My big body would never let me be a delicate *señora*.

I didn't feel like *el major charro* the first day I competed in a real *charreada*. I was so afraid they'd find out I was a woman and beat me up that I didn't sleep for a week. I also was afraid I couldn't stay on the broncos or bulls.

But I needed *dinero* and it was the only way for me to make some fast. It isn't easy because I'm trying to hide that I'm a woman and win some money. I act like a deaf mute so I don't have to talk to anyone. It works.

And the shot of tequila the bosses gave everyone before we competed helped a lot. It gave me a big heart and *mucho valor*. You would have been proud of me. I didn't win the big prizes, but I did get a little *dinero* and tried out some tricks I've been thinking about. *Los hombres* jump on the animals and ride the hell out of them. They holler and bounce around and think they're in control.

I do something different. I pretend the animals are part of me, and I feel that more when I'm on the trail. I even practice this at night in my mind before I go to sleep and sometimes dream about it. I can feel our hearts pounding together and the blood surging through our veins. I smell their fear too. They're more frightened than I am. They just want us off their backs as fast as possible. I don't blame them. But it's a thrill to ride something so wild.

And it's a thrill to be in an arena with people screaming and hoping you'll get thrown or that an animal will gore you. But I get excited because I don't do the expected and break a leg or arm. I don't give the crowd what it wants: blood. Everyone cheers anyway. It's *loca*.

My secret? I don't try and overpower the horses or bulls. I think they feel the difference even before I land on them in the chute. And it's because of what I've learned on the trail from watching all the critters. I swear, Xavier, those animals I ride listen to me and do what I want. I sing to them some of the songs we sang together as kids. They love the cockroach one and seem willing to let me ride them forever. It's the truth! I rarely get bucked off anymore, and now I walk away with some big prize money. Everyone thinks it's because I'm a deaf mute and the animals take pity on me.

Nobody gives me a second look except for the *señoritas*. Don't laugh! They whistle and sometimes throw flowers at me in the ring. *Muy extraño* to have women after me because they think I'm *un hombre*. It doesn't surprise me. Most people want to believe what they see. Don Quixote has taught me that.

I've had some time to read about him again. He does so

many *loca* things that make me laugh. I told you he thought windmills were an army of giants. Maybe he just sees what he wants to but is determined to make life fun. Who knows? Or he could be right and the windmills are giants and a sorcerer changed them into windmills to mix him up.

His book makes me look closely at what's around me, Xavier. I think that's what the voice I mentioned in an earlier letter was trying to show me. Everything can be seen in so many ways. It's changed my feelings about being on the trail. At first I thought I would be bored, but there is so much to see and do every day that I get restless when I'm in a town for long. Life seems too predictable there.

Here, I never tire of watching the wild things around me as we travel north. There are so many that I can't even name all of them. I get glimpses from time to time of osprey, eagles, hawks, snakes, coyotes, rodents, butterflies, frogs, lizards, chipmunks, skunks. For some reason most trust me. Maybe it's because I become like them on the trail. I pee and shit in the open. I swim naked in the streams. I sniff the air for scents that alert me to visitors approaching.

It's *extraordinario* to watch all these *bestia* mate and give birth and hunt for food. It's like the beginning of creation to be here where everything is wild and just trying to survive. Like me. I don't feel so separate from them. We are all after the same thing. *Compatriotas.*

I try to see things the way they might. When I look at the full moon, it's both the moon and a bowl of cream or a map. It changes nightly, always wearing a new garment. It's hard sometimes to say what is real and what isn't. As Don Quixote knows, our eyes play tricks, and so do our other senses. They can't always be trusted.

Sometimes I want Don Quixote's sidekick Sancho to *va-*

yase because he's dull and tries to make his master dull. He wants the *ordinario* just to be *ordinario*. No magic. No enchantment. I don't want Don Quixote to stop having his dreams and following them. I don't want to stop having dreams either. One is of seeing you again. The other is to have my own place someday where I can grow things like our *madre* did and continue to explore what happens to us after we die. Or maybe help us not to die.

You must laugh when you read that last sentence. Me trying to find ways to prevent us from dying after what happened to you. But it isn't just the dying that interests me. It's all the changes animals and plants go through. Humans and frogs and so many other creatures start life as eggs. Maggots feed on dead flesh and later become flies. Girls become women. Boys turn into men. So many transformations happening all the time in nature!

Tonight I made a fire in a pit near a creek. Indians must have built it long ago. It waits for travelers like me to give it life again. Many big rocks planted in a circle and burned black on the inside. I scratched my name onto a couple of them and yours too. I want new travelers to know I was here with my brother.

Yours isn't the only spirit I feel nearby. I can see babies crying. Women at the creek washing clothes. That's what I did earlier today and hung them to dry on the bushes and tree branches. Men passing around a big pipe. I'll bet they sometimes smoked the same thing I do. I've seen it growing wild next to the trail in places. They probably used it to make clothes too.

I don't do that.

I'm going to stay where I am now for a couple of days. Smoke a little and read *Don Quixote* and dream.

You'll laugh and say you're imagining things, Curva, but I found a leather glove flattened on the road. The index finger pointed towards me. The thumb was turned inward. It seemed to be a sign I was on the right track and I would find other signs when I needed them. And I have.

I'm becoming *una mujer dura*. I realize I can live in many worlds. I'm just afraid you might not like the new Curva. She's becoming very different from the girl you once knew.

Curva and Xavier

In the months since the tornado had struck Weed, the town had bustled with activity—trucks carrying lumber roared through the streets, and workers poured new concrete foundations. All day long, tapping hammers and rasping saws had created a symphony of construction sounds as residents slowly rebuilt the damaged structures.

Though tornadoes occurred rarely on the prairies, windstorms visited frequently.

Curva woke one morning in her place outside of town after another dust storm had blown through, chewing grit. Sweeping or cleaning didn't do much good. Another gust followed, and two minutes later a new layer of dirt covered everything. She sat down at the kitchen table with a cup of coffee and tried to outline a map in the fine powder of where she'd started in Mexico and how far she'd come. But the lines kept shifting with each incoming draft. The windows were open, and a breeze wiped out whole areas at once.

Howling coyotes roamed the edge of her property, offering a choral accompaniment and encouragement. The sound reminded Curva of nighttime on the trail. Nothing came between her and all that darkness. She had worn it like a blanket, wrapping it around herself and staring at the stars and constellations while playing Xavier's guitar and singing.

She had gone through all of the songs she could remember her mother crooning. Then she played and sang melodies she'd heard on the radio as a child, making up words she couldn't remember. The sound reverberated in the trees, silencing the wolves and other creatures, drawing the wildlife into the circle of her voice. With the night and the stars as her audience, she had belted out each number, the tunes resonating in her head and chest.

Music had been her salvation, her connection to the living and the dead, especially Xavier. He had seemed most alive to her then, and she had hoped it soothed his spirit and made him less upset with her. Music also helped her to feel again after the numbness that had set in following his funeral, the melodies gradually opening up places in her body that had shut down. Witnessing Xavier's remains being placed in the ground had frozen her in time. She'd been raised to believe the dead weren't really dead but hovered nearby, their souls returning each year for the celebration of *Día de Muertos*. Yet she had seen nothing to celebrate. The person closest to her on this earth was gone, his bones decaying underground.

On the night Curva and Xavier were born, they had fought to stay in their mother's womb, not ready to face life in Tiquicheo, Mexico. It wasn't the town they resisted. It was leaving the womb's close quarters and the warm fluid that embraced them. They also liked being near their mother's heart. Its rhythmic beat echoed throughout their cozy home. But space became more precious in their mother's belly, and they eventually fought each other for every millimeter. They also fought their *madre* when she began having labor pains. They fought the midwife who tried to deliver them. In the end, Curva and Xavier couldn't stop their own birth and burst forth in the middle of the night, holding hands, each refusing to be first or last. While growing up, they did everything together, including bathing, not sure where one of them ended and the other began.

When Curva and Xavier turned fourteen, their parents died. Curva didn't mind her *padre* Manuel leaving this life. A winemaker but not a swimmer, one day Manuel fell into a vat of his favorite *vino* and drowned. Curva went through the motions of mourning him. She wore ruffled black dresses that reached her slender ankles and lit candles for his departed soul, but, secretly, she felt overjoyed. It was such a relief to be free of him.

Manuel had been known for his bad temper, and Curva made it worse by standing up to him, something she frequently did. Actually, she didn't so much stand up to him as stand over him, and that increased his irritation with her. From her early teens, she was as tall as Xavier, who had already reached six foot. This made her feel equal to her *padre*—and to all men—in every way. These extra inches, so unusual for a woman, gave her a unique perspective and helped her to see one source of male power over the centuries. Those extra inches gave bigger men more authority because of their size.

Xavier, now considered the man of the house, had felt differently about his *padre*. The son had expected to step into his father's shoes and take charge of the household, but Curva straightened him out fast. She didn't believe women had to wait on men all their lives, and she could fight as well as any *chico*. After she gave him a couple of black eyes and broke one of his teeth, he stopped trying to run things.

Their *madre* was so grieved by her husband's death that she followed him a few months later. Curva didn't understand how her *madre* could have loved Manual so desperately that she would abandon her *bambinos*. Why did she want to continue with such a difficult man? Her *madre*, always deeply involved in rescuing dying plants and animals, gave in to death's call and couldn't save herself.

Curva's loss of her *madre* shook her deeply. Determined her *madre* would live on through her daughter, Curva committed herself to her mother's important work of promoting the growth of all life.

After burying both parents, Xavier and Curva tried to find odd jobs cleaning shops or picking vegetables, but there weren't many to be had. Even the adults had trouble staying employed because there were so few opportunities. Who was going to hire two *niños?* Thus, they became scavengers, checking out the dump every day for anything that looked sellable. Sometimes they got lucky and found castaway kitchen items that hadn't yet seen their last days—eggbeaters and pots and pans and dishes that they cleaned up, polished, and sold.

With no other family members to call on, they scraped by. Curva kept her mother's garden going with seeds dried from previous years. They had enough vegetables to eat—sweet potatoes, tomatillos, jicama, peppers, tomatoes, green beans, and lettuce. Sometimes Xavier would catch a wild rabbit, skin it, and roast it over an open fire. They feasted for days.

During this time, the two shared a *pasión* for Luis Cardona's novels, especially *Paraíso*. It featured a town called Berumba, and while reading the book, Berumba began to appear in their dreams, offering a lush contrast to their barren village. Berumba conjured up images of trees weighted down by oranges, apples, and bananas. They fell in love with the place and the Pacheco family that founded it. Instead of straggly plants struggling to survive in arid soil, Berumba really was a *paraíso*. And so this world became as real to them as the village where they had grown up.

In their imaginations, Ana Cristina Hernandez and Ernesto Valenzuela Pacheco replaced their own dead parents. Ana Cristina seemed to give birth to all of Berumba; Ernesto Valenzuela fathered most of the children, but not always with his wife.

Ana Cristina, whom Curva came to adore, was an independent woman, though she also carried out the traditional female role of managing the household and raising kids. She ran a successful dairy business, contributing substantially to the family's income and to the town's health. Her cows gave such a prodigious amount of milk each day that Ana Cristina's hired help could barely keep up with the milking required. She resembled the cows somewhat, her own breasts large and still producing, even in middle age. So abundant, they overflowed onto the land, leaving rivers of milk in their wake. Eager to please their owner, who sang to them each night before they went to sleep, her cows also yielded well past their prime.

A fruitful time in Berumba, the place flourished in an era when slow was anything but dull. Life moved at a snail's pace, and sometimes even that seemed too fast for its residents; they wanted time to watch the flowers grow and to sit with one another at the end of a long day's work, recounting in minute detail each aspect of their day, examining these elements as one might a precious jewel.

Berumba residents also held *fiestas* to celebrate anything of consequence (or not of consequence), with singing, dancing, skits, food, and *vino* providing the center of the fun. Berumba's lively presence attracted visitors from all over the world, including Kadeem, a Trinidadian.

Kadeem was a festival in of himself. A calypsonian that played the steel pan, his brown face resembled a cherub, his cheeks dimpled in a constant smile. Though he visited Berumba often over the years, he never seemed to age, somehow embodying what Ernesto Valenzuela Pacheco and Curva both sought: eternal life. Kadeem wore a stovepipe hat he'd made himself, its wide brim adorned with the Trinidadian flag's red, white, and black colors, as was the cape he wore. Built like a draft horse, Kadeem's muscular body resembled a wrestler's, yet he moved like a ballet dancer, appearing not merely to walk but to glide across the land. From the time he was a boy, he pursued what was beyond the horizon, both in the physical world and the one beyond. His desire for knowledge was great, but so was his craving for fun. He somehow managed to marry the two in his work as a musician and traveling salesman.

Some thought Kadeem was in competition with Ernesto Valenzuela Pacheco. They both sold medicines. Ernesto's drugs, however, were viewed as legitimate. He had trained as an apothecary and mixed potions that the medical world agreed were effective. But Kadeem's concoctions had more of an alchemical base and weren't intended for treating the usual ailments. They were meant to emotionally transform the person who had the illness, instilling a powerful impulse to be whole and therefore well. He had read ancient philosophical texts that skirted mainstream thinking. Over intimate late-night suppers, Kadeem passed on this knowledge to Ernesto, who hungrily absorbed it all—the Hermetic treatises on alchemy and magic; the astrological lore that went beyond astronomy. Theosophy.

Luis Cardona's books gave Curva and Xavier much to talk about during their long evenings. They speculated on the characters and the town, piecing together their own version from what they'd read. Both children liked to guess what book the writer would create next and put their names on a waiting list for it at the small local library.

Though Curva and Xavier had much in common, and were also the same height, his facial bones were more pronounced than hers. But they shared similar eye and hair color, and he wore his dark hair long, too. The *mujeres* all were after him. Curva teased him about the women who strolled by their house, hoping to get a glimpse of Xavier. But he would say, Curva, you are my best girl. She believed him. They knew each other like no one else did. How could anything ever separate them?

One day she raced home from Tiquicheo's central plaza after overhearing some of the elderly men talking about their travels on the Old North Trail. Bounding up the stairs to the front door, she yelled, Xavier, Xavier, I have news!

He called from the backyard, I'm in the *jardin*.

Panting, Curva joined him. Getting down on her hands and knees, she yanked weeds from the ground, throwing them on the pile Xavier was making.

What's the big news? he asked.

I heard Juan and his friends talking about the Old North Trail. They traveled it all the way to Canada and back.

Canada?

Sí, I saw it on the map at school. *Muy grande!*

He shivered. Brrrr. You want to go to Canada? It has igloos and crazy people who live in them.

I want to travel the Old North Trail! It will take us to many places. Not just Canada. Who knows where we'll end up? Don't you want adventures, Xavier, like Kadeem?

He shrugged and resumed weeding, digging his fingers into the soil.

But Curva talked about it so much that Xavier finally got excited, too, his eyes growing very big when they discussed the escapades they would have and what they'd take with them—matches, warm clothes, guns, flour, sugar, grains, dried beans, water, a tent. And where would the money come from to buy all these things? They sold their parents' *casa* and used the profits to stake their journey, purchasing a couple of strong young saddle horses and another one to pull the travois they'd made.

Not knowing when and if they would return, the night before they left their home for good, sister and brother visited their parents' graves and solemnly told them of their plans, promising to take good care of each other. A full moon illuminated the cemetery. Curva knelt at her *madre's* grave and kissed the gravestone. Xavier did the same for their *padre*, but Curva didn't join him. She'd had enough of that man. After, the siblings returned to the house for their final night there and packed the rest of their belongings, taking only the necessities.

The next morning, following a *mapa* the elders had given them, they started out. For the first leg of the journey, the *mapa* said to follow a stream for twenty miles and then go north for eight days. They found what once had been a stream, but now it was dried up. Guessing at how many miles they had traveled, by nightfall, they were exhausted. After setting up camp and feeding the animals, they sat around a fire, trying to decipher the ratty piece of paper the old men had said would guide them.

Curva shook her head and said, These marks and instructions don't make sense, *mi hermano.*

Don't worry, he said. We'll figure it out. If those old men could do it, we can, too.

The next morning, they packed up and started off again on their horses, singing to pass the time and sharing stories from their childhood. They also talked about what they might find along the trail. Xavier said, Maybe we'll discover gold.

Laughing, Curva said, And we can build a *casa grande* on a beeg river where we can fish and swim.

Bueno!

The days passed in this way, and they convinced themselves they were making progress. But for directions they depended solely upon the sun's rising and setting as well as the constellations, not realizing they were heading south rather than north. Recalling the promise they'd made to their *padres* to care for one another, they shared plans and fantasies to keep their spirits buoyed. Finally, after climbing a steep hill, Curva stopped her panting horse in the shade of a banyan tree and turned to Xavier: We're lost, *mi hermano.* Those old men gave us bad directions. The stream disappeared long ago.

Xavier nodded and said, Maybe we're under a spell. I've lost track of time. I don't remember how many days we've been traveling.

Curva's horse whinnied and shook its head in the direction of a distant valley visible from the hilltop. Look, she shouted, a village!

Xavier, who had been drowsing in his saddle, stirred. *Una aldea*, he cried, raising his canteen to the heavens. *Gracias*, he said, downing a big slug of water before passing the container to Curva. *Viva, mi hermana*, he said, guiding his horse down the other side of the mesa, Curva and the packhorse following.

With great relief, they approached a town that looked vaguely familiar. Curva said to Xavier, Look, those trees are like the ones we read about in *Paraíso*. So much fruit and I'm so hungry!

Xavier pointed at a large two-story house surrounded by green pastures where cows grazed. *Sí*, I'm hungry too… and thirsty.

As they drew closer, a woman stepped out of the house, wiping one hand on her apron, the other hand shielding the sun from her eyes. She said, I'm Ana. Our family welcomes you! Dinner is getting cold.

Curva cried out, We're in Berumba, Xavier! That must be Ana Cristina Hernandez from the novel we read. I can't believe it!

Nor could Xavier. He whooped and yelled, Berumba. We're no longer lost. Let's eat!

In later years, Curva remembered Berumba as a dreamy, enchanted place. It smelled of sage and other *especias*: cinnamon, cumin, nutmeg. The scent of jasmine wafted through her bedroom window, evoking thoughts of faraway places she had only read about. And the night felt velvety on her skin, as if the moon had poured its creamy substance onto the land. Even the daylight had a silky feel to it, the sun not hard-edged and glaring but caressing her face and bare arms. The many tropical birds—flamingoes, scarlet ibises, parrots, peacocks and swans—seemed like desserts for the eyes, their vibrant colors enlivening the landscape. Their peculiar birdcalls resembled haunted human voices.

This early experience of Berumba branded Curva, leaving a deep impression she couldn't shake. Prior to her time there, life had seemed harsh, as did the barren land where she had grown up. Being in Berumba had awakened a thirst in her for beauty, and she wanted more of the same. The town had shown her not only its tropical abundance but also a more intensified way of living—the residents inhabited each moment as if it were their last. The ambience stayed with her, and she thought of the place often during her travels, so when she later settled in Weed, she longed to recreate Berumba—or something similar.

But Curva's taste of paradise was short-lived. While the Pacheco household flourished in spite of a dark cloud that cast a shadow over parts of the area, the town itself didn't fare as well. Several parties tried to overthrow the Tiburcio Carías Andino regime. The twins joined one of Ernesto Valenzuela Pacheco's sons in defending the Liberal Party, hoping to improve the peasants' living and working conditions. This new pursuit made it necessary for brother and sister to master the art of shooting. Curva and Xavier went up into the hills where they learned how to load and aim a .38 and a rifle. They shot at paper targets of human silhouettes, aiming for the heart and the head.

Sí, mi hermana, Xavier had said. You are good! Better than I am.

Curva playfully pointed her unloaded gun at him. He raised his hands in mock horror. No, no, don't shoot.

She loved the way the rifle kicked when she pulled the trigger; it was like handling something alive. The bullet tore into the target, ripping away the heart. And while she couldn't imagine actually shooting a person, she ended up fighting side by side with the men until a fragment from a stray bullet wounded her. Years later it still lodged in her thigh.

After Curva got shot, Xavier decided they needed to leave the area. He said to her, It would kill me if anything happened to you. I couldn't live. We must get away from here.

She agreed. Watching men injure and sometimes kill each other made her realize what a romantic idea it had been to think she and Xavier could relieve the peasants' struggle. The two of them were like ants fighting an army of giants. She also became aware that Ana Cristina Hernandez and Ernesto Valenzuela Pacheco's interest in developing their businesses added to the town's changes. They put it in contact with the outside world and altered life there forever. The Berumba Curva had once known now mainly existed in her dreams.

Since there was no longer a future for them with the Pachecos, Curva and Xavier decided to move on, alerting their hosts to their departure plans. The trail still called to them, and Kadeem gave them instructions on how to locate it. They planned to depart the following month, and this time they would take a compass.

Sabina and Victor

Caught up in Weed's reconstruction, hammering and sawing where needed, and the demands of her own place, Curva ignored the changes happening to her body. In spite of working long hours at her property and in town, as well as helping to raise Victor, Curva still put on weight. The

67

extra pounds seemed to be concentrated in her breasts and stomach, causing many to gossip about her condition. At Nathan Smart's General Store, the neighbors chattered constantly about the alterations they were witnessing in her. Finally, Curva could no longer deny that she was pregnant, though she refused to think about her condition and continued her life as usual for the nine months it took to incubate a child.

Some speculated that the doctor had inseminated half the town and then fled (fortunately, Victor had the same birthmark as Henry, a butterfly shape on his buttocks like a cattle brand, so he wasn't one of the doctor's offspring), though Curva had dallied at times with the doctor. But she'd always taken precautions with him and her other lovers—and so had the doctor. Many thought that Henry was the father of the unborn child since he and Curva spent so much time together. It's true it didn't take them long to discover each other's bodies, but that happened well after Curva became pregnant.

Rub two dry sticks together and you might get fire; combine a tornado, a mysterious bone, and female genitals and something totally unexpected can happen—not exactly a miraculous conception, but close to it. After nine months, Curva gave birth to a fully formed girl of almost three years of age. She announced immediately *mi nombre es Sabina*. A camera in one hand, a sombrero in the other, and copper-colored hair reaching her shoulders, Sabina formed perfect sentences from the time she was born. Already expert with the camera, she shot whatever crossed her path, as skilled with it as her mother was with a gun.

Curva, who hadn't expected to give birth in her early forties, at first felt fate had played a cruel trick on her, leaving

68

her with this unusual *niña* to raise but no *marido* to help out. At least Curva didn't have to change diapers again as she had with Victor and care for a totally helpless infant, freeing her to tend the greenhouse and grounds. Sabina's independence also allowed Curva to enjoy her daughter as an autonomous being right from the start, not just as someone Curva had given birth to. And while Henry appreciated Curva's continuing help with Victor when she had extra time, he wasn't free himself to offer marriage. He did tell Curva that once he was divorced, they could hook up permanently. However, first he had to locate Olga, and that wouldn't be easy.

Nor would it be easy to convince Curva to marry. Not eager to give up her independence, she preferred walking marriages. A woman invites a man to spend a sweet night with her, but he must leave by daybreak. Besides, though she appreciated Henry's decency, she felt more passion for his son than she did for him. Victor had some bite to him—a little of the devil. But Henry? He was too good and therefore a bit dull. She couldn't imagine herself settling into domestic bliss with anyone, far less Henry.

With Victor spending most days at Curva's place, the two children put new demands on her. Both headstrong, they kept her running from morning until Henry picked up Victor late in the afternoon. They were curious about everything and ignored Curva's attempts to curtail their explorations. Both were impossible to keep inside, even during cold weather.

Curva found them riding the sheep and pigs and calves. They'd get thrown but would climb right back on the animals' backs, ready for another go. She even found the two of them roosting on eggs—after chasing the hens out of the chicken house—and imitating their squawking, though all they produced were scrambled eggs and a sticky mess.

Finally, Curva had to attach ropes to their waists just to keep them on her property, but Victor quickly chewed through them. Nothing kept them restrained for long, and they didn't like anything else to be restricted; they were intent on releasing all the animals and creating chaos. Cows bellowed on the roads, milk straining their udders. Pigs and sheep roamed through the holes Victor and Sabina cut in the fences. Chickens came unmoored from their nests.

A wooden gate Curva constructed across the doorway leading outside didn't last a day. She found pieces of it strewn across the porch. The *niños* had freed themselves, and she found them in the pigpen, rolling in the mud with the pigs, oinking and shrieking.

Curva dragged them to the well, ignoring their shouts of protest—No! No! No! Leave us alone!—took off their clothes, and rinsed off the mud. She needed a dozen eyes and ears, all watching and listening to ensure they didn't harm themselves. No easy task. She ran all day, following them into the fields and beyond, fighting off grasshoppers and flies. Sweat dripped from her forehead and beaded between her breasts.

Chasing kids wasn't what she imagined herself doing at middle age. She always had wanted a life like Suelita Flores. That woman had no trouble, it seemed, having babies and, over the years, bedding down with half of the men in Berumba. Curva wasn't a prostitute like Suelita, but she liked *hombres*—all kinds of them—and she loved Suelita's ability to do as she pleased with as many men as she wanted. Suelita didn't worry about her kids not having a *papá*. Why should

Curva?

Curva threw up her hands and said to Henry, These *bambinos*, they drive me *loca*. He tried to pitch in, taking the kids with him out in the fields and giving Curva a chance to catch up with herself. With some free time, she visited Catherine, Edna, Sophie, and Inez, sharing war stories with them about raising children and laughing about these lively youngsters she was in charge of.

But she couldn't be angry for long with Sabina or Victor, even though her connection to Sabina was different from the one she had with the boy. The pregnancy had happened so mysteriously and unexpectedly that it was difficult for Curva to feel emotionally attached to her daughter. Never a clinging, helpless *bebé*, Sabina's independence from the time she left the womb also created distance between them.

Still, Curva immersed herself in the children's needs and put her greenhouse and other explorations temporarily on hold. Yet at night, before falling asleep, she thought about things she didn't have time for during the day. It puzzled her that while sleep resembled death in that she lost consciousness, she always woke in the morning. Why, then, couldn't humans wake from death in a similar way? Why couldn't they live forever? What was the secret?

The Real People

Inseparable from the beginning, Victor and Sabina seemed more like twins except, technically, Victor was older than Sabina, and they weren't siblings. Though Victor was the elder, Sabina was the leader, her ravenous curiosity the driving force that took them into the world.

Outside, the two *niños* made paths through the abundant prairie grass, taller than they were. Losing themselves

71

in the labyrinths they created, Victor was dependent upon Sabina to find their way out again. They chased field mice and slipped garter snakes into their pockets and chomped on grasshopper legs. Little more than animals themselves, they sniffed the air, sensing the former inland ocean and the dinosaurs that once roamed there. But there was something else they picked up on, another odor they couldn't quite identify.

On the go from dawn till dusk, Sabina and Victor rafted on the sloughs and irrigation ditches, pretending they were pirates on the high seas. Or they lolled in a pasture and listened to the wind in the grass and stared at cloud formations, making up stories about the faces and shapes they saw. They found trees to climb and branches to swing from.

At times, they watched ant colonies carting their booty. They also experimented on the lizards, cutting off their tails to see if they'd grow back. And they swung from a rope in the hayloft, landing in piles of newly mown hay. Haystacks had other attractions, making excellent huts that they burrowed into. When they tired of being moles, they climbed to the top and rolled down the sides, trying to see who could do it the fastest.

They also liked to catch mice and put them in their pockets. Then they ran back to the house and barged inside: Look, Curva, they said. Touch them.

Curva shrank back in mock horror: With my bare hands? They might bite me.

Tittering, they said, Come on, Curva. They're nice. Look! They won't hurt you.

She could see the animals' little bodies moving under their trousers, squirming, squeaking, and quivering. Then they scurried up Sabina's and Victor's backs, making the two of them laugh even louder. The mice poked their heads through the openings between their shirt buttons and twitched their noses, trembling with terror.

Okay, let them go now, *mis bambinos*, Curva said, clapping her hands together. *Pronto.* And she had shooed away the frightened little creatures, sending them all back into the fields.

One day, Sabina and Victor went farther than usual and in a new direction. The land no longer produced much except for intermittent patches of straggly grass, and the earth had turned sandy in places. Victor called out, Let's go back. But Sabina—walking in the lead, wearing a pair of Victor's shorts and one of her own blouses—ignored him. She marched into this new territory. He followed, hesitantly.

Suddenly, Sabina began to sink. Reaching out for Victor, she screamed, Help. She didn't understand why the land was swallowing her. The clammy mixture of wet earth and sand gripped her bare legs, pulling her under. The clearly defined mountains in the distance and the prairies themselves tilted and swirled. Nothing appeared solid; nothing held together. Even Victor was a blur, his features indistinct. For the first time she realized that life could end in minutes. There was nothing she could do about it except watch.

Victor stood there, staring. He thought his friend was playing a joke and laughed out loud, his mirth merging with her shrieks.

Face contorted in fear, she tried to grab him, waving her hands like windmills. Pull me out, she said, unable to move her legs without a great effort. But he could see that the nearby earth was dangerous. If he tried to help, he'd get sucked in too.

73

Frightened now, he also started screaming. Sabina's legs were no longer visible, and it wouldn't take long for the ground to claim all of her. Certain he was seeing the last of his friend, he yelled as loudly as he could, their voices rolling across the prairies like tumbling tumbleweeds, picking up speed and force. They bumped into Billie One Eye, who was working nearby with tribal members, teaching youngsters how to carve totems. He cocked his ear, recognizing the cry for help. Holding the shovel in front of him like a spear, he took off in the direction of the shrieks, quickly reaching the two children.

Sabina's upper body was still above ground, and her arms flapped frantically, resembling chicken wings and equally as useless in this situation: she could neither fly nor help herself. But her screams quieted when she saw Billie.

He placed the shovel's handle near her hands: Grab it, kid, and hold tight, he said.

She did as she was told, and Billie pulled her out of the bog to safety. She held onto his legs, afraid to let go, wet sand clinging to her skin.

Sabina seemed somehow familiar to Billie. He knew she was Curva's daughter, though he had only seen her from afar. But he recognized something in her of *Ni-tsi-ta-pi-ksi*, the real people, a name the Blackfoot had given themselves instead of what the Whites called them: Blackfoot. Sabina was one of the few individuals he knew, outside of his mother, whose hair was red, like his own. And she had Sighing Turtle's sky blue eyes, now blurred with tears. It startled him to see something of his mother in this girl, who was looking up at him adoringly.

Once their hysterics quieted, Billie took the two children back to Curva's place, shooing them on ahead, using the shovel as a walking stick. But Sabina wanted to hold his hand, still frightened over her brush with death. She masked her fear with questions, lots of them, wanting to know about the recently discovered bones, and whom they belonged to, and why they were there, and what exactly is a Blackfoot burial ground, and couldn't she help him with it?

Sabina hopped along, trying to keep up with his longer strides, unable to take her eyes off him. His red hair shimmered like polished copper in the sun, and the black eye patch made him look like a pirate. Sabina wondered what he hid beneath it.

Victor trailed behind, sulking, kicking at clods of dirt, angry that he hadn't been able to save his friend. He whistled between the spaces in his teeth, and did a cartwheel or two, trying to get Sabina's attention, but she was too caught up in admiring Billie to notice Victor.

When they arrived at Curva's, they found her weeding the vegetable patch next to the house. A paisley scarf kept her long hair off her face. Billie explained what had happened, stuttering a little and shuffling his feet. His face turned the color of flame when Curva threw her arms around him and thanked him profusely for rescuing her daughter. She smelled smoke in his hair and sweat on his body and felt a stiffening in Billie's groin.

Bones will be bones.

Sabina ran into the house and grabbed her camera. But by the time she appeared again, Billie had left. Curva was sitting on the porch, looking dazed, and Victor was chasing some chickens around the yard, flapping his arms and imitating their squawking. The girl aimed her camera and caught the look on Curva's face, a cross between desire and bliss.

The Weedites and Curva

Though her neighbors didn't object outwardly to the illegitimate *niña* she'd borne or to Curva carrying on with Henry, they gossiped plenty in private about both. When the sewing circle met at Catherine Hawkins's house, she served tea in china cups her mother had brought from England as part of her trousseau. Along with the tea and cookies, Catherine also served up the latest Curva rumors, her lips quivering as if fighting a smile. She said, I saw her in the woods one day, naked, fondling herself. The woman has no shame!

While sipping her tea, pinky curled like a piglet's tail, Inez Wilson raised her eyebrows and told the others that Curva bedded down at Henry's place some nights. Or else he did at hers.

Edna MacGregor clucked her tongue and blurted out, What kind of example are Curva and Henry setting for the children? Such loose behavior.

Sweat beading on her upper lip, Catherine ran the tip of her tongue along her lower lip, forgetting the cup and saucer she was holding, her fingers slackening. Both fell to the floor and shattered. Catherine shrieked: Oh my god, Mother would turn over in the grave if she knew. All she sacrificed to bring that china with her!

Sophie Smart, who had been sitting quietly, drinking her tea, said, There's more, my friends. I've heard that Curva has been slipping out at night to see Billie One Eye at the greenhouse and the burial ground.

Edna gasped: An Indian lover? That's the limit! What would Catherine's mother say to that?

Catherine rolled her eyes in response and said, Mother would die a second time.

Dropping to her hands and knees, Catherine began collecting the fine porcelain shards from under the table, trying to piece them together. Sophie joined her, the two women face to face in that small space. Her curly mop in disarray, Sophie hissed, How can she let Billie touch her?

Catherine's eyes glazed over. She was unable to respond because she envied Curva's freedom to carry on as she did.

Later, Catherine and Sophie glanced at the other women, curious to see how they were reacting. But no one wanted to speak out too harshly against Curva, so the ladies gave her a lot of slack. The women had a strong motivation to protect Curva: her greenhouse, a tropical paradise that was expanding before their eyes. Never before had they witnessed something so fertile. They remembered the dried-out seed Curva had shown them, one she had brought with her from Mexico. It had turned into a dwarf avocado tree almost overnight and produced strange fruit they had never seen before. Her greenhouse tomatoes began as ordinary garden varieties but became gigantic—as big as bowling balls.

The structure itself seemed to be a living thing. The women didn't know what to make of it. So they approached the greenhouse with reverence because it was beyond their understanding. They wanted to be near the place, yet they also feared it—feared what it might do to them. If strange phenomena happened within its boundaries to plants and other things, what might it do to humans who strayed too close?

Of course, Curva's lustiness also attracted them, as well as her infectious laugh. Both offered hope that they too could escape from their mundane lives and find the delight she did in what seemed to be trivial things. They

77

had never seen anyone else get so excited about bee colonies. Even ants fascinated the woman to no end. Inez stumbled on Curva crouched by the side of the road, charting the track of a long line of marching ants. An hour later, after shopping at the Smart's store, Inez reported that Curva was still there. And those phantom streams that at times mysteriously appeared and disappeared in Curva's presence caused them to jump and hop around to avoid getting their feet wet. Before she showed up in Weed, their days had been drab and uneventful. Now they couldn't imagine life without her.

If Curva was aware of these women's conversations and her own role at the center of their circle, she didn't let on when she saw them. Nor did they say anything to her. Though they felt she had crossed a forbidden line by carrying on with an Indian, they envied her boldness and lived vicariously through her. It was one more thing she could pull off that they couldn't. They protected her uniqueness—the impulse to follow her own desires—and viewed Curva as one of them. If they had to, they would fight for her till the end. Anything that threatened her freedom likewise jeopardized their futures. Before she had arrived, they didn't think they had much of a future outside of the usual routines. Now they saw a glimmer of hope. It was no surprise, then, that any time their men talked of reining in Curva, the women withheld their sexual favors until their partners saw the light.

A Visitor

One night, Curva was sipping a glass of dandelion wine at her kitchen table after dinner, dreamily trailing her fingers through the dust on its surface left from another windstorm, watching them create an image. Sabina was in bed, sleeping. Dios let out a low growl and whimpered, cowering under Curva's skirt. Manuel and Pedro huddled in their cage, shivering. She glanced around the room, wondering what was upsetting the animals, and patted the trembling dog. She said, It's just the wind, Dios. The parrots shrieked, Wind, wind!

Some branches knocked against the window, and Curva rose, ready to pick up a gun. But before she could do so, Xavier, accompanied by a strong wind, strode through the front door, though it wasn't *día de los muertos*. Curva froze, unable to do anything but stare at her *hermano*. Death hadn't changed him at all. If anything, it had made him more handsome and vital.

Dios slunk into the bedroom, tail between his legs. The dog had faced wolverines, bears, and worse on the trail, but ghosts? They didn't have a scent, leaving Dios confused and scared. Manuel and Pedro screeched Ghost, ghost!

Xavier threw back his head and laughed. *Buenas tardes, mi hermana*, he said, as if they'd parted only yesterday and not twenty years before. He wrapped his arms around Curva and held her close. She slowly melted in his embrace, her heart beating wildly. His arms seemed weightless, as light as silk against her skin, and he smelled of the earth after rainfall on a warm humid day. She sighed, tucking her face into his neck and soaking up his scent, afraid to look at his face for fear he would disappear.

Shivering, Curva pulled away so she could see him better, still unable to believe Xavier was actually in her *casa*. She stared at him, stunned, not comprehending what she was seeing. Her brother. Over the years he'd appeared often in her dreams, but this was the first time he'd materialized in waking life. Death may not have changed him fundamentally, but his hair had grown, now longer than hers, and it had grey streaks at the temples. His face had wrinkles, too, and was weathered from the sun. She took some comfort from knowing that everyone and everything aged, dead or living, except, it seemed, for Kadeem the Trinidadian.

Xavier also brought the odor of newly mown grass with him. The smell filled the room, though none grew near Curva's house. It reminded her of the lawn that surrounded their family home, the one they'd sold to fund their travels. Whenever Xavier had mowed it, the scent filled the place for hours afterward.

Curva recalled that when the people in their village had celebrated *día de los muertos*, many spoke of their departed family members as if they were actually present. Some believed they saw them swirling among the living, part of the colors and smells and sounds. Curva had liked that idea then, and she still did, though Xavier's appearance stirred many questions about death and immortality.

Her voice shaking, she asked, Why has it taken you so long to visit me?

He stood there, staring at her, his eyes still the same hazel shade, except now they were darkened by sorrow. He said, I was trying to protect you, *mi hermana*.

From what? she said, turning away, afraid to look too deeply into their depths. I don't need your protection, Xavier. As you see, I've done well for myself.

Sí, muy bien. I've done well too, don't you think?

I didn't think being dead was an achievement.

Xavier laughed: For some it might be.

You didn't answer my question. What were you protecting me from?

Me! I thought it would make you too sad.

But I'm sad anyway. A visit would have made me feel better.

So I'm here at last. Do you feel better?

Sí. Mucho. Tell me about where you've been all these years, *mi hermano.*

He twirled and did a modified soft shoe. I've been busy performing in Hades. Singing. Dancing. They need *mucho* entertainment. I'm a popular guy there.

Curva looked puzzled: Hades?

Sí, Hades. You know I was never a believer. So they love me in Hades. I can stay there forever if I want. It's better than the alternative.

Hell?

Sí, that place. They don't let you leave the pit. Xavier looked around: It's been a long time, no?

Manuel and Pedro cawed, Long time, and Dios crept back into the room, sniffing Xavier's trousers. Xavier opened cupboards, the dog at his heels, examining the contents within. He took a fat book from its shelf, studied the cover, and asked, Who is this Don Quixote?

A *muy* famous knight. He's a little *loca* but he makes me laugh.

I need some laughs. Maybe I'll read it.

He put the book back on the shelf and looked inside the fridge. You live well here, *mi hermana.* Plenty to eat. May I? He gestured at a covered bowl.

Sí, she said. But why are you visiting now?

He said, I've been starving for too long, Curva—for food, for you. I knew it would hurt you to see me again, but I couldn't stay away any longer.

The lights flickered several times before going out. Curva could barely see Xavier's shadowy form by the fridge. He didn't seem to notice they were in darkness and took the bowl, placing it on the counter by the sink. Curva lit the kerosene lamp she kept on the table for emergencies and joined him.

¿Las cucharas? He motioned at the cupboards.

The spoons are in that drawer, right behind you, Curva said.

Xavier opened the drawer and laughed. Baby chicks were hatching there, eggs swaddled in wool she'd taken from the sheep. Curva held the lamp above them.

Look! Xavier said, pointing at a tiny beak poking through one of the creamy white shells.

They both stared at the new life cracking the casing, creating a zigzag in the egg's surface. They smiled at each other and then roared with laughter.

The tension Curva was feeling at this surprise visit began dissolving. They were young again, caring for the animals her parents kept on their land—a cow, some chickens, a few pigs, and, of course, cats and dogs, all strays.

It was difficult to absorb: This was her brother prowling her kitchen, back from the dead—back from somewhere. How had he escaped his fate and appeared in her kitchen as if he had been alive the whole time? She wanted to pelt him with questions, but it didn't seem the right time to do it. His appearance reinforced her notion that life didn't necessarily end with the body's death. What more she could learn from him, only time would tell.

For now, he was here, and he was hungry. Famished by the looks of him. His clothes hung from his lanky frame, several sizes too big.

Curva took a pan from the pantry and cracked her chickens' three-yoked eggs into it, scrambling them. They reminded her that she and Xavier were both born of one egg. Some were fertile; some were not. She lit one of the burners and shook the pan back and forth until the eggs were set. Then she slid them onto a plate, found a fork in one of the drawers, and set everything on the table, next to the image she had created in the dust.

Xavier ate as if he had a bottomless hole to fill, inhaling the eggs and bread she gave him. It didn't take long for him to empty the contents of her fridge and cupboards. He gobbled everything in sight; if there had been more to eat, he would have finished that, too. She felt as if a strong prairie wind had struck her, leaving her breathless.

He put the dirty dishes in the sink and asked, You live alone?

Sí. But I have *muchos visitantes*. And I help care for a friend's *niño*. She didn't mention that Victor sometimes felt like her own or that she had a daughter herself. It might be too much for him to digest after all they had once shared both inside and outside of the womb.

You look the same, Curva. Are you still my best girl?

She wanted to say yes. Yet it had been a long time since they'd sworn their loyalty to each other as teenagers and experienced so many intimacies together. It had seemed normal then to curl up in each other's arms and pour out their hearts.

Much had happened in the meantime. Curva had known many men, not just Xavier. A couple of them she'd even loved. These romances taught her the difference between fondness for a sibling and ardor for a mature adult lover. No longer innocent, she couldn't in all honesty answer affirmatively.

Curva moved away from Xavier: I'm your sister, Xavier.

I can't be your girlfriend anymore.

He frowned and clenched his fists. The lights came on, flooding the room and chasing away the shadows. Now there was no place to hide.

He moved closer to Curva and said, I thought we made a promise to each other.

I'm no longer your best girl. We were too young to know any better. Our parents were gone. We were all we had. We did things we shouldn't have done.

And you have someone better now?

No, I've grown up.

And I haven't?

You died.

Curva couldn't bear the stricken look on Xavier's face. It was as if he hadn't known he was dead till she told him. Under the electric light's glare, he shrank to the size of a six-year-old, the same boy who'd clung to her in the night after a bad dream. Someone was chasing me, Curva. A bad man. He wanted my head. Curva had held him in her arms, crooning in his ear till he again fell asleep.

And then Xavier left as suddenly as he had arrived. The yard lit up mysteriously when his shade passed through it, and the coyotes yowled in unison. Dios sniffed the air. Manuel and Pedro screeched, Gone.

Curva glanced at what was left of the image she had unconsciously made in the dust on her kitchen table. The outline resembled Xavier's face. At one time she would have been overjoyed by this strange phenomenon. She would also have been thrilled by his visit. But she felt his appearance had an ominous cast to it. Having the dead turn up wasn't the problem; she welcomed that. Yet she didn't welcome a brother who was stuck in the past and still wanted to be her future.

Curva & Billie

Ecstatic moans vibrated Curva's greenhouse glass, causing the whole structure to levitate. The townspeople had grown so used to strange things generating from her nursery that they ignored the latest phenomenon, though they couldn't overlook for long the relationship that was blooming there.

Nor could they ignore the spectacle of Curva and Billie fornicating in Billie's tent trailer near the Indian remains, another trysting place. There was even some discussion among the more conservative Weedites of apprehending the couple for lewd behavior, but they didn't have grounds for such a charge. Whether inside or outside Billie's trailer, the couple had their rights. Yet everyone wondered how the two of them could bobble like that surrounded by the dead. It seemed unnatural somehow. Bizarre.

Yet for Curva and Billie, it was the most normal thing to do, especially during the warm fall nights. The weather begged them to be outside, under the moon in all its transmutations, making an offering of themselves to the ancestors, to the gods, and to the night itself. The earth clung to their naked bodies, and for days afterward they found stray pieces of dirt they'd missed while bathing. Curva put some in her mouth and chewed, certain she could taste Billie's seed, the slightly salty flavor embedded now in the rich soil.

It wasn't just Billie and Curva's outrageous behavior that caused consternation among the locals. They were still reeling from having Blackfoot burial bones in their midst. The idea that an Indian community had once thrived on this land made them feel less clean, less Caucasian. Indians had been invisible to them for so long, even though they lived nearby, it was difficult to make the shift and actually see them. Were they human? Yes, of course. But were they Canadian? That rankled.

Many Weedites had either immigrated to Canada, acquiring citizenship themselves, or were the offspring of immigrants. But the Indians just assumed they belonged there without proving it by passing citizenship tests. It wasn't right. Nor was it right for their ancestors' bones to reside near real Canadians' remains. It was too intimate. Like being married, for God's sake.

Unaware of her neighbors' concerns, on the night after Xavier's visit, Curva popped into Billie's tent trailer at the burial ground. She undressed and, stooping a little, rubbed her erect nipples against Billie's naked chest. Do you mind me being taller than you, Bee-lee, she asked.

He shook his head, his tongue following the path of darker skin around her teats: It just gives me more of you to enjoy.

It doesn't make you feel less of a man?

He looked up at her, puzzled. Does it make you feel less of a woman?

No! she laughed. I feel more *mujer*. There's more of me!

Billie shrugged, his hands stroking her breasts, and said, Height isn't what makes a man. Or a woman. It's how you act in the world. Your deeds. I know a lot of tall men who aren't manly.

We're getting too serious, Bee-lee. See if you can catch me.

Curva ran out the door, and, giggling like kids, the two

chased each other, naked, around the burial mounds, careful not to step on the ancestral remains.

Did he catch her? You bet.

Leading her back to the trailer, Billie took longer than Curva to disrobe, still bashful at having a woman see him in the nude. His sisters had teased him when he was younger because he was scrawny. Now, whenever he exposed his body, he could still hear their shrill laughter, and it made him self-conscious.

Don't be shy, Bee-lee, Curva said, and they lowered themselves onto the sleeping pad, its coverings rumpled. Billie kissed her from head to toe, stopping at times to savor a particularly tender spot—the back of her knees, the curve of her elbow, the bushy area covering her cunt. Curva groaned with pleasure and shivered. You scare me, Bee-lee, she said. You make me feel good all over, not just in my *concha*. I think you really like women. A lot of men don't. They just want to *chingarse*.

After sex, they huddled together. Curva nuzzled his neck and entwined her legs with his. Fully relaxed, Billie's fingers combed her tousled hair, and he told her about the vision quest he had undertaken at thirteen and his disappointment at not experiencing a major revelation. He felt he'd failed at becoming a real man. Stroking his arm, she corrected him. No, no, Bee-lee! Your art is filled with visions. The animals you recreate live in the wood you carve. I've heard them breathe and growl. They're alive!

He hadn't thought of his art that way and thanked her, though he had his doubts. And so did his father, who still visited Billie in dreams, wearing the ceremonial dress he had worn as chief. Dropping in from the land of shadows, he couldn't let his son forget who really was the leader.

That disclosure led to Curva telling Billie about Xavier and his visit. Billie didn't seem surprised her dead brother had made an appearance. I see my father all the time, he said, adjusting the black patch on his right eye and caressing it. I guess my father still thinks he's chief. Maybe he is chief in the shadow world. Or maybe he's trying to prepare me for the next life.

Curva said, Maybe Xavier also is preparing me for the next life. Do you believe there's life beyond this one? She played with Billie's ponytail, twining it around her index finger.

Billie nodded. Death doesn't stop the dead from being part of the community. They think they can help us from the other side.

But your father isn't helping you. Tell him to *vayase*, Curva growled. You're the beeg chief now. But I'd like to know how these dead people travel between worlds. Do you think they understand?

Billie sat up. No. They just act the way they always did in life, pursuing what they want. That powerful impulse propels them, dead or alive. You don't know my father. He's not so easy to get rid of, especially now that he's dead.

Si, sometimes the dead don't know when to die. Maybe it's so boring where they are—the place you call the shadow world—they have to leave and visit us. That Xavier. I think the only reason he wanted to see me was to fill his stomach!

Curva laughed, though it sounded more like a growl. Then that turned into one of her belly laughs. It gathered resonance and echoed over the plains, ricocheting between the Rockies and landing on the other side, knocking loose some rocks and scaring a herd of mountain goats.

She rose and slipped on her clothes, flicking away a feeling of being watched. Curva shuddered as a sudden breeze swept through the tent, reminding her of Xavier's earlier visit and suggesting he wasn't far away.

Curva on the Old North Trail

Hola, mi estimado Xavier,

I'm now in America, but there was no sign saying *Hasta la Vista Curva,* and no one in the States said welcome *señorita.* I guess I crossed at a secret place. No *federales* saw me.

It took me *mucho tiempo* to get here. At least five years. Maybe more. You know me: I have trouble keeping track of time.

I wandered into a town that had a good rodeo—Las Cruces. Lots of prize money. It's in a place they call New Me-he-co, but there are lots of *gringos* who only speak *inglés.* It's hard to get used to the language and for them to understand me. In the shops, I tried out a lot of the words I've learned from reading *Don Quixote.* I even strung together some of them. I was buying grain for the road and said, "Too much sanity may be madness—and maddest of all: to see life as it is, and not as it should be!"

Everyone laughed at me. I cursed at them in Spanish, and some Spanish Americans clapped their hands. They understood me.

This is a different world from what I left behind. No *mariachis.* No *fiestas.* I cannot understand these people, Xavier, and they make no attempt to understand me. On the trail, the animals and I speak the same language. We are *simpatico.*

People here seem *muy serio.* I need to hear your laugh again, Xavier. You have the best laugh, so big and round and hearty. Just to hear it makes me laugh too.

There are lots of rodeos in the States, but American *charros* don't like competing with a woman, and I'm sure they would hate losing to one. So I'm already getting a name for myself, busting broncos as Xavier. I can thank you for putting lots of money in my pocket. I can make enough to take me a long way on the trail.

I did run into some trouble at one of the contests. I was in the chutes, getting ready to ride. An American cowboy ran his hand over my crotch. He must be one of those men who love other men. What a shock it was for him to find no *polla*, but he couldn't make a fuss. *Charros* don't like *hombres* who love *hombres*. We exchanged surprised looks that said everything.

What a relief it is to compete in sharpshooting contests. I can be myself then. People come just to see Curva Peligrosa do her tricks. They say I handle a gun like someone named Annie Oakley. I say I only do what comes naturally.

The Calgary Stampede is my goal. Everyone says it's the biggest rodeo around. Then I'll leave the trail for good and quit competing. Buy myself a little farm. Stop pretending I'm you.

But it will be hard to leave the trail for good. Life on it is simple and pure. Like Berumba when we first arrived. I have little sense of time passing except for the changing seasons and nightfall. I don't want to live in clock time, anyway, just counting off the days and years I have left. Why remind myself I'll join you one day in the same place? But if you're there waiting for me, I won't dread it so much.

It's always a shock entering a town and seeing how other people live. Or don't. They get married. Have kids. Work. Most of the women stay home and take care of *bambinos* and drink tea. But they don't have *aventuras grandes* that let them know they're really alive. They don't have *mucho* to look forward to except more more more of the same.

I met one woman in Las Cruces when I was buying supplies for the trail. I was dressed as Curva then. She saw all the bags of flour, sacks of dried beans, and other things I'd bought and asked if I had a restaurant. I said no. I just have a *hermano* with a beeg appetite. Her eyes got the size of tortillas and she watched me pile everything onto the travois.

On the trail I feel I'm in a cocoon like the butterflies I love. I can feel myself changing every day from the girl who was so *inocente* into a *mujer independiente*. I hardly recognize myself.

What will I be when I leave it?

I bought a goat in Las Cruces so I can have goat milk. It also obligingly chews through the bushes that often bar my way. I call it Don Quixote. I like the sound of that name, and Don Quixote is an old goat anyway.

I thought I saw him and Sancho yesterday on their beat-up horses. I tried to catch up with them, but they kept disappearing in the trees. I finally gave up and read more of their stories last night so I could meet them in my dreams. I hope to see you there too, *mi hermano.*

Curva and the Stranger

Curva collected hydras and planarians from nearby sloughs and slipped them into an aquarium where she could study them. She removed one of the planarians she'd named Cupcake from the water, placed it on a work table in the greenhouse, and cut it into pieces, murmuring *lo siento, lo siento,* Cupcake. After, she gently placed the dissected flatworm back in the tank, and every day she watched its prog-

91

ress in producing several little cupcakes, all fully formed, the process taking just a few weeks.

These creatures' ability to recreate themselves fed Curva's imagination. They seemed ageless in that they could continue to replicate. She realized humans did something similar when they had children and passed on their characteristics from one generation to another. She assumed she had done something similar with Sabina. But the hydras and planarians seemed able to not only reproduce but also to continue living indefinitely. Curva wondered how these creatures appeared almost ageless while humans—definitely more complicated—were not.

Curva mused on her experiments while wringing the necks of two chickens she planned to cook for dinner. She was standing in the yard, plucking their feathers and ripping out their guts, when she noticed the progress of a small plane as it dropped out of the sky, bumped across the field, and skidded to a halt in a cloud of dust next to her house. The sun reflected off its metallic surface, making it gleam and creating a halo around the plane. It looked like something from outer space.

Her first thought was, Oh my god, Xavier's learned how to fly and wants me to join him.

She wiped her blood-spattered hands on the flour sack she used as an apron and headed toward the pasture, expecting either her brother or some god to climb out of the machine. When the pilot did appear, he wasn't a god, nor was he Xavier, but he was different from *los hombres* she saw every day in their soiled flannel *camisas* and baggy *pantalones*.

Wearing neatly pressed khaki slacks and a jacket, he climbed out of the cockpit, an immaculate white Stetson planted squarely on his head. He wore a red kerchief around his neck, his skin tanned and weather-beaten—Hollywood's idea of a cowboy.

The two of them reached the fence separating her house from the field at about the same time. He tipped his hat, reached out his other hand, and said, My name's Shirley.

Shirley?

He laughed. Yeah, Shirley. Grandpa's name. Those Englishmen had weird ideas.

Curva nodded: *Sí*.

He waved his hand at the house. Nice spread.

She felt herself blushing, something she hadn't done since she was an *adolescente*. He smelled of aftershave and wealth, speaking with the confidence of someone used to being in charge and having his way. A *funcionario*. It wasn't her world, and she felt unsure of herself. At a loss for words.

Cat got your tongue? he asked and smirked, looking her up and down, his white teeth dazzling against his skin. His eyes lingered on Curva's breasts, making her blush even more from both anger and embarrassment. The heat from her face seeped into her whole body until she felt she was on fire. He reminded her of one of the *lobos* that occasionally turned up in her yard. She wished she were carrying a gun or that Dios were there, but the dog had gone to school with Sabina.

Curva backed away from the fence, relieved that barbed wire separated them.

He laughed again. Don't worry, I won't bite. I'm from Montana. Sweetgrass. Have a big ranch there and I'm interested in buying more land. He extended his arms: I need to spread out. I've been meeting with your neighbors. Know of anything around here that's for sale?

She should have known he was an *americano*. She'd run

into many during her travels. Most of them she liked, but some hit her the wrong way. Shirley was one of those. Normally unflappable and self-assured, Curva found herself momentarily stumbling over *inglés* words. This smooth-talking stranger's male authority made her feel flustered. She fiddled with her apron hem, which had come loose, and bleated, Land?

Yeah. That stuff you're standing on. I want some. I also want the oil that comes with it. He motioned to the plane and said, Mind me parking here while I mosey around a bit?

Her confidence returning, Curva shrugged her shoulders, blurting out, Parking it is no *problema*. But your beeg flying machine might not be here when you get back.

My "beeg" flying machine? You gonna sell it? He took a package of Marlboros from his pocket and lit one. The cigarette dangled from one corner of his mouth, and smoke curled around his head.

Now back in control, Curva said, Maybe I'll take it for a spin.

Sucking deeply on the cigarette, he asked, Have a pilot's license?

Pointing at the sky, she said, No one will ask for my license up there.

Shirley laughed. Want a ride? I'll let you steer.

Curva regretted her boldness. She didn't want to go up in the air with him, even though she wished she could fly like her *pájaros*. Planes passed overhead now and then, and she always wondered what it would be like to soar among the clouds and leave the earth behind.

But concerns about this outsider buying up a lot of land and developing it held her back. Curva had seen big cities and understood the dangers of progress. She also often lamented the fate of Berumba. When she first visited the town, she had found it enchanting—suffused with joy and delight. The residents took pleasure in the simple tasks of growing, preparing, and consuming food. Even though men and women worked hard, they infused their chores with play, singing and dancing in the fields, creating *fiestas* wherever they went, finding time to pleasure each other between the rows of corn. Every moment became an eternity, and they refused to live by clock time. People hardly thought of it passing. Nor did they seem to age.

But Berumba and its inhabitants had lost their innocence because strangers like Shirley had appeared, sparking contact with the outside world and upending the bucolic community. Curva still mourned its passing. Buying up land would only be the beginning. The next thing would be expansion and trains. People would come from all over to settle in Weed, starting new businesses, causing friction with existing establishments and complicating everyone's lives. Her little Eden would no longer exist. Let the *americano* bring progress somewhere else.

She said, I thought you were looking for land.

Plenty of time for that. First things first. If the little lady wants a ride, I'm all for seeing she gets one. Does the little lady have a name?

Angry at being called a little lady—she was as tall as he and around the same age—she felt her face flame again and refused to speak. "Little lady" were the words the *americano* had used when she was bidding for the farm. Shirley was the same *hombre* that had tried to buy the property she now owned.

Sounds like the cat has got her tongue, he said, staring at her intently. He motioned at the plane: You ready for some fun?

Curva turned away, concerned about the desire this brash visitor stirred in her. I have other things to do, she said.

Ah, come on. You've got a few minutes to spare. Let me take you for an outing. You won't regret it. Is there a gate so you don't get your pretty self caught on this barbed wire?

Her pretty self? As much as Curva distrusted this man and his motives, her head was in a whirl at being treated like a *señorita*. It scared her because she liked his attention, but she also was determined to resist him. Yet the thought of following the butterflies' migratory path and experiencing flight herself weakened her resolve.

She pointed to the other end of the field.

He said, Meet you there.

After untying the apron and dropping it to the ground, she found herself at the gate, passing through it to the other side. Hand on her elbow, Shirley guided Curva to the plane's interior. Most men were intimidated by her height and treated her as if she were one of them, so this gesture was a new experience. Curva almost pulled away, but she liked the warmth from his *mano* on her skin. And it wasn't unpleasant to feel protected, even if he was an untrustworthy *americano* lusting after the land.

As they took off, the plane rocked back and forth several times, the motion making Curva's stomach lurch. The turbulence gave her a good jostling, throwing her onto Shirley's lap, her flailing arm knocking off his Stetson. He groped Curva's leg and grabbed a breast. Curva slapped at his hand and fell back into her seat, enjoying the game in spite of herself. He laughed, though it sounded more like a growl, and pointed outside.

Curva wasn't prepared for the view. The clouds swirled

around them at times, then broke to reveal the landscape far below. She could look down on people and animals moving in the fields, the land a pastel patchwork of pastures that blended into the foothills. She gasped as they approached the snow-capped tips of the Rockies, on the same level as the plane. She didn't need to think about gutting chickens or watching the *niños* or working in the greenhouse. She could have stayed there forever, time suspended. Did eternal life feel like this?

Shirley interrupted her reverie. Where's this greenhouse I've heard so much about?

Greenhouse?

Hell, everyone I've run into is talking about someone named Curva and her greenhouse. They say it's constantly changing shape.

Curva let loose with one of her belly laughs. It shook the plane even harder than the wind gusts, this time jolting Shirley from his seat and into Curva's arms. He looked startled, his composure shaken. With no one at the wheel, the plane flipped. The two of them fumbled at each other, trying to right the lurching craft, the ground suddenly looming. Shirley cursed, grabbing the wheel, and wrestled with the aircraft until it leveled again.

A little close for comfort, he said, his voice shaking, strands from his carefully Brylcreemed hair flopping onto his forehead. You okay? he asked.

Curva didn't hear his question. The ride reminded her of when the tornado had picked up her outhouse and hurled it through the air. She hadn't felt fear then. It had happened too fast for her to feel anything except excitement in the pit of her stomach, not unlike sexual arousal. Nor was she frightened when the *avion* went topsy-turvy. Something in her thrilled at being out of control, neither here nor there, at the mercy of fate and natural forces.

It's why the Old North Trail had appealed to her so much. While traveling on it, she had to react moment by moment to whatever crossed her path, and there was always something unexpected or threatening happening. Like the rattlesnake she surprised one day, sunning on the trail. Without thinking, she'd grabbed its tail and flung it into the bushes. Later, she chastised herself for being so reckless: Curva, Curva. What you did was *loca*. That *serpiente* could have killed you with its poison.

Shirley's voice interrupted her thoughts: You're a cool one, all right. I think you like being tossed around like a salad.

Curva glanced at him, realizing she'd run into another rattler and needed to be careful how she handled him. Nothing would be sacred to the *americano*. He would take, take, take and leave nothing in return.

She looked out the window again. They were now passing over her greenhouse. Excited, she pointed at the roof glinting in the sun. There it is, she said, the famous *cristal* house.

It attracted light like a jewel. The sun struck the slick surface from many angles, making it appear to be floating, its facade reflecting the surrounding sky, clouds, and mountains.

So that's it, Shirley said, circling the building. He flew over several times. You think she's inside it?

Curva pressed her face against the window, thinking she caught a glimpse of herself on the *tierra* below or maybe inside the structure itself. She shrugged her shoulders and said, You never know with Curva. She could be anywhere.

Shirley guided the plane for one last pass, appearing reluctant to leave. I didn't realize it was so close to your place, he said.

Curva just smiled and changed the subject. Let's fly over the town, she said. I want to see the Blackfoot burial ground.

Burial ground? In town? He laughed. Is the land for sale? Maybe I'll buy it.

You crazy? The Indians have the government on their side. The burial ground belongs to them now. It's shaken up the whole town.

She pointed to the earth that was dug up and piled in mounds. There, she said. See it?

He nodded, turning the wheel so they could loop over it again.

Seeing the heaps of dirt from this height helped Curva to understand Billie's *pasión* for those bones and his desire to preserve them. It was clearer from the air that they belonged there as much as Weed's newer structures or residents did. A door to the past, the bones not only gave Billie's ancestors the importance they deserved, but they also promised a future that embraced the Blackfoot as well as an earlier age. And all were part of the collective memory, indigenous or not.

Shirley nudged her. Hey, old girl, getting airsick?

She nodded and let out a hearty laugh, the reverberations making the plane rock and roll again. Shirley clung to the wheel until the turbulence lessened and let out a deep breath. You know, you've got powerful lungs, woman.

They passed over the town one more time, and the school doors opened. Curva watched all of the *niños* pile out. She saw Sabina and Victor running down the road, heading for her place. Curva usually provided them with target practice after school.

Land this thing, Curva said. I've got things to do.

At your service, he said, banking the plane and making a wide circle. The unexpected tilt caused Curva to cling to her seat, and she whooped.

Shirley said, You'll wake the dead.

You mean I'm in heaven now?

As close to it as you're likely to get, he said.

I'll be in heaven before you ever get there.

Shirley leaned over and kissed her full on the mouth, forcing his tongue between her teeth. She'd had better kisses. This one was too wet. But she felt a little thrill anyway to be in the sky with this powerful stranger and didn't pull away. Nor did she slap him.

When they landed, she didn't wait for him to help her out of the plane but jumped to the ground herself, Shirley following. She said, People around here don't care much for strangers trying to buy up their land.

Curva turned away and strode off, disappearing minutes later inside the greenhouse.

He took off his Stetson and scratched his head, muttering, You don't say.

Curva in Motion

The ride in Shirley's plane not only gave Curva a new perspective, but it also put her in motion in other ways. She needed to reach her neighbors before Shirley did. Curva wasn't going to let this *gringo* carry out his plan without a fight. One way to deal with snakes was to get down in the grass with them, to monitor their movements. She intended to keep a close eye on the *americano*.

The next day, a Saturday, Curva, headed into town wearing dark *gauchos*, a white shirt with billowing sleeves, and a royal blue poncho. Speeding over the gravel roads in her

100

battered pickup, stones pinging against the rusted exterior, Dios in the passenger seat, she pretended she was piloting a plane. Clouds of dust followed her.

Curva hoped to catch many of her neighbors doing their weekly shopping or hanging out at the Odd Fellows Hall. Later, she planned to bring Billie and his workers a lunch of enchiladas she had made. Recalling how fresh everything had looked from the plane, she sang

De colores, de colores se visten los campos en la primavera
De colores, de colores son los pajaritos que vienen de afuera
De colores, de colores es el arco iris que vemos lucir
Y por eso los grandes amores de muchos colores me gustan a mí
Y por eso los grandes amores de muchos colores me gustan a mí[3]

It wasn't just the feeling of renewal in the air and the respite from the long winter. She literally felt lighter, and, of course, she was. She didn't need to wear as many layers of clothing. She had more bounce to her step, and the days were getting lighter, too, the sky not darkening until well after 9 p.m. All of her plants, inside and outside the greenhouse, perked up as well, receiving more hours of sunshine each day, responding to her ministrations of fertilizer and water and song. It was time to leave hibernation.

Not that Curva hibernated exactly; she was too active for that. But she did live differently during the winter. She confined herself primarily to her farm, minding the greenhouse and animals, her trips to town limited to shopping,

---

3 All the colors, all the colors, oh how they dress up the countryside in springtime, All the colors, all the colors of birdies, oh how they come back to us outside, All the colors, all the colors in rainbows we see shining bright in the sky, And that's why a great love of the colors makes me feel like singing so joyfully, And that's why a great love of the colors makes me feel like singing so joyfully.

the occasional Saturday night dance, and practicing her midwifery and healing arts. Now it felt good to be flying over the country roads, free of winter's weight and restrictions. She didn't have to constantly dig out her truck and create pathways to her front steps, greenhouse, outhouse, or barn. Nor did she need to slow for ice patches.

At Smart's General Store, Curva skidded to a stop. Her truck shuddered and rattled, all of its parts settling. Curva switched off the ignition and slid out the door, patting the exterior as if it were a horse. She waved at Inez Wilson, who carried a shopping bag and was wearing a rumpled floral housedress. Curva flashed her gold tooth, and the two women stopped to chat, commenting on the weather and the previous Saturday night dance, laughing at some remembrance. She leaned over and whispered in Inez's ear, swinging her own hips and gesturing to them. The two laughed uproariously.

From inside the store, Nathan Smart hollered, The bloody clocks have stopped again. Curva's nearby. It wasn't just Smart's Store that felt the effect. In houses up and down the block, not only did clocks stop, but also watches slid off people's wrists, some breaking on brittle floors. Their interiors scattered under furniture along with dust balls, waiting to be collected and reassembled. Time temporarily stood still.

And that was fine with Curva. If everyone could get lost in the present, then Shirley didn't have a chance, and she could stop worrying about him buying up land. But if all the Weedites could think of were future profits, of the *dinero* earned by sale and development, then the blight that had destroyed Berumba would hit Weed. However, she knew how fickle time could be and how transitory her powers were. Neither Curva nor anyone could control it. So she

102

spoke to everybody inside and outside Smart's General Store, as well as at the Odd Fellows Hall, warning her neighbors with passionate conviction that while Shirley's offer might sound good, they would end up losing not just their land but also their souls.

He wants to take over our lives, she shouted, her face flushed. He'll bring in his wealthy oil people, and they'll rule everything. You might have more money in your pockets, but you won't have peace of mind again.

They all stared at her, partially taking in what she was saying. Later, they gathered in small groups, chewing over her words, not sure whom to trust, the *americano* or the *mexicano*. Though she had lived in their midst for a few years, some still felt uncertain about Curva, and Shirley had stirred up their earlier concerns by calling her a wetback—an illegal alien. Since most were aware of her unusual abilities, some Weedites didn't want to offend her even if she wasn't legal, especially the more adventurous women that had sought her out. They weren't going to rat on her. They told their husbands that selling their oil rights could cause women to conduct a mass strike—in the bedroom. Those who had befriended Curva didn't want to lose her midwifery skills or access to her kitchen and greenhouse. In her presence, they always felt more alive. But others, the more conservative townspeople, refused to let this former stranger from Mexico determine their futures. If they wanted to sell their mineral rights or land to the *americano*, they would, Curva be damned.

Upset that many hadn't heard her pleas, Curva sought comfort from Billie. She drove straight to the burial ground and parked next to his truck. She liked watching him separate the tribal bones from the dinosaur relics, a way for him to reclaim his tribe's past. She believed Billie and the bones held a key to something she was searching for. Her earlier encounter with the bones fornicating and dancing at midnight in the graveyard showed they were still filled with life, even in their most frangible state. They also reminded her of the many lives that had gone before, human and otherwise. It was important not to forget that period. Otherwise, the prairies had no depth, no history, no roots.

But the bones also possessed another kind of life, and that's what intrigued her the most. During the night, they changed positions, surprising even Billie and his workers. As for the fossils, they, too, didn't always remain in one place, puzzling everyone that had observed them. Yet there were many times when the bones didn't reorganize themselves. Death seemed as unpredictable as life and even more intriguing.

For the Blackfoot, preserving these bones was essential to their identity. Because their present culture had been so diminished, their ancestors' bones surfacing from under the soil helped to define them. Like the bones, much was underground or otherwise out of sight—their rituals, beliefs, and customs disparaged outside of the reservation. But Curva knew from her work with plants how much happened beneath the surface, invisible but powerful. The roots, the plant's lifeline, worked in the dark to absorb nutrients from the soil that were then passed along to leaves, vegetables, and flowers. They in turn converted sunlight into energy that stimulated the ongoing process. This dynamic helped her to appreciate Billie's belief in a land of the dead. The bones were a bridge between the mortal world and what was beyond. These remains also behaved like plant roots for the lives that continued above ground, bringing nourishment through visions and dreams and other visits.

Curva found Billie kneeling over a depression in the earth, his hair tied back in a ponytail, his overalls coated with dirt.

Are you digging yourself a grave, Bee-lee?

He glanced up at her, motioning for her to come closer and gesturing excitedly at the ground, a smile breaking across his face: Look at what I've found!

Curva fell on her knees next to him and stared at the assemblage of stone scrapers, chisels, arrowheads, knives, and pottery fragments. She whistled and said, Your ancestors took all these treasures with them to the grave?

Billie nodded: They must have felt they needed them wherever they were going. I know I'd feel better if I weren't buried alone. We've been finding jewelry, tools, and food alongside the bones.

Curva said, I guess taking their precious possessions made them feel there really was an afterlife.

Billie gave a thumbs up and said, But they didn't all have personal things buried with them. Sometimes the bones were laid to rest alone in bundles or baskets. He paused before saying, Maybe they were the outcasts.

Your face looks like a dark cloud just landed on it, Bee-lee.

He pulled a scarlet handkerchief from his shirt pocket and wiped his forehead before answering. You know what I'm thinking. Outcast. Those feelings never go away.

You're not an outcast to me.

Billie stared at the mounds, looking pensive, and waved his hand. There's a whole miniature world here. The remains have been placed inside these mounds—all in different positions. On their backs. On their sides. Face down. Sitting. It's amazing!

No wonder I can't pull you away from here, Bee-lee. It appears these remains complete the family you've always wanted.

Maybe. Now if I could just get them to speak. What stories they would tell! Raids. Rapes. Betrayals. Hunting tales. Love triangles.

You can tell their tales in the wonderful murals you showed me.

He slapped his thigh. Of course! I never thought of that.

Curva sat on the ground, knees bent, arms wrapped around her legs, and said, We live as if we're in a tomb already.

Whaddya mean?

In our homes we surround ourselves with things we love, just like your ancestors did when they died. It's as if we are really dead in life, and the things we have make the days bearable.

Billie nodded: So our ancestors were just trying to continue their lives in the next world.

Curva laughed. I want to continue my life in this world. You know me: I want everything. But if I have to go, I want enchiladas buried with me. And lots of dandelion wine. Maybe a copy of *Don Quixote*. In *español*. It must get boring in the grave. I think that's why Xavier visits me.

You'd find something to make it interesting.

Sí, some bones! You know me and *huesos*, Bee-lee. Especially yours. It drives me *loca!*

She pushed herself off the ground, picked up the container of enchiladas, and rotated her hips like a belly dancer. Nodding at the tent, she said, Let's go have lunch. I'm hungry.

But the enchiladas had to wait.

After, they lay in each other's arms, Billie stroking Curva's hair and back, kissing her closed eyes. Curva moaned: You hit all the right notes, Bee-lee. It's hard to believe you haven't had more women in your life.

She gazed at him and touched the black eye covering. You've been inside my dark patch, she said, touching her bush. But you haven't let me see behind yours. What's hidden there?

Billie pulled away and said, I don't like to remember how I lost that eye.

Curva stroked his back and gave him fish kisses where her fingers had been. I know what you mean, she said. I don't like to think about all the development that's going to happen here once Shirley starts buying leases and drilling for oil. No one seems to understand. She shivers.

Billie turns to her and says, Could I offer you some tasty enchiladas? They're guaranteed to chase away any concerns.

Curva laughs and says, You know the way to a woman's heart, Bee-lee.

Two

Bone Song

Raven found a clam
after the flood and
discovered humans
inside. He let them
out, shell cracking.

Billie One Eye

Billie didn't have just one cowlick; he had at least ten. They all flew in different directions, following their own laws, defying any attempts to be greased in place. They made him even more self-conscious about the blue eyes and red hair he'd inherited from his mother, along with his father's darker skin. His strange appearance made Billie stand out on the reservation—or off. It also made it difficult for Billie's father to accept his son fully, though the father felt differently towards Billie's three sisters because they didn't resemble their mother.

Billie's mother was a Scot whom the Blackfoot had named Sighing Turtle. She had left her children when Billie was eight because her husband was uncommunicative and the tribe had never fully embraced her. She represented the world outside the rez—the one that rejected them—and served as a constant reminder of their imagined inferiority. While she had tried to help all the children learn how to read and write after school, tutoring the slower ones, it only alienated Sighing Turtle further. Soon men and women were complaining: Who does that bitch think she is, they hissed, filling our kids' heads with her highfalutin' ideas? As a result, Billie's father also spurned her, making it impossible for Sighing Turtle to remain.

The situation created many conflicts for Billie. The other boys had made cracks about Sighing Turtle. Robin Falling Star had called her a whore, extending the word so it sounded like "whoooo-her." Billie's friends also teased him mercilessly about his cowlicks: Hey, Billie, ya got bird feathers growin' outta your head. Billie struck out blindly with his fists. A lousy fighter, he was unable to defend himself properly and constantly got the worst of it.

That's how he lost his right eye in the schoolyard when he was ten. He'd been fighting again, arms flailing, pelting the air. The boys had crowded around Billie, and he dove into their midst, hearing only the clatter of shoes scuffling against hard-packed dirt, grunts, and fists popping off bone. He had punched wildly, stumbling and falling onto a stick one of the other boys happened to be holding. At least that was the story Billie's schoolmates had given, and everyone more or less believed it.

Except Billie. He knew that Robin had poked him on purpose. They'd been rivals since Billie beat him at casting "arrows," plain sticks they hurled like darts, trying to outdistance each other—one thing Billie excelled at. Robin and the others were also out to get him because Billie's dad was the tribal chief. They wanted to cut Billie down to size. With the whole group against him, it would only make matters worse if Billie squealed.

His teacher, a nun, had rushed him to the hospital in the city, but it was too late. He lost the right eye, though he gained the others' respect for not blabbing. Being one-eyed gave Billie some status, as did the black eye patch he now wore, imparting a slightly menacing look. Subsequently, the guys left him alone, feeling guilty for their part in the fight, but Billie never let down his guard.

Losing an eye was no small thing: It altered how he viewed his surroundings, reducing his peripheral vision, at least on one side, and giving him a skewed perspective. He felt certain something was constantly rushing at him from his right side, so he developed a kind of twitch, frequently jerking his head to the right, hoping he'd spot his attacker before he struck.

After the incident, Billie became more of a loner. He avoided Robin and his group or he hung out with the older boys who accepted him more. Or he played arrows with his three sisters, all younger than he. Other times he sprawled on the prairie grass, watching the clouds change shape and imagining new places to explore. A hole had opened inside him that he liked to burrow into, temporarily forgetting his feelings of isolation.

Stampede

In early July, the Calgary Stampede—the annual rodeo and fair that attracted people from all over the world—started. Each year, Billie trekked to the festivities with his tribe. They traveled the Blackfoot trail in the old manner, using horses to pull wagons loaded with tepees and supplies for the week, camping along the way. It was a great holiday, a chance to escape the rez and enjoy a featured role at the exhibition. They set up their teepees in the Blackfoot Village at the fairgrounds, near the entrance, providing a Wild West atmosphere. In return, they received free passes to all the rides and the grandstand.

Billie loved to wander through the exhibit halls, gawking at the arts and crafts on display. He especially liked the drawings and paintings, marveling at how the artists could create something on a piece of paper or canvas that hadn't existed before. When he tried to do something similar, using a pencil to draw an image, he felt frustrated, unable to make anything recognizable appear on the page. A few squiggly lines didn't add up to much. They resembled the stick figures his ancestors had drawn on rocks to describe a hunt they'd made—or some other scene. He wanted to do better than those old-time drawings.

The exhibition halls also dazzled him with their unusual smells and sights and sounds: a blend of scratchy country-western records playing in the background, Hank Williams belting out "I'm so lonesome I could cry"; objects clanking together and dropping; and human voices buzzing. He watched salesmen demonstrate potato peelers and slicers, toasters, Mixmasters, and other things he'd never seen before. The Blackfoot lived pretty basic lives, just getting by, and everyone was poor. No one had much, except for discarded items the white people gave them—clothes and appliances and gadgets that had outgrown their usefulness, most of which the Indians couldn't use either.

Billie hadn't thought of himself as poor before. He believed the way he lived was normal, that the rez was the world: everything he needed had seemed to be there. But this year, he understood how mistaken he'd been. Another realm existed outside of what he'd known all of his life—maybe more than one realm. He liked what he saw.

The peddlers' products intrigued Billie, as did the sellers, so sure of themselves and skilled at the patter they'd developed. "Step right up, ladies and gentlemen! Come in closer, little lady: you'll catch cold standing back there all by yourself. I'm going to show you something today that will change your life. Gentlemen, have your wallets ready so you don't lose out on this great buy...."

They talked non-stop, not considering each word carefully as Billie did. He felt shy with people he didn't know. The salesmen's self-confidence drew him in, their voices honey, dripping with sweetness and promise. Billie just wished he had money to buy these things. He wanted to take the shimmering icons home to worship.

After he spent hours wandering about the exhibitions,

he attended the rodeo. He stood right up against the wire fence so he wouldn't miss anything, staring with his one eye through a diamond-shaped gap. The bulls and steers shot out of the chutes, riders flailing on their backs, one hand holding the rope circling the animals' bodies, the other trying to balance the rider and appearing to grasp the air for support. Neither the rope nor the air had much to offer. The riders hurtled through space, landing in a humbled heap on the ground. The uninjured riders stood up, brushed off their jeans and shirts, planted their Stetsons squarely on their heads, and slunk off so the next victim could take his turn.

So much depended on the luck of the draw—the ride you'd been given. It was difficult to outride an unbroken animal. A few people did it, many of them Indians that outshined the cowpokes. The rodeo was the one area where they could excel. And that kept Billie glued to the fence until the last rider had plunged into the arena and taken his chances. He identified with those that did succeed. Their triumph gave him hope.

Billie also liked the Stampede because it was one of the few times when his father wore his ceremonial clothes, including a feathered headdress that reached his knees. Billie and the other tribal members dressed like "Indians" in their traditional buckskin and beaded moccasins, performing in the streets and at the Stampede grounds. Billie's favorite was the chicken dance, the performers imitating prairie chickens mating. The good ones could make their feather bustle and headgear vibrate so fast that they resembled frenzied chickens. But not Billie. He had two left feet, and he never could get the movements right. Worse, his red hair and black eye patch caused Stampede visitors to stare at him and ignore the others.

Still, during these times, he felt that being a Blackfoot was something to be proud of. He liked seeing his father sitting tall on his horse, assuming the official status of chief during the daily parades. The animal tossed its head, decorated with a beaded halter and mantle, its mane and tail also woven with a rainbow of multi-colored beads. Both man and horse seemed transformed by the decorations and gave Billie someone to look up to and admire, not just to fear.

Vision Quest

At thirteen, Billie longed to go on a vision quest. He'd heard his father and his father's friends talk about their vision quests. In preparation, they had purified themselves by burning sage, cedar, and sweetgrass. Then they had gone off alone into nature and fasted for four days, having neither food nor water. They prayed, smoked a sacred pipe, and presented gifts to the spirits, hoping to be rewarded with a vision or a voice from the spirit world that would guide their future lives.

But gathering their medicine bundle together was equally important. It involved killing an animal—usually a deer because its skin was strong, soft, and durable—and skinning it. The men used part of the hide, filling it with a collection of symbolic objects that might include an unusual rock, a strand of hair, a feather, a bird's beak, an animal skin, or sweetgrass—items related to their vision quest that could evoke their guardian spirit. It helped if they got instructions in a vision about what to put in their bundles. Yet Billie knew that not all did, and most men made it up as they went along.

The rite was no longer popular among Billie's friends, but that only increased its appeal for him. Since he'd been marked from birth as different, a half-breed outcast, he chose to do things his friends weren't doing. Hoping to bolster his Blackfoot heritage, he was attracted to many rituals the other guys laughed at. Besides, with only one eye, Billie needed all the extra vision he could get. Thus he set off alone to a remote area, hoping to fast until he contacted the spirit world.

At the end of his quest, he wanted to return with his own medicine bundle containing magic charms to protect him from further harm. It would prove his manhood and give him stature within the tribe.

And acceptance.

He hoped.

Before leaving on his quest, Billie snuck into the ramshackle shed behind the house and found his father's medicine bundle, tucked inside his fishing tackle. The light was too dim to see much, so he fingered the supple, well-worn hide that held his father's medicine. Billie was unable to associate the soft surface with the man who seemed made of granite. The tribal chief never showed any emotion towards Billie, shunning his son just as he had turned against Sighing Turtle.

Billie froze as the door hinges squeaked and a shadow fell across him. The chief whacked Billie on the head, snatched the bundle from his hands, and snarled, Beat it. Billie didn't wait around for another wallop and lit out across the fields, still feeling the sting of his father's fingers. But the man's strong reaction roused Billie's curiosity even more. What was he protecting? Maybe he kept his heart in that smooth purse. Or perhaps his father's guardian spirit lived inside the bundle and his father was afraid of losing it. Billie also wanted his own protector, certain that if he'd had one when he was younger, he might never have lost his eye.

Early the next morning, he wrote a note to his family that said "GON ON VISIN QEUST," headed to the horse pasture, and borrowed his father's mare. After putting a halter on the horse's head and throwing a blanket over its body, he tried to leap on its back, imitating Indians he'd seen in movies that seemed to be the real thing.

Instead of landing on the horse, Billie flew over it, hitting the ground with a thud. He'd stuffed his satchel with a jacket, tobacco, cigarette papers, and matches—lacking a pipe, he'd need to use cigarettes in its place for sacred smoke—and it cushioned his fall. Luckily, it was just before dawn, and no one else was there to witness his humiliation. After a few more failed attempts at being a real Indian, he finally led the animal to the corral fence and climbed it, mounting that way.

Mid-July, the weather was warm, so at least he wouldn't freeze. Billie guided the horse over the prairies toward the foothills as *Natosi*, the sun, made its ascent for the day, lighting the fields and causing the grain to glow. He understood why his forefathers had worshipped the sun. It transformed the appearance of things—changing night into day, wheat into gold. It even made the distant snow-capped mountains peaks appear lit from within until gradually all of them became illuminated, the sky tinged a powdery pink. The sight reminded him of how much he loved the earth and everything on it.

He rode until *Natosi* was high in the sky, finally settling in a valley near the Bow River where the prairie grass was taller than Billie in places and cottonwood trees competed for space. After tethering the horse in an area where it could graze, he spread his blanket on a huge, flat rock he planned to sleep on that was near the water. Then he took off his clothes and stepped into a pool that gradually became deeper. Rough stones cut into the soles of his feet, making him holler, as did the biting cold water.

He forced himself to dip all of his body, including his head, startled to find himself eyeball to eyeball with *Ksisk-staki*, a beaver that Billie must have disturbed with all of his yelling. Viewing it underwater distorted the size of the beaver's eyes and protruding front teeth, making them appear much larger, turning the animal into a monster. Billie scrabbled for shore, stumbling and tripping on slippery rocks, climbing finally onto dry land. The beaver took off in the opposite direction towards its dam.

Billie lay on the rock he'd chosen, his heartbeat returning to a familiar trot and not a gallop, letting the sun dry and purify his body. Its rays played on the surface of his skin, heating it, filling him with warmth. Eyes closed, he idly fingered his penis, enjoying his casual strokes. It stiffened, becoming a focus of pleasure.

He tried to forget the fright he'd just had, wanting to clear his mind and prepare for a vision. But the more Billie struggled to be empty and receptive, the more he was flooded with images. He didn't see monsters from the deep but a cluster of naked women, young and old, slender and voluptuous, indigenous and white, so vivid he was convinced they were real. They called to him, offering their breasts, their pubic areas resembling furry animals—soft, velvety, and welcoming, containing good medicine.

He forgot his reason for being there and spent the afternoon in this altered state, bathed in fantasies of being buried in the bosoms of these women, sucking on their nipples. Their fingers touched him all over, urging him to

117

one orgasm after another. Before he knew it, the sun was hovering over the horizon, resembling the tip of his own flaming penis. His hands were worn out, unable to produce another drop, his semen seeping into the dry prairie soil and drying in a crust on the rock. Never had he been so aroused. Or so spent.

Feeling weak from his exertion and lack of food or drink, he managed to dress and move the horse to a better grazing area. Then he wrapped himself in the blanket and sat cross-legged on the rock, remembering his purpose for being there. He sent prayers to the sky, the sun, the moon, and the earth, asking for a vision and a guardian spirit. Everyone, he was sure, requested a vision and a guardian spirit. But he also wanted his sight returned and to fly.

To help him focus, he took the tobacco and cigarette papers from his bag and rolled a cigarette, lit it, and puffed furiously, hoping a vision might materialize from the smoke. But it just made him lightheaded and a bit woozy.

Before dark fully descended, he built a fire within a circle of stones he'd arranged on the large rock, using tumbleweed and sagebrush to start it, feeding the blaze with some logs he'd found nearby. The flames would keep away any dangerous animals. Within its embrace, he felt safe, protected from black bears, or coyotes, or wolves—or whatever else lurked out there, including the underwater monster that had scared him so.

A squall blew in abruptly and tore at him from all sides, shrieking like a banshee. Lightning streaked across the sky, zipping up and down and back and forth. Thunder immediately followed, shaking the ground, a downpour not far behind. The fire hissed and spit before fizzling out.

Billie felt fully exposed on his rock, and he remembered

how dangerous lightning could be on the prairies: Anyone sitting or standing in open space could become a lightning rod. One of his father's friends had been killed that way, fried by a bolt. Hugging the boulder and absorbing the heat it still retained from the sun, Billie flattened himself on his stomach underneath the horse blanket, rain pelting his back. He wondered if he should jump on the horse and make a run for home.

The animal whinnied and snorted. Spooked by the electrical storm, the horse reared and tore at its tether, snapping it easily, and took off. The sound of galloping hooves hitting the earth echoed hollowly in the distance. The boy's only companion, and his ride, had fled.

The night darkened, closing in around him. Billie was sure he heard growls and rustlings, making him jittery. Huddling under the sodden blanket, he waited for a voice to speak from the darkness in response to his vision quest. But all he heard was the rain attacking the hard ground, his own thudding heart, and the river's constant babbling in the background. It sounded like many voices all speaking at once, none making any sense.

Later, after the rain stopped, cumulus clouds drifted to the outer edges of the night sky. They resembled a fringe of white hair on a bald pate, lit up by *Kokomi-kisomman*, an almost-full moon. Shivering, Billie rolled over and stared at the stars piercing the darkness. Satellites streaked across the sky. A boundless universe beckoned, making earthbound creatures seem plodding, dull, and unimaginative. Out there in the stratosphere was where he wanted to be. But the earth held him captive—the rock unyielding beneath him, the blanket reeking of horse sweat. He was a magnet for whatever creatures lurked in the shadows. Except now everything was a shadow, Billie included.

Eventually he couldn't fight off sleep and sank into a dreamless slumber. A growl woke him at dawn, so loud that he sat up, startled, shivering from cold and fear, forgetting where he was. Another growl slashed him. Billie jumped off the rock and grabbed a stick, flailing out in all directions. At least he'd go down fighting. The next growl sounded so close that he couldn't separate it from himself. Relieved and feeling foolish, he realized it was his own empty stomach he was hearing, howling for food.

Billie was grateful to see the sun return to the sky and to leave the night behind. He decided to keep himself busy, hoping to forget the hunger burning a hole within. First he hung his damp clothes and blanket on some bushes to dry. Then he spread out his tobacco, cigarette papers, and matches in the sun. Hoping to avoid a repeat of the previous night, Billie made himself a more comfortable bed. Using his knife, he slashed a stack of thick pine branches from nearby trees and spread them on the rock, interweaving them, planning to use the brush both as mattress and cover in case it rained again. He could burrow inside the branches, an animal himself.

The sun nibbled away at the morning chill, making the day more inviting. He decided to hunt something whose skin he could dry and use for his medicine bag, maybe an elk or a deer or a coyote. Billie wanted a bigger bundle than his father's to prove he was one of the *Ni-tsi-ta-pi-ksi*—the real people.

After getting dressed and smoking a cigarette for breakfast, Billie was ready for the hunt. He sharpened his knife on a stone and stabbed the air with it a few times before tucking it into his waistband and puffing out his chest. Then he remembered to make up a few good hunting prayers, chanting them while he danced around the boulder he used for a bed, primed and ready to hunt.

There was one problem: The sun had gathered Billie's potential victims within its cloak of light, and there wasn't anything to hunt. All the animals he'd heard in the night had completely disappeared, as if inhaled by *Natosi's* rays. Occasionally a mouse zipped through the tall grass, or a snake. A few lizards posed on nearby rocks, sunning themselves, their heads jerking back and forth, watching for predators. None appeared.

Then Billie remembered the beaver he'd seen in the river, but there was no way he could trap it. The animal had looked too ferocious underwater. Besides, all the beaver spirits and the government officials would hound him till the end of his days if Billie killed a major emblem of Canada —a rodent.

He followed the river upstream, hoping to find a few thirsty creatures he could take by surprise. He'd heard the men bragging about things they'd slain and listened to their descriptions of holding down an animal with one hand and piercing between its ribs with a knife. These stories were so familiar he was sure he could do it himself. Blindfolded.

The sun passed the mid-day point, making its descent, and the sky was clouding up, but still no luck. Billie collected some rocks and feathers and bones to put in his bundle, yet he still hadn't found an appropriate animal to kill. Desperate, he chased a few rabbits, but they all got away.

Then he spotted a squirrel. Moving quickly, he pounced on it, trapping it under his body. It wouldn't make much of a bundle, but it would be better than nothing. The squirrel chattered and squirmed beneath him, trying to escape. Billie huddled over the animal, not sure what to do next. His knife was tucked into his waistband, difficult to reach in this position without releasing the squirrel. If he wanted to kill it, he'd have to squash the animal with his full body weight and hope it would suffocate quickly.

He could smell the creature's fear and feel its body trembling beneath his own. The squirrel's fear became Billie's, its thundering heart inseparable from the boy's, vibrating the earth beneath them. He let the squirrel go. It scampered up a tree, chattering in protest, not resting until it reached the highest branches. There it crouched, black eyes alert, like bullets aimed at Billie. He watched the animal, his heartbeat returning to normal, relieved he hadn't killed it.

When Billie was just eleven, he'd quenched his taste for carnage, hoping to impress his father, who had given him a BB gun. Billie knocked off birds right and left, briefly earning his father's praise. But after killing a magpie one day, he'd heard massive chirping from a nearby tree. He'd climbed it and found the bird's nest and its babies. Realizing they wouldn't survive without their mother, he swore then he would never slay another living creature.

Billie shook off this painful memory. The rain came suddenly, big drops the size of quarters. He raced back to his makeshift camp and burst into a clearing, surprising a coyote hunched over a rabbit. The coyote, frightened by Billie's sudden appearance and blood dripping from its mouth, bolted, heading off into the bush, leaving its prey behind.

And that's how Billie ended up with a skin to hold his medicine bundle. Since rabbits were so fertile, he also kept the tail for good luck. The well-known fertility of rabbits would guarantee his own sexual potency. Later, when he told his father and the others about his adventure, the story would shift somewhat. It was he who killed the rabbit, not the coyote.

That night, exhausted, his matches safely stowed under the rock that was now his bed, Billie slept soundly, tucked into his nest of branches, too tired and hungry to be afraid. He dreamt he was a bird, waiting for his parents to bring him food. He woke with his mouth open—parched, expectant. No one appeared with food, but the wind visited, whirling around him, rustling the trees and scudding the clouds across the still moonlit sky, sounding like a long drawn-out moan.

He went back to sleep, sinking into an erotic dream that ended in ejaculation. It woke him. The sound of water splashing over rocks in the river made him aware of how thirsty he was, but he couldn't break his fast, though he did manage to dredge up saliva and wet his mouth with it.

The sky gradually lightened. He'd now spent two nights there and was beginning to doubt he'd have a vision or find a guardian spirit. While *Naa-to-yi-ta-piiksi*, the spirit beings, chose not to appear to just anyone and Billie may have undertaken this torture for nothing, it still seemed worth the effort. He hoped it would show the others in his tribe that he was one of them. He also longed to be one of the *Minipoka*, the favored children on the rez.

To pass the time until he received a vision, he sat on his rock and carved shapes out of pieces of wood he'd found by the river, gift offerings to the spirits—dogs, men, women, children, horses. By the end of the day, he had numerous figures surrounding him, his own village. And he was the chief. Billie also carved himself a pipe because the rain had ruined his cigarette papers. It would be a sacred pipe much

123

like one the elders passed around their ceremonial circle, their heads wreathed in its smoke.

Since it had turned cool, he built a fire. Then he put tobacco in his pipe and lit up, swallowing the smoke rather than inhaling it, pretending it was food, holding it inside as long as possible, wanting to feel full again. Gasping for air, he finally released a big puff that hovered over his village, mingling with the campfire smoke. That's when he saw the beaver standing nearby, its bright beady eyes staring at Billie. Certain the pipe had given him a vision, he sucked in another mouthful, hoping for a clear image of his totem animal and guiding spirit. He couldn't help feeling disappointed, though. Beavers seemed so common. He'd anticipated something more exotic, even a badger with its white streaks and long neck.

Then Billie realized this wasn't a vision. It wasn't his guardian spirit. It was the real thing. And it was spitting mad. The beaver planted itself in front of him, baring its big teeth, more menacing on land than underwater. It thumped its tail on the ground and hissed.

Billie saw his visitor eyeing the villagers he'd carved; it didn't take him long to figure out what had happened: He'd used the beaver's store of wood for his fires and the figures he'd created. Within minutes, the beaver made wood shavings out of the village, ruining Billie's gift offerings. And then it waddled back to the river, leaving Billie with only his smoldering pipe.

He took a couple more puffs to steady his nerves, afraid to exhale the smoke for fear he'd really have a vision, though reality was turning out to be stranger than dreams. He dumped the wood chips onto the fire, getting some satisfaction from seeing them ignite and illuminate the darkness.

After lowering himself onto the rock, Billie stared at the heavens. The Milky Way made him think of his semen, planted in the dirt around the rock. The wind would pick it up over time and scatter his seed far and wide, carrying his spirit with it. He finally fell into a dreamless sleep, still cradling the warm pipe in his hand. He was holding it when he woke to an overcast morning. For a moment, he couldn't recall where he was or what had happened before dropping off. The night had passed through him like a spirit itself, invisible, stealthy, leaving not a mark, though it left him feeling disoriented. Hearing the river's burbling, Billie recalled his visitor. The idea of being stalked by a beaver seemed laughable in the daylight. But in the dark, it had been frightening. He looked around now to be sure he was alone.

Famished, he felt like a tree hollowed out by lightning, the taste of smoke lingering in his mouth. He didn't have the strength to go far that day, and he wondered how he'd return to the rez without his father's horse to ride. But he didn't want to think about it. If the horse hadn't found its way home, Billie was going to be in big trouble.

Brushing aside these potential difficulties, Billie concentrated on getting through this last day. He had to fill the time and his thoughts with something other than fried flat bread or berry soup or smoked meat. Sitting cross-legged on the ground, he picked up a stick and began scratching out images in the dirt. Doodling. Not paying much attention to what he drew. *Ponoko-mitta*, horses. *Iniiksii*, buffalo. *Imitaa*, dogs. Realizing his hand was actually producing something recognizable, Billie really got into it. He sketched whatever came to mind. The images tumbled out, telling a story if he'd had time to study them. They reminded him of the many legends he'd heard the *Napi* tell about the Indians and their ways; these stories poured out of him onto the earth. He recalled the art he'd seen at the Stampede and longed for paper and paints so he could add color to his scenes. Shadows and depth. Make them permanent.

Billie felt he'd touched on something unexpected. He still couldn't see out of his right eye. And he hadn't had a vision. Yet he felt nourished by these pictures that flooded him and now surrounded his rock. But when he looked them over, wanting to understand them better, the rain started. There was nothing he could do. The big drops came faster and faster, washing away his work.

He remembered his grandfather saying how fleeting the things of the earth were. This explained why the Indians relied upon oral history rather than writing to pass on their culture. As long as humans could transmit the stories and the art, little else mattered. If humans no longer existed, then writing and art were useless. Who would see them?

That night, curled up in his nest, feeling lightheaded from the lack of food, his body seemed as buoyant as a bird's. Billie was sure he could fly without much effort, expecting the next waft of wind to carry him away. Instead, it separated the clouds, exposing *Kokomi-kosomm*, which was gradually being eaten away to a quarter of its size. He thought he must be hallucinating or finally having a vision. The moon had been perfectly full earlier when it first came out, casting a milky glow over everything. He felt like a cat, so thirsty he wanted to lap up every milky pool in sight.

Now the great-globe-of-milk-in-the-sky gradually disappeared until everything was cast in darkness. He was too dulled by hunger to feel much fear. Still, the sight gave Billie goose bumps, but then that made him think of plucked turkey skin, roasted until it was brown and crisp, making him salivate.

Billie took the moon's disappearance as a sign: Since the moon was fading away, he decided something familiar in his life was also about to vanish, replaced by something else. At that moment, buoyant and somewhat delirious, he feared it was himself.

Huddled in his nest of branches, he felt like a speck in the universe. Out of tobacco, he couldn't console himself with a puff on his pipe. Lying on his side, Billie curled into a ball and sucked on the pipe stem. From the north, a sheet of rose- and green-colored light fell from the sky, a huge waterfall of light descending to the earth—the northern lights. Later, the moon, a stealthy cat, gradually crept back to its rightful place in the heavens.

Billie woke suddenly to hot breath on his face and slobber. Afraid to open his eyes, he lay there, still curled up, clinging to the pipe, wondering where his knife was. He'd forgotten to tuck it into his waistband before crawling into his nest. Defenseless, he felt his heart rattle his rib cage, attempting to escape. Billie tried to ignore his visitor by thinking about food, but he couldn't. Something brushed against his arm, and he opened his one good eye. A dark shape loomed above him, blocking out the moon. Billie was certain that any minute he'd become some animal's midnight snack. The shape moved away, into the clearing. Even in the dim moonlight, Billie could make out a horse's body. Rope still dangling from its halter, the mare he'd borrowed had returned.

When Billie left for home the next day, though he'd managed to create his own medicine bundle and had survived in the wilds on his own, he felt he'd failed his vision quest. He believed he returned with no vision to brag about. No voices. He also didn't think he'd found a guardian spirit. But worst of all, he still was blind in one eye.

The Coast

Not long after returning from his vision quest, Billie made friends with Henry, a white kid, at a local swimming hole. They hit it off and hung out together for a while. But Henry couldn't take Billie home with him (his parents didn't want any "injuns" in their house), and the Blackfoot weren't keen on having a white kid on their land. So they met in the fields outside of Weed or at the Bow River. Billie taught Henry how to cast arrows. Henry quickly caught onto the game and excelled at it.

Billie also showed Henry where he'd gone for his vision quest, pointing out the dam where the beaver lived and the large, flat rock where he'd hung out. They fished together in the river, using Henry's fancy pole and the flashy lures he used, taking home brown and rainbow trout. Billie believed he was the better fisherman, though Henry didn't think so.

Henry claimed that more than half of the fish they caught one Saturday were his. Look, he said, it's my pole!

Billie said, Hell they are. They went for my worms, not what you bought at a store.

The boys took a few half-hearted punches at each other, none of them doing much damage, before Henry stomped off, flinging cuss words over his shoulder.

It wasn't long after this encounter when Billie took off for the Coast.

At fifteen, eager to see the world, Billie dropped out of high school and walked most of the way to the nearest city, Calgary, hitching the occasional ride. He carried a backpack that held most of his worldly goods—a change of clothes; $50 he'd taken from the stash his father kept inside an empty Players' tobacco can; his medicine bundle; colored pencils; a pad of paper; tobacco and cigarette papers; a rabbit's tail that guaranteed good luck and sexual potency; his father's Swiss army knife; and a tattered packet of letters from his mother Sighing Turtle.

Sighing Turtle had written to Billie and his three younger sisters over the years, describing her new life on the Coast. She lived with a bunch of artists and had taken up weaving and quilt making. Billie had kept the letters, but the correspondence stopped when Billie was twelve, and he had never learned why.

He had slept with the letters under his pillow, next to his medicine bundle, and now he hoped to track down the woman who had sent them. He wanted to learn why she had taken off without any explanation. But he also wanted to see her again, the parent to whom he felt a deep connection. No wonder, then, that Billie left behind his father and his siblings without a word of explanation.

In Calgary, Billie found the railroad station and hid in one of the freight cars carrying grain that was heading for Vancouver. Feeling like a fugitive, he concealed himself among the kernels, grateful for the hypnotic whirring of wheels that lulled him to sleep. He awoke when the train pulled into the Canadian National Railway Station, hungry but excited to see his first big city.

Vancouver overwhelmed him. All the people swarming the sidewalks. The towering buildings. The concrete. Everything seemed crunched together. But what affected him most was the nearby ocean. He'd never seen it before except in pictures, and they hadn't prepared him for the sea's power. Forgetting his hunger, he sat mesmerized for hours and watched brazen waves break over the rocks, sending frothy spray high into the air. Water landed on Billie and penetrated his jacket. This was more impressive than *Natosi*, the sun, or at least its equal.

Overcome by all these new things, Billie could hardly talk. He left the ocean, but when he tried to ask directions for a place to stay, the English words refused to form in his mouth. He found himself reverting to his native language. Eventually a Mountie took pity on him and brought Billie to a homeless shelter where he had dinner with other lost souls lined up with their tin plates. The bedraggled male servers filled them with stew, tossing a slice of white bread on top to soak up the juices. Later, Billie flopped among the bedbugs and readied himself to search for his mother.

But where to begin? Billie could barely read the well-worn address on the last letter—some place in Kitsilano. He was sure the word had an indigenous reference, and at first he thought his mother was living on another reserve. In a way he was right. One of the shelter workers told Billie there had once been a reserve south of the beach called Kitsilano, but it was currently home to old estates and single-family structures that had been converted to rooming houses. And the Coast Salish village of Snauq had been located on the shore of False Creek, now taken over by office and apartment buildings.

While wandering Vancouver's streets, Billie found a map of the city in a trashcan and plotted his route to the address on the envelope, which took him across the Burrard Street Bridge. He hugged the rail, afraid of falling off and into the water below or of being hit by a car speeding by. He'd seen cars before, but at home they poked along. Everyone and everything here seemed in a rush, racing into some future he wasn't part of. Horns blared. Metal and concrete dominated. He felt totally out of his depth.

Billie finally found the address on the envelope. It was a three-story house with only a hint of paint left on the weathered exterior. He climbed the porch steps, took a deep breath, and rang the doorbell. No answer, though he could hear someone clomping around inside. He pushed the buzzer again. The door flew open, and Billie almost fell across the threshold. No vacancies, the guy said. He resembled a wrestler, his biceps bulging out of his t-shirt, his head bald.

Billie stared at the wooden floorboards. I'm not looking for a room. I'm looking for my mother. He shoved the envelope into the man's hands. It read Fiona, Sighing Turtle's English name, and it had the Kitsilano return address on it. Billie said, See? She lived here.

Well, she don't any more, buster. No sighing turtles here. Just a bunch of frogs! *Parlez-vous francais?* He laughed at his own joke, and tossed the envelope at Billie, shutting the door in his face. Billie could hear him telling someone inside the house JUST FROGS, and another voice joined in the laughter. Billie didn't get the joke.

He knocked again. This time a woman answered the door. She wore a muumuu that made her look even larger. Yeah, she said. You looking for a frog? She glanced behind her and laughed.

Do you know someone named Fiona MacLeod?

Sure it's Fiona and not Frog? Only Fiona I know is long dead.

Billie felt a little lightheaded. She knew a dead Fiona? Maybe it was his mother. He hadn't considered she might

131

be dead. He asked, How long ago?

No sense getting all concerned about a dumb dog, the woman said, waving at some flies that zipped past her. The beggars. Get away, you. It was a stray. The dog tag said Fiona. So we just called him that.

Him?

Can you beat it? A male dog with a female name.

Relieved, Billie thanked her and backed away, clutching the envelope in his hand, almost tumbling backwards down the steps. He caught himself just in time and trod down the street, feeling he was on a fool's mission. He'd never find his mother here. About to cross the street and find his way back to the shelter, he spotted a phone booth. Maybe his mum was listed in the telephone book. He entered the cubicle and looked through the directory, not sure how to use it. He searched first under Sighing Turtle, but that didn't produce anything. Then he looked under Fiona. Nothing. Finally he found MacLeod. Hundreds were listed and none had Fiona for a first name. He felt defeated. He didn't have the money to call all of the MacLeods. It was hopeless.

Tired of Vancouver and depressed about not finding his mother, Billie just wanted to leave that urban hell. He asked a friendly shelter worker if he would drop him off at the city limits. After hemming and hawing about it being out of his way, the guy finally said okay, and the two set off. Once there, the worker stopped the car, and Billie climbed out, slinging his backpack over one shoulder. Billie thanked him for the ride and started hitchhiking up the coast.

Eventually an older man driving a rusty station wagon stopped and called out, I'm heading for the Squamish reserve. Want a lift?

132

Billie grabbed his bag and climbed into the front seat. Two grungy mutts prowled the back seat and yapped at him. The man said, I'm Joe, and stuck out a gnarled hand. Billie shook it and said, Billie.

Don't mind the dogs, Joe said. They think this is their car. I'm their driver.

Billie laughed. I get it. Joe made him feel at ease immediately, as if they had known each other for years.

Joe said, You going far?

I don't know where I'm going, Billie said. Then he told the man where he was from and what he'd been doing in Vancouver: I thought sure I'd find my mother, but she must be dead. Saying the words made the possibility real, and he felt even more alone in the world.

Joe cleared his throat: You're welcome to stay on the Squamish reserve with me and my wife. You remind me of myself at your age. A fire destroyed our place. Both parents died. I was on my own.

And that began Billie's education. Joe had a house painting and handyman business. The white townsfolk hired him when they had jobs. Joe took Billie on as an apprentice, teaching him carpentry—how to work with his hands. But in the evenings and on weekends, Joe did traditional art and taught the boy everything he knew about making sculptures, masks, totem poles, and paintings.

Billie and the *Ni-tsi-ta-pi-ksi*

When he was thirty years old and still living on the Squamish reserve, Billie dreamed one night of a dark cloud passing over the sun. He awoke shivering. Then he broke out in a sweat, believing it foreshadowed his father's death. Billie had thought he might take over as chief when his

133

father died, hoping to pass on what he'd learned from Joe and others at the Squamish Nation. It was different from the Plains bands where he'd spent his youth. The Squamish regularly worked in nearby towns and were more involved in the world than the Blackfoot. Nor did they think of themselves as second-class citizens. For Billie, it had been like visiting another country with new customs, language, and beliefs.

But he hadn't expected to become chief so soon. Could he plant these positive values in his own tribal members? He knew that people, even the *Sitsika*, needed to change with the times. They couldn't remain in a rut of their own making. Yet he also knew that making changes would be an uphill struggle. Leading them out of their swamp might take more skill than he had. Still, he was willing to try. He felt if he could help them recognize their worth, then they wouldn't need him or anyone else. They could save themselves.

It turned out his dream had predicted his father's death. One of his siblings sent a telegram about the burial service that had been planned. During the intervening years, Billie had visited the rez several times to catch up with family and tribal members, sharing some of his Squamish Nation experiences. His three sisters now lived with their husbands, and each had a slew of kids. They called him Uncle Billie, and he liked being part of their lives. Now he was willing to take a leadership role, though his approach would be different from his father's. Billie packed up, said his emotional goodbyes to Joe, Doris, and the many friends he'd made there, and returned to Alberta for good.

Robin Falling Star, Billie's old foe, had other ideas about who would replace the chief. The person who had damaged Billie's eye, Robin also wanted to be in charge. In Billie's absence, he had hung around with Billie's old man, gaining his favor. He oversaw the chief's purification ceremony before his death and arranged the subsequent service—along with Billie's sisters. So when Billie drove onto the reserve in a truck with B.C. license plates, pulling up to the former leader's house, Robin stood on the porch. His eyes narrowed, and he spat tobacco in Billie's direction. Assuming Billie had taken off for good, Robin didn't anticipate what happened next.

Billie stepped into the chief's house, carrying his suitcases. Many of his earlier insecurities had vanished, and he strode into the room with new confidence, not fearful any longer of what people thought of him. Robin followed. Billie said, I'll take over now, Robin, setting his bags on the floor. I want to spend some time alone with my father and give him a proper sendoff.

Robin stood there, his mouth hanging open, eying Billie from top to bottom. A black patch hid the eye Robin had blinded, but Billie's other eye stared at him until Robin had to turn away. This wasn't the same Billie who had run off at fifteen. This man had broad shoulders and muscular arms. He spread his legs wide, hands on his hips, and acted as if he already were chief, appearing determined to claim his father's mantle, something Robin hadn't expected.

Later, at the gravesite, Robin started a whispering campaign. While Billie gave offerings of tobacco, food, and his father's medicine bag, placing them in the plain wooden box to help the corpse in its journey to the spirit world, Robin claimed to anyone willing to listen that Billie was not a full-blooded Blackfoot. His mother's a Scot, Robin said, raising his shoulders and frowning in scorn, spitting on the ground, as if Scots were vermin. Robin also spread the word that Billie was not a real man. He'll be after your sons,

Robin said, nodding at Billie. He's going to destroy our tribe.

Meanwhile, Billie addressed the crowd gathered there by quoting Chief Crowfoot. He reminded everyone that in the late 1800s, Crowfoot had been a much-admired leader. He went on: That great chief had said, What is life? It is the flash of a firefly in the night. It is the breath of the buffalo in the wintertime. It is the little shadow which runs across the grass and loses itself in the sunset.

Billie continued, expressing his own beliefs now: Life is fleeting, but while we're here, we want to show the world we have something important to offer. We must interact with those outside the reserve and expand our knowledge of the world around us.

He looked at those gathered there. Some watched him attentively. Others stared at the ground. He went on, hoping his words might make a difference: The kids need to learn trades or get a higher education. My life wouldn't have improved if I had stayed put and not gone to the Coast.

No one had heard Billie's father speak so passionately of what the future might hold for the Blackfoot. The former chief had not been much of a speaker or a commander. Poverty, alcoholism, and ignorance had kept them and their leader rooted in a destructive way of life. Now Billie offered a different perspective. He opened his arms wide and whispered, forcing them to listen closely, *Ni Kso Ko Wa* means we are all related, but we don't act as if we are. I want us to own this idea. Let's help each other discover what we're capable of.

A buzz swirled through the group. A few listeners felt excited by Billie's words, nodding their heads in assent and nudging each other, but many also feared where he might lead them. They weren't used to being challenged. Nor did they believe themselves capable of something more, though Billie actually thought they could create a better future together. Yet not all rallied to his call. Some shook their heads and shuffled off, grumbling to each other about the foolish upstart and his fanciful ideas. They couldn't conceive of changing.

But those who heard Billie's plea allowed his words to plant a seed in their brains. They wanted a better life for themselves and their children. They also were impressed with the way he had conducted the burial ceremony. He had concluded it by saying, My father's spirit has left his body and is traveling westward across the prairie grass, over the Bow River, and into the mountains. It ascends the mountains to the high clouds where a bright light will guide it to the place where loved ones wait to embrace it. The spirit lives forever.

The day following the burial, Billie called a council meeting and invited those attending to talk about their tribal history. Each spoke of his past experiences. Adam Stillwater told of his childhood living off the rez at a Christian Boarding School. He often got the strap or his head shaven if he did something the nuns didn't like. Adam said, They forbid the kids to speak their language. If they did, *Bam*. Out came the strap and those bitches were strong. Boy did it sting the hands and other places. They wanted to prove our ways were bad—our dress, our language, our beliefs. All things 'Indian.' The treaties said the government had to make sure we got an education. They wanted to 'civilize' us: 'kill the Indian and save the man'. Many nodded their heads, remembering the pain of those times themselves.

Billie took over from Adam, reminding those gathered

that they didn't want to repeat this earlier "schooling." They wanted to learn from this terrible time and make sure that in the future they controlled their children and what they learned. He said, We can have our own schools, taught by our people, not by white nuns. Our children can learn their own language and customs as well as things that will help them compete off the rez. We can control our own destinies.

These words resonated with many, but they still needed to be convinced that this young, one-eyed man could actually lead them into such a future. And Robin resisted Billie every step of the way, continuing to attack his credibility. He's the white man's puppet, Robin said. Look, he deserted his father and his people when he took off to the Coast. Now he's returned with all these big ideas and wants us to fit into that world. It will be worse than the Christian boarding schools.

Robin attracted a limited audience for his accusations There also were rumblings among those who hadn't been big fans of Billie's father and weren't eager for his son to be in charge, even though Billie was totally unlike the former chief. But they didn't have enough clout to change many minds, and Robin Falling Star began losing favor, living out the meaning of his name.

Billie showed his wisdom when, during a subsequent council meeting, he said to Robin, I need someone to help me build my house and make sure the tribe makes some progress. Will you give me a hand?

Totally thrown off guard, Robin stared at the floor, not wanting to give Billie the satisfaction of looking him in the eye. The other tribal members watched silently, waiting for Robin's response. He shrugged and said, Yeah, I guess I could do that.

The log cabin Billie built for himself with Robin's help

symbolized his distinctiveness. The tribal members watched them construct it from trees that fringed the rez. Billie made it up as he went along, the whole thing shaped like one of the ships he had admired on the Coast, his own ark. The place grew unpredictably and included a lookout tower; it stood out among the surrounding shacks, and not just because of its unusual shape. He'd learned well from his Squamish friend Joe the pleasures of repairing things, so he never let his house get rundown. He kept the exterior primed, and he immediately replaced any chipped or loose chinking.

The interior also defied expectations. There was no living room or kitchen per se, just one big space he filled with a mixture of things he loved. A wood-burning stove that he used for heat and cooking stood in the center. He resisted gas or electricity, preferring to keep some of the old ways alive. Kerosene lamps and candles lit the cabin. His one concession was running water rather than an old-fashioned pump in the kitchen.

The lookout tower had a large skylight where he could study the constellations. A mattress on the floor served as his bed. Staring at the night sky reminded him of his vision quest. He realized now it had started him on his own personal path. When he'd left that morning alone on his father's horse, Billie had dared to pursue a dream and to seek a connection with *Naa-to-yi-ta-piiksi*, the spirit beings. He also affirmed his manhood, though he hadn't thought so at the time.

Three

Bone Song

Such a long
time from
sun up

till sun
down. So
much can

happen in
the empty
spaces

Curva on the Old North Trail

Hola, mi estimado Xavier,

It doesn't feel like it at times but I'm making progress. Today I left Fort Sumner. I stopped for the Pioneer Days Rodeo and competed with the locals. It reminded me of our *fiestas* at home. Music. Dancing. Lots of tasty food. And good animals to ride that paid me well. I hope the money will keep me on the trail until the next rodeo stop. Maybe Albuquerque. Maybe Santa Fe. I'll need to hibernate until spring in one of those places. I'll try out more experiments then to find a special potion that will prolong this life. Maybe it will even bring you back from the dead.

Last winter I mixed dog and horse pee with semen I collected from a walking marriage I had one night in Fort Sumner. I added herbs I found along the trail and had dried to use later. Stirred it all together and brought it to a boil. Let it sit for a week. Then I fed some to all my animals and myself. It knocked us out for three months. We slept like bears do. Not stirring. And I awakened full of energy, ready for the trail, but with a bad taste in my mouth. Couldn't death be seen as a kind of hibernation?

I know, you'll think I'm crazy to keep trying all these brews. I can hear you saying *Curva, you'll kill yourself one day.* But traveling this trail is an experiment. It's taught me a lot about nature's many cycles. Life returns in the spring. Why can't animals return after death? We're nature too.

But I started to tell you about the big *fiesta* here. Two Indians came up to me after the sharpshooting contest I won. I had seen them earlier at each event that day, pushing to the front of the crowds. They shook my hand and said, You're the best shooter we've ever seen.

The old man must have been over 100. His face looked like cracked dry earth and his gray hair hung in long braids tied with bright red ribbon.

I bowed and said *Muchas gracias, señores.* I'm from Meh-hi-co and I'm traveling the Old North Trail.

The Old North Trail! they said. That made them very excited. They motioned for me to sit down with them at a nearby table. They knew the trail well, and the older man told me about its beginnings. He said, Long ago a great tribe had lived along the eastern side of the Rocky Mountains. He waved one hand in the air and continued: North and south, up and down they went so many times they made a trail from Canada to Mexico. Many other tribes followed them, and the path became deeply rutted from all the movement back and forth. Some used it to trade goods. Some were on a sacred mission. Some just wanted to explore new lands.

I said I was on a kind of mission, heading to Canada, and asked for any tips. They told me the main trail comes close to the city of Helena in Montana and gave me a rough map to follow. They said I would see a lone pine tree on Crow Lodge River that marks the trail. Towns have grown up right on the passage in some places, cutting it off. But they said the trail continues on the other side.

I would never have known how to pick up the trail again if I hadn't run into these Indians. They may have saved my life!

I said *Muchas gracias* and shook their hands. Then the old man gave me a gift. He took his medicine bundle from around his neck and said, You shoot better than a man so you should have your own medicine bag. Its good spirits will protect you on your journey. Just call them if you get lost or need help. They'll come. Don't worry. I'll die soon, and I want this bag to give you a long life.

My heart went boom boom when he hung it around my neck. I touched the soft hide that held the sacred objects. It felt like a living thing, pulsing against my skin. I know these bundles are sacred to their owners, and I take the gift seriously.

The old man and his friend shuffled away. Dazed, I returned to the camp and carefully opened my gift. I was surprised that such ordinary things could have so much power: Seeds (I'll have to plant them someday so I can see what they are). Pinecones. Rocks. Animal teeth and claws. Tobacco. Beads. An arrowhead.

I wear the bundle around my neck and hope its magic works for me. I can use some when the trail disappears at times and it's easy to lose my way.

Billie & Curva

Billie felt blindsided by Curva. She had crept up on his blind side before he could find his balance, snaring him in her lusty lovemaking and delicious cooking. His experience with women had been limited to ones he'd met while at the Coast and on the Squamish reserve. His sisters also offered him limited insight into the opposite sex, as did those tribal women he'd known all his life that seemed like sisters to him.

Curva was anything but a sister. Untamed and unpredictable, she was an animal that couldn't be fully domesticated and like no other woman he'd known. It made her even more appealing to Billie. She insisted on being free of unnecessary restraints. Bold, she challenged him to be more of a man because she was so much of a woman. He had to reach deep to match her, and he almost didn't make it.

Still, she was fascinated by his ability to create art. She

143

said, Bee-lee, it's magic, pure magic, and watched like an entranced child while he worked. Look, she said, things seem to come alive from your touch.

This conversation took place in Billie's big, rust-colored barn. He'd turned it into a workspace where he and Robin showed some of the rez kids how to do a variety of things, from simple carpentry—chairs, cradles, tables—to carving animals, spoons, bowls, and more. Hammers, saws, chisels, gouges, clamps, vises, rasps, and other tools Billie had brought with him from the Coast, competed for space with paint-splattered surfaces, brushes, cans of colored paint, huge rolls of paper, and additional art supplies. Small figures in every possible posture that he had carved from wood—human and animal—roosted on any available space. Curva flitted from one thing to the next, touching and studying each item.

She asked, If you're the beeg chief, do your people mind you working so much in here?

Billie laughed: Being chief is not so big. I lead more by giving everyone a vision of what we could do if we pulled together. Building a museum to feature Blackfoot history and those ancient bones will be a big step for us.

Since returning to the Blackfoot reserve from his travels, Billie had focused on his artwork, his main source of income, though he now also was spending more time at the burial ground. Because of his work ethic, Billie had become a model for the tribal members of a successful, committed worker, just as Joe had been for Billie.

Curva held a small carving of a bison Billie had made and whistled approvingly.

Billie laughed and said, It's Joe you should be thanking. He taught me everything I know about this stuff.

Joe? Curva asked.

Yeah. The Squamish man I've mentioned. He rescued me when I was just a kid and became like a second father to me. My spiritual father.

Curva stopped where Billie was working and stroked his back. She said, Now I remember. Joe must have shown you how to contact the spirits through art. You're constructing another world with all these things. You give life in your art!

Billie hadn't thought of his creations in that way before, though he did lose himself in the materials and at times felt the spirits communicated with him through them. He sensed their presence nearby, and the creatures he sculpted even seemed to move slightly. Their limbs trembled and their eyes followed his gestures. This happened also in the paintings he did and the totem poles he carved. If the art allowed the spirits to talk to him, to let him know they were awake and watching, then maybe his creations did point to something beyond the surface of ordinary life. This vital communication with the beyond made Billie even more eager to be working in his barn as well as the burial ground. He felt he was an important link.

As much as Billie enjoyed his time with Curva, Henry had become a problem. They couldn't avoid running into each other in town, though the last time they'd said more than a terse hello was years earlier when they'd fought over the fish they'd caught.

Now Billie was doing more than sharing a fishing pole with Henry. They were sharing a woman. And Billie didn't like it any more than he had when they'd gone fishing together. Billie had his own pole now and didn't need anything from Henry, including a woman. It became the one dark spot in his involvement with Curva.

Billie tried not to think about it. He filled his days with plans for the burial ground, working with the bones, and making art. He also thought about ideas he had for a museum of dinosaur bones and Blackfoot history he was designing with the help of a Native architect, a man that shared Billie's vision. Billie also planned to record the tribe's history in a mural, a task that would take him a lifetime.

One afternoon, Billie was working on a small totem at the burial ground when Victor turned up. The boy stood there, fidgeting, watching Billie flash the knife over the wood surface. A blizzard of tiny chips flew everywhere, some landing in Victor's hair.

I came to help out with the bones, he said, shaking the chips out of his hair.

Billie glanced at Victor, recognizing the planes of Henry's angular face in the boys' features—the same jutting jaw. Victor was already tall for his age and lanky. His straw-colored hair flopped over his forehead, cut, it appeared, by either Henry or Curva.

Billie stopped whittling and cleared his throat before speaking. Sorry. Only Indians can handle them. You got a name?

Victor stared at his saddle shoes. They were badly scuffed. He scratched his name in the dirt with the toe of one shoe. There, he said.

Billie looked down. The boy had written "Satan." You're pretty famous, all right.

Victor blushed and turned away.

Who named you Satan, guy? Billie picked up his carving knife again and attacked the wood.

My mother, Victor said, swinging a chain he'd found on

146

the road. It was about three foot long.

Your mother, eh, Billie blurted out. I hear she didn't hang around long after she had you.

Billie felt like kicking himself for what he'd said. The kid didn't need to hear his mother hadn't wanted him; he already knew that. Maybe Billie was seeing something of himself in Victor, though he had been a lot older when Sighing Turtle left. That had given Billie plenty of time to get attached to her. Victor didn't have a chance to hang out with Olga, his mother, except when he was in her womb, but Billie supposed that was long enough to feel a strong connection.

Victor flicked the chain against the outside of Billie's trailer and spit in the dirt. My dad and Curva are raising me.

They are, eh? Do they call you Satan?

Victor ducked his head. It's my nickname. I picked it.

Billie stopped carving for a minute and looked up. What's this Satan guy got that you want?

I just like the way the word sounds. And I heard he was supposed to be the prince of this world. I wouldn't mind being a prince. Victor stood up straight and flung aside an imaginary cape, almost looking like a prince in that moment.

Billie could understand the boy's desire to be something special. He'd had the same kind of longings when he was young. He still did at times. Many of the bones he was protecting belonged to his warrior ancestors. Thinking about the courage it had taken to attack other bands as well as whites made him feel inadequate in comparison. He never could get the hang of bows and arrows. And guns scared him. He had to admit it was one of the things about Curva that intrigued him, her ease with firearms and her total lack of fear in their presence. He'd watched her practice target shooting, shaking a little in his boots whenever he heard a shot.

Now he swiped at a long strand of hair that dangled in front of his one good eye and said, Victor's a pretty good name too. It's an even better name than Satan. It means you're the winner. Satan's a loser.

Victor glared at Billie and asked, How could he be a loser if he's prince of the world?

He's only prince of the underworld. Of evil. Haven't you ever heard the expression 'Get thee behind me, Satan'? You don't want to be tempting everyone to do bad things, do you?

Billie grabbed his whetstone and sharpened his knife.

Victor screwed up his forehead, thinking, before he said, It depends. Sometimes you have to do bad things to make things right again. He looked at his chain. Victor had planned to use it to tie up Billie. But now that he was there, he realized how foolish he'd been. Billie was a man. Victor could never overpower him. He was just a boy trying to be a man. Trying to be scary. It wasn't working.

Victor dropped the chain and faced Billie. It's about Curva. Me and Dad don't like her hanging around you or your kind.

Billie dropped the knife on the bench he was sitting on and leaned forward, elbows on his knees, hands dangling. You don't, eh. What about Curva? Doesn't she have a say?

Victor stared at the knife, wishing he had one like it. Billie's initials were carved into the handle. Victor said, We have first claim on her.

Billie hooted. Have you told her that?

She doesn't listen to me.

Billie picked up the knife and started whittling again. He

148

glanced up and said, Well, she doesn't listen to me either. Billie hated the anguished look that crossed Victor's face. No wonder the boy wanted to be known as Satan. Victor hadn't been victorious after all. Here Victor had gone on a mission to rescue the woman who had been like a mother to him and he'd failed.

Billie didn't have the heart to tell Victor that neither Billie nor Henry nor Victor had any claim on Curva. She had her own way of doing things, and there wasn't a man around who could keep her under wraps for long. Billie had figured that out soon enough. As an Indian, he'd become used to leftovers, so he didn't feel so bad knowing he'd never have her to himself completely. But Sabina spent more time hanging out with him than she did with Curva, eager to learn all she could about the Blackfoot and his art. He had her daughter's heart, and that counted for something.

Curva & Sabina

On a warm summer day, Curva rode one of her horses to town, arriving breathless. Hair windblown, face flushed, a few drops of sweat on her forehead, she called out *Hola* and waved at Billie, reining in the horse and swinging one gaucho-clad leg over the saddle before jumping to the ground. I brought lunch, Curva said. She took a large pot from the saddlebag and opened it: Tamales. The real thing!

She carried it to where Billie was working, and the pungent scent of corn and pork and green chilies followed her. The food still warm, the mouthwatering smell of spicy sauce floated on a breeze, finding its way into the pores and nostrils of each person there. It caused Billie and the other men to almost levitate in anticipation. Even the bones quivered, sounding like castanets. Shouting *Olé*, Curva responded to their rhythms and rotated her hips, practicing a belly-dance move.

Before long she was leading a conga line of workers around the perimeter of the burial ground, tamales temporarily forgotten. Some of the skeletons followed, kicking up dust clouds that swirled behind them like miniature cyclones. The other bones kept up their rhythmic beat. Sabina watched, intrigued by Curva's ability to enliven the usual routine with her cooking, wine, and high spirits. She could make a party out of any occasion and draw people to herself.

Busy taking photographs, Sabina didn't join the dancers. But later, after the workers had devoured the tamales and they were all lounging on the ground, soaking up the midday sun, Sabina crept close to Curva, wanting to inhale some of her vitality and warmth. She leaned against her mother, who unconsciously embraced the girl, idly stroking her bare arm. Curva said, Bee-lee, you haven't told me exactly what you're doing here with the bones!

Sabina stood up and stretched. Billie removed a tobacco pouch and cigarette papers from his shirt pocket and rolled a cigarette, one eyebrow raised, carefully tucking in all of the loose threads of tobacco. After lighting it, he took a few puffs and said, We do rituals. Re-consecrate the burial ground.

Curva sat with her legs spread out in front of her and asked, What rituals?

Billie said, We make a fire. Spread smoke over the remains. Sing songs in *Siksika*. He sucked on the cigarette and blew a series of smoke rings that hovered over them before dissolving. Then he chuckled and said, The bones don't talk back.

Why use smoke? Curva asked.

He shrugged, glanced at her, and said, The smoke from

the fire brought people together for meals. Warmth. Story-telling. Their bones remember that. We believe it purifies them.

Curva nodded, remembering the many campfires she had stoked on the trail and how much pleasure they had given her, the smoke a living presence. The fires had stirred something primitive in her. Flames stabbed the dark and constantly changed shape. Mesmerizing. And the fire was alive. It spoke—snapping and crackling and spitting.

Si, I understand, she said.

As for Sabina, her experience with quicksand didn't slow her down or stop her explorations, though she was now more aware of the emotion fear. The experience of being sucked up by the earth hovered, a ghostly presence waiting to pounce. Occasionally, Sabina thought about the bog that had almost swallowed her. When she did, it held both fear and fascination. She took her camera one day and photographed the area, being careful not to get sucked in again. Still, the possibility of entering the earth stirred her imagination: there could be a whole world under there. She vowed one day to learn more about it.

Sabina also hung out with Billie at the burial ground, photographing the bones. Being the official photographer made her feel important. It also gave her a chance to examine skeletons up close and take pictures of them. Previously, all the skeletons she'd encountered remained clothed in flesh: the farm animals she and Curva had buried were still recognizable as the creatures they had been while alive.

Bones stripped of covering were different. Sabina had to imagine what the person they had supported might have been like. Bones alone were just bones. They didn't vary all

151

that much. Of course, some were bigger and shaped differently, and the colors weren't all the same, varying from stark to muddy white, a few having a yellowish tinge. Yet overall, they had the same structure—ribs were ribs no matter what species. The same with hands or feet. Oddly, they didn't give her nightmares. They seemed natural somehow.

It did amaze her that all of the skeletons held different positions, reminding her of the alphabet. The letters seemed alive to her, twisting themselves into various shapes. So did the bones and the positions they took. It was as if they were trying to say something. She thought her photos might help them to speak.

Sabina's Mentors

There was much to see and do within Weed's radius and beyond, especially in the summer when long days free of school constraints presented infinite opportunities for adventure, and the horizon seemed to blend into the sky, offering endless vistas.

Sabina and Victor wondered what lurked past that horizon, to the west in British Columbia, past the distant mountains, longing to visit there one day. They had heard the siblings Ian and Edna MacGregor tell stories, describing a lush landscape that existed on the other side of the Rockies. It was unlike the umber and burnt sierra prairie grasses surrounding Weed. Ian had said oranges hung from trees there, and everything was greener, increasing its appeal to the youngsters.

Books flooded Ian and Edna's house, piled haphazardly on tables, shelves, bookcases, chairs, beds, the floor. Sabina had never seen so many. All those pages covered with text seemed a little forbidding. Words she hadn't seen before.

Still, she liked looking at the colorful book jackets.

Sabina also liked hearing how Ian and Edna had moved to Weed from Scotland. Their parents had died of a fever that had killed countless Highlanders. A rainbow appeared at their parents' burial. Edna and Ian had thought it was a sign. Look, Edna had said. The other end of the rainbow is pointing to Canada. So they used their inheritance to migrate to Alberta. They had been eligible for a homestead, and the Weed school hired Edna as a teacher.

Ian intrigued Sabina. Tufts of hair fringed his bald spot, and he had a long white beard he stroked as if it were a pet. She liked the way he spoke, the burrs at the edge of his words—their chewy quality. She asked him why he had so many books.

He paused and thought for a minute. I love words, he said. I'm a writer, you know. Children's books. Like Lewis Carroll. Have you ever heard of him?

She shook her head.

Well, you have now. Every lass should read his book— *Alice in Wonderland*. I'll give you a copy to take home with you.

An amateur photographer, Ian also developed photographs for the townspeople, and when he saw Sabina wearing her ever-present camera around her neck, he offered to print her pictures without charge. Once she saw the prints, she noticed that framing the skeletons with her camera gave them importance. The camera lens functioned as a kind of eye, and the way that eye framed the bones elevated them into another category. Instead of just being objects, they now took on a larger significance because they were isolated from their original setting. The photograph also gave them layers of meaning if she were only able to decipher their significance.

She asked Ian what he thought they were saying.

He said, Lass, you've got me. They just look like bones.

Disappointed, Sabina hoped Billie could help her get to the bottom of what she was sensing about them.

But Ian MacGregor was valuable in other ways.

On Sabina's eighth birthday, he took her into his darkroom, a former storeroom, and taught her how to use it. She quickly learned the right way to handle the different chemical washes and got excited every time her images appeared on the negatives. At times, she liked the negatives better than the actual prints. Everything looked backwards, the original image turned inside out. It was like seeing the insides of whatever she'd shot. There also was something about the predominantly dark quality of the negative that attracted Sabina. Even the darkroom fascinated her, its safe light giving everything a weird orangey-red glow.

Excited, she climbed onto a stool and clipped more negatives to a clothesline that ran from one end of the room to the other. Ian patted her shoulder, nodding, Aye, lass, you've got it now. Good work!

Sabina liked poking about other rooms in the house after they finished developing prints. She followed Edna around the kitchen. When she wasn't teaching in the tiny red schoolhouse, Edna canned preserves or made baked goods, her shoulder-length hair, threaded with gray, hooked behind her ears, face puckered in concentration. Sabina liked adding cinnamon and sugar to the rolls and biting into them when they were still warm.

Edna asked, Would you like some hot tea with that roll, lass?

Sabina nodded, watching Edna pour the amber liquid

into a flowered china cup. Sabina added cream and three teaspoons of sugar, stirring until it turned the color of muddy water. Then she held the cup in both hands, sipping and listening with Edna to Amos and Andy on the radio. The two of them laughed together at Kingfish's jokes.

After, she joined Edna in the living room. They both sat in deeply padded, floral-covered armchairs, reading. Edna helped Sabina with words she didn't understand, something that Curva had trouble doing because of her limited English skills. Unlike Curva, whose lively personality overwhelmed Sabina at times, Edna offered a more settled maternal presence.

Sabina chose books that had some pictures, like the *Book of Knowledge*, though she was learning how to grasp words on her own. When she read about how long it would take to reach the moon, Sabina wanted to be the first woman to travel there.

At times, Ian joined Edna and Sabina, settling his bulky body in a rocker by the large bay window overlooking the main street, glasses parked on his nose. He chewed snuff, the wad making his cheeks balloon out, and spat it into a spittoon next to his chair. Then he returned to the book he was reading, a collection of Robert Burns' poems. Lines of verse drifted from his mouth and seemed to hover in the air and change shape like clouds.

Periodically, he glanced up, gazing out at the townspeople mingling on the street. Billie One Eye stepped out of Smart's General Store and climbed into his truck, carrying a grocery bag. It was the first time Ian had noticed that Billie and Sabina had similar hair color. He filed away the observation, not thinking too much about it. Ian had heard it said that Billie's Scottish mother was a redhead. It both-

155

ered him to think that a fellow countrywoman had taken up with an Indian.

Ian was even more uncomfortable to be living in the same town as some Indian bones. He didn't know why the government insisted on protecting the Indian remains. And he didn't know why he was so down on them. Ian didn't think of himself as racist—he certainly didn't object to Curva's presence. But the Blackfoot got under his skin, insisting the burial ground belonged to them. They acted as if they owned the land now, treating those who weren't tribal members as trespassers. That idea upset him.

Ian had talked to Nathan Smart about taking up a petition to have the dead moved to the reservation where they belonged. Nathan had collected signatures from customers. But the plan fizzled out when Ian gave them to the Indian agent for the area. The government guy had said they couldn't overturn a statute with a petition, and the law supported Billie and his tribe.

Ian glanced at Sabina, wondering why she didn't resemble her mother more. A handsome woman, she had taken the town by storm, and he didn't know quite what to think of her. Friendly? Aye. Lively? Definitely. Mysterious? That, too. A puzzle overall. It surprised him how easily she had inserted herself into the community. She became indispensable in no time. And it wasn't only her good wine and healing arts. She made people feel better just being around her. It affected everyone, even Ian. Of course, her ample hips and breasts made her popular with the men as well.

But Curva's house didn't have many books, so the MacGregor place opened up another world to Sabina. She found it amazing that these scratches on the page, letters that morphed into words, could have such an impact on her brain and be so filled with life. She had started reading *Alice in Wonderland*, and the world in those pages soon became Sabina's as well. She was Alice falling down the rabbit hole and being transformed in that underground world, reminiscent of her own rabbit hole experience when the earth tried to swallow her. She felt Alice was showing what marvelous things might be lurking there, though it wasn't just the words' literal meaning that entranced her. Images of the Cheshire cat and the Hatter and the Queen of Hearts were as vivid as any she captured with her camera, and they lived within her now.

But Billie's art also was gripping, and Sabina soon was a frequent visitor to his place as well. He took her with him to the reserve in his rattling old truck, held together with wire and rope, to pick up tools and supplies for his work at the burial ground. That's when she saw the things he made that filled his spacious barn.

The first time Sabina entered it, she felt a little like Alice in Wonderland. She hadn't fallen down a rabbit hole, but she had crossed into another world. Masks of various sizes covered one wall, some resembling birds, foxes, or wolves. Others had more human features, but the dramatic slashes of vivid colors and the boldly painted eyes frightened her. They seemed to watch everything she did, and she thought they were whispering to her. Sabina didn't want to hear what they were saying and turned away.

Billie said, You know, some people think the animal's spirit enters them when they wear the masks.

Sabina shivered. To her, the masks themselves seemed real. She moved away and stared instead at the whitewashed wall where Billie had started a mural. So far, he had only blocked in colors and a few shadowy figures.

Sabina asked him what the painting was about and he grunted.

I wish I knew, he said. A history, I think, of the Blackfoot.

The impact of vivid images inside the barn finally drove Sabina outside. She approached the wooden totem poles planted there, but they also unnerved her. Some—the wolves and ravens and bears—had glaring eyes and fangs for teeth. Their gaping mouths seemed to be calling out something, all speaking at once. They looked animated and angry. Sabina covered her ears, afraid of what they might be saying

From the corner of her eye, Sabina thought she saw something move and spun around, hoping to catch the totems in motion. But they all were lined up, still as sentries, just as before. She couldn't resist getting closer to them. One wolf looked partly human, its arms pressed close to its body and only four fingers showing. No thumb. Beneath it a bird-like being stared at her. She didn't immediately recognize all of the animals carved into the many-layered totems because the images merged, though she thought she saw a deer, a wolf, and a raven. Another had a fish and a bear. Was that an eye twitching in fear? Some movement within the totems themselves? She could sense the animals' desire to be freed and how frantic they must feel to be confined in the wood.

She ran back inside the barn and asked Billie if he could free them, but he just laughed. They don't need me to free them, he said. Their spirits are everywhere, not just in the totem pole.

Sabina wasn't convinced the animals weren't somehow locked up in his designs. She wished Victor were there. He would have some ideas for setting the animals loose. She had asked him to go with her to Billie's, but he had scrunched up his face and said no thanks, twisting his body into the shape of a pretzel. Then he stuck out his tongue and, pretending he was choking, said, I have better things to do than hang out with Indians.

Sabina knew some of the villagers shunned the Blackfoot, so she wasn't surprised when her best friend acted this way. Still, she felt bad for Billie; she didn't see what was wrong with having him for a friend. Except for having one eye, he didn't seem any different from other people she knew. And Curva liked him. A lot.

So did Sabina. She thrived in Curva's triangle, feeling a special kinship with Billie. If anyone had asked her, she would have said Billie was her real father. It wasn't just the hair color. Nor was it because he'd saved Sabina's life. Something else linked them aside from his affair with Curva, though Sabina wasn't sure yet what it was.

Curva on the Old North Trail

Hola, mi estimado Xavier,

I don't know what day it is. Time swirls around me like snowflakes. And snow covers everything, falling from the sky in huge pieces. They whirl in the wind. If I listen carefully I can hear them land. They cling to everything they touch—kisses from heaven. The gods must be very passionate to send so many at once. They know a lonely *mujer* is here, longing for their touch. For any touch.

I got on the trail too early this spring and ran into snowstorms. The bad weather made me stay in one place for days at a time. Dios keeps me warm during long stormy nights. When the wind swoops through the mountains and wails like a hundred bad spirits, Dios yowls back. I join him—another animal.

159

It feels good to let loose like the dog. The wind carries my voice so far I can hear it come back to me. I pretend it's an *amiga* I haven't seen in a long time. I pretend it's you.

Writing you gives me something to do at night besides howling at the moon and gibbering at Dios, the parrots, the horses, and the goat. It's also a good way to practice my English. I want to leave something behind if I die here. My words might give heart to other adventurers. They'll know a woman traveled on this trail and lived to tell about it.

It's been snowing for days now. I wear my leather coat all the time. It's lined with sheep's wool and the smell underneath it is *muy mal*. Several layers of socks protect my feet inside fleece-lined boots. I'm grateful the sheep have given up their warmth for my sake. They're the most useful of animals.

I've hunkered down in the tent. Dios and I go out only to get more firewood and to feed the horses. They look at me with big sad eyes because it's hard for them to graze with so much snow covering the ground. We're low on hay but I can't let them down. That thought keeps me going. They depend on me to make it out of here. And I depend on them for everything.

I finally had to get some food for Dios and me. A vulture was circling while I was hunting for game. We're all in the same boat doing our best to stay alive. I've never liked the alternative—being put six feet under.

I had better luck hunting than the vulture did. Shot a fat rabbit and skinned it. I even drank its hot blood and that warmed me. I guess some people would find drinking blood disgusting, but I've been doing many things I didn't think I ever would. Survival has stripped me down to the basics. I did manage to light a fire and roast the meat so at least I ate it

cooked. I'm not completely savage. Not yet. But I like flirt-
ing with the animal part of myself and feel a deep kinship
with the wild creatures around me.

At times I've drunk my own urine when I was low on
water. Seriously, Xavier. You would do it, too, if you had to.
We didn't have rain and I hadn't seen a river, creek, or a lake
for days. I pretended it was lemon juice and almost believed
it. Warm lemon juice. Or dandelion wine. The color is the
same. I was so thirsty anything would have tasted good.

The rabbit's warm blood reminds me of *vino rojo* which
I haven't had in some time. I pretend that's what it is. I can
make anything taste the way I want it to. Urine. Blood. It's
all a game to me. How much I can fool myself. I learned
this from Don Quixote. Most people get through their
whole life this way.

You're the only one who understands why I've picked
such a hard existence for myself. You shared my excitement
about following this trail from one end to the other. If we
didn't do anything else in life we could say we had done
that.

This trail has become my life. Our life.

Dead Man's Polka

Curva slipped out to the greenhouse after breakfast as
soon as Sabina had left for school. She made her way between the raised beds she'd planted, fertilizing her sunflowers, lilacs, snapdragons, zinnias, tomatoes, *Cannabis,* and
so much more, caressing their leaves and singing softly to
them. She also put grain in the bird feeders.

In the midst of this activity, something made Curva shiver.
She looked around, thinking she'd left open the door. Then
she thought she heard someone tapping on the glass and

wondered if Henry had stopped by, perhaps taking a lunch break. Or maybe Billie?

Pushing aside some large fronds, she saw no one there. *Hola*, she called out. No one answered. Oh Curva, she said to herself. You're imagining things!

She continued with nurturing her flora and fauna. Bent over a pepper plant, she sang to it. Some words from *Bésame Mucho* came to mind, and she began humming it—Xavier's favorite song. A familiar baritone joined in. It could only belong to one person. The two of them had sung this song together many times.

Xavier, you dog. Where are you?

Right before your eyes, *mi amor*.

Curva spun around, face to face with one of her parrots. She said, You're not Xavier!

No, it's not the parrot. It's me, your *hermano*.

Where are you?

Right behind you. Watching over you. I'm always behind you, *mi hermana*, always watching over you.

Curva headed for the workbench. She set down her tools, a trowel and a clipper, and wiped her soiled hands on her *gauchos*. Okay, Xavier. Stop hiding. You're acting like a *niño*.

I'm not hiding. I'm here.

The greenhouse vibrated with the richness of his voice, booming out another verse of "*Bésame Mucho*," though Curva still couldn't figure out just where it was coming from. The sound seemed to materialize out of thin air, a part of the plants and flowers.

After he stopped singing, Xavier said, Is that what your lovers sing to you?

They're *mis amigos*, Xavier. I've a right to have *amigos*.

I've a right to be jealous.

What do you expect from me? I'm your *hermana*, not your *novia*.

I don't want to lose you, Curva. You're all I have. It's cold in the grave. There aren't any pretty *muchachas* there. Besides, you promised....

Curva set down a clipper she was using to prune the plants and poked her fingers into a clay pot filled with soil. She said, I don't like you spying on me like this.

You don't want me to visit anymore?

Visit, *sí*, but not like a *fantasma*.

Then how?

She extended her arms and lowered her voice several levels so it resembled an *hombre*: Like a man, Xavier.

I can't be like a man. I am a man.

Stamping her foot, she said, If you're a man, then face me! Don't act like my shadow.

Like this, Curva? He stepped into a pool of sunlight pouring through the glass windows, wearing a blinding white zoot suit, his long hair slicked back into a ducktail. Laughing, he asked, You like? It's the new me, he said, swinging a long gold chain, one end attached to his waist-band, the other to a pocket. A lit cigarette dangled from his mouth.

What's with you? Curva said.

I wanted a new look. I got tired of dark, gloomy colors. They're for the grave. Don't you think *blanco* suits me? He took a drag from the cigarette and sucked in deeply, the smoke curling out of his nostrils. Then he flicked the butt onto the ground and crushed it under the heel of his white shoe.

You look like an *ángel* in that all-white get up, Curva said. Where are the wings?

Wings are for those with no imagination. I don't need them. He did a soft shoe, spinning around in the spotlight and bowing to the row of plants in front of him.

Curva applauded. You weren't much for dancing when you were alive. Why this sudden interest?

It's boring being dead. I watch a lot of movies. Fred Astaire. Gene Kelly. They've taught me a few tricks. Come dance with me.

Dance? I have work to do. Sabina will be back any time. Don't you scare her!

Don't you want her to meet your brother? I haven't met her father yet.

Neither have I! Scoot now, Xavier. I have *mucho* to do.

You've become too serious, Curva. In Mexico, you never put work before play. You need some fun. Come on. Let me show you the dead man's polka.

Dead man's polka? Are you serious?

Deadly.

Xavier grabbed Curva's arm and planted her hands on his shoulders, his on her hips, and they flung themselves around the greenhouse to an imaginary band playing *norteña* music, the two them shrieking giddily. The birds screeched in unison, wings fluttering frantically, darting into the eaves. Plants and flowers swayed on their stalks, doing their own modified dance.

Xavier and Curva tripped over a low bed of newly planted bulbs the size of a freshly dug grave, landing in soft soil that flared around them. Curva found herself in Xavier's arms and pulled away. To cover her dismay, she howled, My *bambinos!* We've uprooted them all. But she was talking to herself. The earth had reclaimed Xavier. The only sign he'd been there was the chain attached to his keys, now looped around

Curva's neck like a noose.

Sabina and Victor To the Rescue

The image of animals trapped inside Billie's totems haunted Sabina for weeks. In dreams she heard them baying, howling, and yowling, tightly curled up and unable to move, their eyes wildly rolling. She could feel their inability to escape captivity. Finally, she told Victor about her visits to Billie's place and her concern about what she'd seen. We need to free them, she said. I wake at night and they're calling to me.

Victor didn't like his friend to be so upset, so he promised to help her. He said, Let's go there when Billie's at the burial ground. He doesn't need to know we've been snooping.

Though he wouldn't admit it to Sabina, he was curious to see where Billie lived and all of the things he had made.

Sabina felt bad to be doing something behind Billie's back, but her concern for the animals came first. She and Victor took off after breakfast, riding Curva's horse bareback. Sabina sat in front, holding the reins; Victor rode behind, fingers inserted in her jeans' belt loops. They flew over the country road, leaving a plume of dust behind them.

Billie's place was on the reserve's outskirts. On the way, Sabina and Victor saw several abandoned, rusted autos that appeared to be planted in the earth, car parts and other debris scattered around them. Victor wanted to climb inside the vehicles and pretend he could drive, but Sabina said, No, the animals need us.

The tribal members had seen Sabina with Billie enough times on the reservation that they wouldn't question her being there. Still, she glanced around, hoping no one was watching. She and Victor even walked the last couple of

165

miles, leading the horse, not wanting the dust trail to give them away. Once at Billie's place, Victor grabbed the reins and tied the animal to a fencepost. Then he joined Sabina, who was staring at the totems.

Holy cow, Victor said, they're weird.

Sabina shivered. I know. They give me the willies.

They give me more than the willies, he said.

See what I mean, Sabina said. The animals aren't happy.

Victor nodded and said, Maybe the totem pole is just a shell and they're caught inside.

Quivering, Sabina said, They must be frightened too— and starving.

Victor could feel what it must be like for the animals trapped there, but Sabina's distress also urged him on. He wanted to free the creatures for her, but he also hoped to win over his friend from Billie and his kind.

First, though, Victor needed a tool to break into the totems. Retrieving an ax from a nearby woodpile, Victor lifted it over his head and aimed it at one of the posts, striking a wolf between its ears.

Sabina seemed to awaken from a dream, realizing the destruction she had set in motion. She screamed, Stop.

But Victor didn't hear her. He was freeing the animals. He remembered Billie's remarks about needing to be victorious, and now he was. He liked the thudding sound the ax made as it hit the wood, giving him the strength to strike again and again. Parts of the totems flew in many directions: hands and feet, eyes and ears, wings and claws.

If there were animals inside the totems, they wouldn't be there long. He expected to see them dashing across the fields or flying in the sky. But this wouldn't be his only good deed that day. He'd leave some fine firewood for Billie.

Though distressed by the carnage, Sabina couldn't stop shooting the shattered totems with her camera, hoping to catch a glimpse of the creatures before they ran away. But she also wanted to capture the expression on Victor's face—his brows pinched together in concentration, cheeks flushed, eyes filled with rapture. Never had he been so absorbed by something since she'd known him.

He didn't notice Sabina.

He didn't notice the horse's whinnying.

He didn't notice Billie's arrival in his pickup.

The children froze; their feet felt encased in concrete. They couldn't run or speak. The horse did it for them, letting out a shrill whinny and stomping its hooves.

Billie stepped out of the truck and planted himself in front of the children, his face as fierce as one of his animal masks. You got an explanation for this? he asked, motioning towards the destruction. Wood shards littered the ground where only ruined totems now stood, some chopped in half, others splintered into many pieces.

Sabina tried to respond, but her throat had closed and she couldn't form words. When she and Victor had taken off for Billie's place, releasing the animals had made sense to her then, though she didn't know how they would do it. Now she could see how mistaken they'd been. In horror, she stared at the destroyed remains. No creatures were trapped inside the wood. No voices called out to her for help. Though Victor had been the one to swing the ax, she knew he had done it to please her, and she was just as guilty.

Fists clenched, Billie walked over to what was left of his totems, his face the color of red clay. He stood motionless for several minutes, taking in the destruction. Then he shook his head and squeezed his eyes shut, flinging the ax as far as he could. It cleaved the earth where it landed, clanking against something hard.

Billie opened his eyes and said, Get outta here! He motioned to the horse and went to see if he'd broken the ax blade. Leaning over, he felt what the ax had hit, his fingers gradually exposing what was there. His work at the burial ground had prepared him for what he found: petrified bone. The remains of prehistoric animals were also on the rez.

Billie and Henry

Henry's door flew open before Billie could knock. Victor tried to block the entrance. Go away, he said, my dad's not here.

Billie glanced at the pickup sitting in the driveway.

He's not, eh? I think I'll see for myself.

Billie hollered, Henry, I need to talk to you. Your kid's causing trouble on the rez.

Victor ran outside.

Billie stood there, holding the screen door open, listening, waiting, remembering his former friendship with Henry. The competitiveness between them. The lies they told each other about the number and size of fish they'd caught. Billie's envy of this white man who could go anywhere he wanted. Billie had always felt like an interloper whenever he left the rez and still did at times. The townspeople had stared at him, even feared him, though it was Billie who felt the most concern. He was afraid someone would tell him to get back where he belonged. Off the reserve, he had few rights.

Henry approached from the barn. Straw stuck to his coveralls, and his big hands hung limply at his sides as if disconnected from his body.

What's up? Henry said.

Billie avoided Henry's eyes, uncomfortable because they each shared Curva. Clearing his throat, he said, Your boy came to my place when I wasn't there and destroyed my totems.

Henry swiped at flies that were circling his head. Victor? Who told you that?

No one needed to tell me. I saw it with my own eyes.

This time Billie looked at Henry directly and was surprised that the other man was studying him intently.

Henry frowned. What do you expect me to do about it?

Teach your boy some manners and respect for others' property. Those totems are irreplaceable. It's as if he chopped me up in little pieces. I could report him to the Mounties.

Henry spit. The glob landed next to Billie's boot. You have a witness?

Sabina. She was with him.

Henry grunted and said, Does Curva know?

She knows. Billie kicked at the dirt with his toe and sent up a miniature cyclone cloud.

Henry frowned. I don't have any money to give you.

I don't want your money. I think your boy's trying to get even with me for something. I don't want any more trouble from him.

Victor's a good kid.

He calls himself Satan. That ain't so good.

Satan?

Billie told Henry about Victor's visit to the burial ground and their conversation.

Henry scratched his head. Where'd the kid get those ideas?

Billie shrugged and said, He doesn't want me hanging

out with Curva.

Henry stared at the ground, avoiding Billie's eyes. That isn't his business.

He thinks it is.

Henry glanced at Billie. She's been like a mother to him.

I know.

Henry said, You can't blame him for not wanting to share her.

I don't like sharing her either, Billie said, and headed for his truck. He stopped before he reached it and looked back. Henry was still standing there, and their eyes met. Billie said, I think we need to stop fishing in the same stream. We aren't kids any more.

It's up to Curva to make a choice, Henry said.

Billie climbed into his truck and gunned the engine. The exhaust shot out a burst of smoke. It settled around Henry's shoulders like a shroud before dissolving. Henry brushed at his clothes, but he couldn't get rid of the straw and soot that clung to him.

Curva on the Old North Trail

Hola, mi estimado Xavier,

The campfire slithers across the rocks and sizzles the fish I caught this afternoon—trout. Your favorite. Dios is standing watch. He already ate his share raw. I took out all the bones before I gave him any. He knows he'll get leftovers too.

The smell is drawing some of the locals. Squirrels. Rabbits. Deer. I can hear the other animals in the underbrush cracking boughs and the squirrels flying from branch to branch watching. They keep their distance but they're curious. I see them at times peering through the scrub. Their

170

eyes are bright as baubles, and their noses twitch when they smell the food sizzling on my campfire.

Today I woke in the dark. It was so warm I hadn't put up the tent the night before. Manuel and Pedro were screeching Get up! Get up. Dios was licking my face, and for a moment I thought I was in bed with a man. But it was the dog and just as I was ready to have a big one. I had gone to sleep thinking about my horse Alanzo's huge organ.

That horse can't seem to keep it out of sight and dangles it for no reason. Drives me crazy. Sometimes I use other things and pretend I'm riding Alanzo's cock. You used to laugh when I talked like this, *mi hermano*. You liked me to tell you such things.

Then Dios growled and started barking like he was *loca*. I knew he had heard something. I picked up my .38 just in case and shined my flashlight around. Sure enough, a mother black bear and her two cubs had crept into our camp and were making off with some fish I'd hung from a branch. I didn't have the heart to shoot. All they were after was food.

Then Dios started whining and barking again. It made me wonder if something else was out there. Maybe raccoons. Maybe Don Quixote. Maybe you. And the parrots kept ruffling their feathers and pacing in their cage. I decided I'd better hide. I threw on some clothes and stuffed my sleeping bag so it looked like I was still inside. Then Dios and I crept behind some big boulders not far away, waiting and watching. I had my rifle and .38 ready with plenty of ammunition.

Dios tried to growl. I muzzled him. The fire's glow gave enough light that I made out two *hombres* creeping across the clearing and over to my sleeping bag. I thought it was Don Quixote and Sancho until I saw the moon glint off their gun barrels. I took aim with my rifle and shot each in the leg. Their guns flew out of their hands. The *bandidos* yelled and collapsed on the ground, clutching their legs, cursing. What the hell, they shouted. I sent Dios to pick up their weapons and he brought them to me.

You would have been proud of the way I strode into the camp and pointed my .38 at them. They put their hands in the air. *Mis amigos*, I said. I have something you want?

They just moaned. I motioned for them to move to a nearby tree and made them sit with their backs pressed to it while I tied them up. Dios kept them busy, snarling and nipping, while I made some tight knots and asked how they'd found me. The *bandidos* said they'd followed me after I won a big rodeo purse.

I packed up our camp and got the horses ready to leave. We took off at dawn and left my visitors swearing at each other. But it was a close call, and I'll need to be more careful now about covering my tracks. It's strange to think I have something that others want to steal.

Curva and Ana Cristina Hernandez

Curva felt as if her own heart had been pierced when Billie had told her about the children's vandalism. His art seemed as palpable as the things in her greenhouse, and she had grown as attached to his work as to her own creations. She would never forget his furrowed brow and the way his voice had caught when he described what they had done.

Seeking an appropriate punishment for Sabina and Victor, Curva had discussed what to do with the two men, but they weren't much help. Billie didn't feel it was his place to discipline Henry's son or Curva's daughter. Henry just threw up his hands and asked Curva to take care of it.

And she did. She didn't want to inhibit their curiosity, but she wanted to teach them a lesson, so Curva told them they couldn't have contact outside of school hours for a while. They howled, and Sabina threatened to run away; Victor said he would join her. They said they would take off on the Old North Trail and never return.

Curva knew it wasn't an idle threat. Both had expressed an interest in finding the trail, especially after hearing so many stories about it. Speaking in the gravelly voice that made their spines tingle, Curva had often told of her adventures along it. When she described her travels, she seemed another person entirely, not the woman who cooked their meals or washed their clothes. She appeared capable of anything: skinning animals and roasting them over a fire as skillfully as she later prepared their hides for use. It was the one time when they sat still and listened, enthralled with the world Curva depicted in such detail.

Once, she had recounted setting up camp in a large cave during a snowstorm, only to find she had company—a black bear rolled up in a tight ball, hibernating. The children had stared at her intently, the bear suddenly in their midst, her words capturing its musky smell and rasping breath. Their eyes wide, they had listened to her say she had little choice but to spend the night there. It was either that or freeze in a snowdrift. The bear didn't wake up, and Curva escaped the next morning, the sun already melting the snow.

These stories whetted Sabina and Victor's appetite for exploring, and more than once they had secretly discussed setting off on their own to find the trail. Aware of their interest, Curva reminded them of the poisonous snakes and hungry mountain lions she'd frequently run into, as well as the *banditos* that roamed there.

173

They got the message.

With Sabina and Victor safely in school, Curva had more time to spend in the greenhouse, a place where she could lose herself. The interior was so lush it was like being in the tropics. The calming sound of the fountain flowed over her, and, for a moment, she was back in her mother's womb with Xavier, holding his hand, listening to the burbling, both of them awash in amniotic fluids.

The hothouse had expanded, and one section was now a habitat for Monarch butterflies. Their eggs hatched in a protective wire cage Curva had built so she could watch them evolve. Inside it, she hung branches for the pupa to latch onto and regularly replenished the milkweed, giving the caterpillars plenty of food. She studied the cylindrical chrysalises that dangled from branches. They resembled tiny lanterns, the orange and black butterfly designs already visible in some beneath the opaque skin. Others looked like jade jewels.

Curva felt akin to these amazing insects, joining in spirit their regular migration to Mexico and back, feeling as if they carried some part of her native country with them. Those she didn't release in late August resumed their cycle in her nursery. Living through winter would have been difficult if she hadn't had the butterflies to commune with or the comforting oasis she'd created there. When the resident butterflies emerged and flew freely in the greenhouse, nectar plants—sunflowers, lilacs, snapdragons, and zinnias—kept the insects busy feeding, laying eggs, and hatching.

The children joined her whenever the butterflies emerged from the pupae. Watching this transformation always moved Curva deeply. She felt the insects held a clue to immortality. She also believed the process they went through was like the human life cycle: the fertilized egg is planted in a woman's womb. After children are born, they resemble the caterpillar, eating and creeping; when they die, they're like the dormant pupa in its chrysalis. Then the soul leaves its cast-off body the way the butterfly emerges from its chrysalis—rebirth after death, a never-ending succession.

This whole process seemed miraculous to her. So did the transformation of dried-up seeds she'd planted. They eventually sprouted and became plants that produced more seeds—a continuous cycle. But her intense feelings about the butterflies were more complex than having an emotional response to witnessing new life. She knew that most of them would leave soon, just as she would one day leave the earth. So while they seemed an emblem of immortality in many ways, they also represented death: they didn't live long, and they stayed in her greenhouse only a short time. Curva always felt that something of herself had flown off when they left the safety of her garden. It made her want to keep them close for as long as possible.

Curva was working in her sanctuary one day when she came across Ana Cristina Hernandez smelling the herbs Curva had planted. Though she was used to unexpected callers from her past, Curva was surprised by this visit from her former employer. Curva rushed over to the woman and embraced her, inhaling the scent of mold and lavender. Curva said, *Mi amiga*, it's wonderful to see you!

Bowed from age, her face crumpled, a burgundy shawl draped over her frail shoulders, Ana Cristina said, And to see you, *mi amiga*. I've been hearing about this greenhouse of yours. I had to see it for myself.

Curva took her arm and said, I'll show you everything.

Ana Cristina said, *Gracias*, but I can find my way.

Almost blind, she used her extraordinary senses to move around the place, hands hovering over flowers and plants. She seemed to feel them into existence and herself as well, capturing their very essence through her fingertips, sniffing and inhaling, listening intensely to them. Then she bent over an ailing bird. *Cheep cheep cheep*, Ana Cristina said and cupped it in her hands, bringing it close to her ear so she could hear the bird's response. It's suffering from lack of will to live, she said.

Lack of will to live? Curva looked at the bird and then at Ana Cristina. How do you know that?

It told me. The bird doesn't like being holed up.

But if I freed it, the poor thing might die. It gets cold out there.

It needs its freedom, Curva, just as you do.

Given how hard she had worked to make the environment nurturing, Curva was shocked that the greenhouse might seem like a prison to the wild things she had collected there. Not only did she provide food for flora and fauna, she also assumed the shelter protected some of its inhabitants from the unpredictable world outside. It hadn't occurred to her that a benevolent act might have such negative consequences.

Ana Cristina blew on the bird's feathers, her breath enlivening the creature. The feathers twitched; its normal breathing resumed. Before long, it spread its wings and flew a few feet. Ana Cristina opened the door and shooed it out. Off with you, she said, and it soared into the prairie dusk.

Curva watched the bird fly away, silhouetted against the sky, and said, I can't bear seeing all of the birds leave!

They don't have to leave, Ana Cristina said. The rest seem

176

happy here. Just that one bird was not well.

Relieved, Curva looked around the greenhouse. Knowing she could walk into it at any time and be surrounded by this tropical island, filled with the sights and sounds of her native land, sustained her through the long, hard winters. When the snow piled up in drifts outside, she could completely lose herself in this spot—digging into the grainy soil and tending to her plants and creatures. Neither day nor night mattered, neither past nor present. Time folded in on itself.

Her heart stirring, Curva glanced at Ana Cristina, now hunched over the orchids, almost drinking them in. Ana Cristina had welcomed Curva into her household when she was only a girl. Offering advice. Taking Curva under her own comforting wing. Curva had learned then that the attachment between Xavier and herself was wrong. She remembered Ana Cristina saying, If you do it with your brother, you could give birth to a pigeon, you know, or a cross between a cat and a dog. Either way, it would be cursed from birth. And then Ana Christina had given Curva lessons on how to protect herself from unwanted *bebés*.

When Curva had told Xavier about Ana Cristina's warning, he had laughed. She's just superstitious, he said. If you get pregnant, we'll have a beautiful normal *niño* or *niña*. Just like us.

But Curva became uneasy about their closeness. She didn't have any scruples about sex; it seemed perfectly natural to her. Yet if she had a child with her brother, it might be abnormal and suffer needlessly. Everyone would look for signs that the *niño* was marked in some way. No one would let Curva or Xavier forget the circumstances surrounding the birth. Curva also knew that as the child's mother,

177

she would bear the most responsibility. Not only would she have a child to nurse and care for, but she'd also be judged for making a baby outside of marriage—and with her own brother.

Too young to be buried under motherhood's responsibilities, Curva refused to give up her dreams of returning to the Old North Trail—of traveling its length. She wanted adventure. Something more than a conventional life. From that moment, she became determined no man would trap her.

Ana Cristina had been right all those years ago. Curva watched her straighten up, a surge of affection welling up for the woman who was so like her own *madre*. Ana Cristina groaned: My bones have gotten rusty. She stood in silence, her hands fluttering at her side, unable to find a place where they could settle comfortably. Curva saw many new lines in the other woman's face, and the flesh sagged. Curva moved closer and stroked her arm: it felt like fine tissue paper. Then Ana Cristina's fingers traveled over Curva's features, picking up on the determined set to her jaw and how weathered her skin had become. She no longer was an innocent young thing under her employer's protection and needing guidance. Curva was a woman herself now.

Berumba

After the civil war started, violence in Berumba increased. Lawless bands of hungry fighters caused mayhem at times, looting and pillaging. Residents had to defend themselves from intruders. The conflict made remaining there impossible, so Curva and Xavier planned to return to the Old North Trail. For protection, they both carried a weapon at all times.

A few nights before their departure, Curva was sitting on

a wicker rocker in the Pacheco courtyard, taking a break after dinner, knitting a pair of socks. The light had almost left the sky, and the only sounds were the birds' call to sleep. Protected by a brick wall six-foot high, the large patio included a fishpond, a rose garden, weeping willows, and a row of tall bushes that lined the enclosure.

Lulled by the tranquility and the hypnotic sound of her knitting needles clicking together, Curva dozed off. Some rustling in the bushes next to the wall awakened her. Since invaders recently had been caught scaling the barrier, her first instinct was to reach for a gun. Though groggy, she slipped her .38 out of the knitting bag, pointed it at whoever was moving in the shadows, and pulled the trigger. She heard a sharp intake of breath and a groan.

Then nothing.

Upon hearing gunfire, the Pachecos and their visitors crowded into the courtyard, asking what had happened, their voices buzzing around her like flies. Curva tucked the weapon into her bag again and told them she had stopped a thief from running off with the family's wealth.

A couple of men dove into the bushes and dragged out a limp body. *Cristo santo,* one of them said, *es Xavier. Muerto!*

Curva fainted.

The men called for someone to help Curva, who was slumped over in the chair. Ana Cristina heard the cries from the kitchen, grabbed a kitchen towel, dipped it in cool water, rushed to the courtyard, and pressed it to Curva's forehead, fanning her face and clucking over the young woman.

When Curva came to, she had to accept what she'd done. Her beloved *hermano* was *muerto* and from Curva's bullet. Xavier stared at her from his prone position on the ground,

179

his neck at an odd angle, his look accusing. Someone low-ered the dead man's lids, covered his body with a white sheet, and carried it into the house. His blood seeped through the wrapper.

Curva sat there, stunned. Too shaken to cry. Too shocked to do anything but rock back and forth, jabbing herself over and over with a knitting needle until she drew blood. Ana Cristina gently took the needle from Curva and dropped it on the ground, pulled the girl to her feet, and led her into the couple's bedroom, away from the bloodstained patio. Then Ana Cristina told the men to place Xavier's corpse in the big center hall.

Curva spent a restless night in the Pacheco's bed, haunted by the killing. Her *madre* and *padre* invaded her dreams, wail-ing and calling out Xavier's name. Curva joined their lament, as did the surrounding walls, tears seeping from everywhere and creating meandering streams on the bedroom floor.

The next morning, both Ana Cristina and Curva prepared Xavier for his final viewing and for the grave. Using a fra-grant soap made of rose petals, the two women washed ev-ery inch of Xavier's skin lovingly, respectfully, including his penis—erect even in death. It made them both laugh in the midst of this solemn ritual. The laughter turned into wails, their copious tears baptizing him. His once vibrant skin felt like marble, as if he'd been carved by a sculptor and now lived on as art.

Ernesto Valenzuela Pacheco gave Ana Cristina his wedding suit for Xavier's burial, and the women placed a blood red rose in the lapel. The smell of roses lingered in the air for days afterward, and from then on, that sweet scent would remind Curva of that painful day. Grieving deeply and drowning in guilt, she envied Xavier's dark sleep. He was free now of the daily troubles many people faced—conflicts, hunger, suffering. There also was something mysterious and opaque about death that attracted her. Darkness cloaked everything on the other side, allowing only occasional glimpses of what was beyond. She looked forward to *Los Dios de los Muertos*, hoping Xavier might visit her then.

Soon after Xavier's burial, Curva began gathering supplies she would need on the trail—food, water, tent, axe, utensils—and said goodbye to the Pachecos. No one had asked her to leave. Ana Cristina admired Curva's shooting skills so much that she wanted the girl to stay and protect the place. But Curva couldn't bear walking into that courtyard. Each time she did, the scene repeated itself—Xavier lying on the ground, blood pooling around his body. She had to get as far away as possible. And she had to complete this journey they had undertaken together.

After packing up her few possessions, Curva strapped them onto the travois that another horse pulled, saddled her mount, and headed north, weighed down with a severe melancholy. She felt if she could reach the Old North Trail again and continue their aborted quest, she could keep Xavier close to her. They had started this adventure together; they would end it together as well.

Curva on the Old North Trail

Hola, mi estimado Xavier,

It's so quiet I can hear the trees inhale and the stars sing. My own breathing and heartbeat sound so loud it scares me. I feel like the only human left on earth.

But the silence also can be bitter and piercing. It weighs on me like a heavy blanket covering everything. Even the air has pores.

At night I can hear different animals stirring in the brush and circling the campsite—lynx, wolves. They growl. Yowl. They're my audience. I sing to them and they hoot and howl in response.

Sometimes I just talk for hours about anything that comes to mind. Don Quixote. Sancho. Kadeem. Ana Cristina Hernandez. Ernesto Valenzuela Pacheco. You. Life on the trail. I open my heart and Manuel and Pedro talk back. It's like being in an echo chamber. Their words comfort me. They feel like food in my mouth that I chew on. It helps to ease the loneliness and saves me from going *loca* at times.

Despite coming into this world with a companion, you, I now spend long periods of time alone. You must be thinking, You, Curva, okay without someone to talk to? Yes, *mi hermano*, me! The longer I'm on the trail, the easier it gets.

Your death still pierces me, so I convince myself you're with me, sharing this adventure. Or I tell myself a story that makes me feel better. I pretend one of the rebels killed you, and I refuse to leave Berumba before I track down your killer.

I even give the murderer a name—Mario René Berrios. Grey threads his hair and his scraggly beard. Do you remember the *hombre?* I find him in Suelita Flores's arms, sucking on her nipples. In my fantasy I stride into the room, draw my .38, and aim it at the man's head. Suelita screams, Get out Curva. This isn't your business.

It is my business. He killed Xavier.

The man tumbles out of the bed. His eyes search for an exit. He dives at the open window, and as he flies through space, I take aim. The bullet enters his rear end and leaves through the top of his head so he doesn't shed a drop of blood in Suelita's room.

He has sons, you know, Suelita says. They won't rest until they avenge their father's death. You'd better leave the country fast.

I drop the gun into my leather shoulder bag and say, *Hasta luego, mi amiga.*

As much as I believe this story sometimes, I know I was the one to kill you, not the rebels. I will never forgive myself for that.

Still, I occasionally feel Mario René Berrios' sons *are* chasing me, and I must keep moving so they don't catch up. These stories I tell myself have lots of power. At times, they seem more real than life itself, just as Berumba became a real place after we read the novel about it. Remember? Don Quixote also seems actual to me. He lives in my mind now, and I'll never get rid of him. Nor do I want to.

Today the skies opened and instead of rain it snowed, even though it's nearly the end of May. Now it has stopped and the sun has come out. Everything has awakened after a long slumber, and the snow melts almost as quickly as it fell. Dios has been chasing rabbits and his tail. Running in circles.

And I've been chasing Dios through the trees. Snow falls from the boughs. Dios barks. I pretend to bark too and then laugh, feeling like a girl again. I'm relieved to see the blue sky and feel the sun's warmth. The dog and I ended up rolling together down a slope that had a thin layer of snow. Underneath it, new growth is trying to take hold.

Billie and Curva

Billie felt he'd been stabbed in the gut when he saw his totems lying in ruins. It was as if he himself had been blud-

183

geoned, and it took time to recover from Sabina and Victor's action. Though Sabina's guilt-filled explanations helped him to understand why they had done it, having these two children attack him so personally awakened his old feelings of inadequacy, leftovers from when he was a child. For days afterward, he spent hours picking up totem shards, often pausing over a particular one—a raven's beak, an owl's luminous eyes, a bear's paw—and realized little was salvageable.

With his totems ruined, Billie was more determined than ever to create something enduring. The museum he had envisioned would answer that need if he could ever find the money to build it. The place would preserve the tribe's cultural treasures, and visitors would finally learn about Billie's world, its influence continuing long after he had left this earth.

On nights when Curva stayed at his place on the rez, Billie shared his plans with her. She got caught up in his ideas for the cultural center and encouraged him to include a replica of the Old North Trail. Maybe Sabina could get Ian to help her create a 3-D film of vegetation and animal life that was prevalent on the trail. They could show it in the museum's theater, and visitors wearing 3-D goggles could trek the trail without leaving their seats.

Curva entertained Billie by mimicking the various animal sounds she'd heard on her travels—growling and howling, snorting and screeching. She lunged, and he cowered on the mattress, feigning fear of the wilder animals. She also made up background music for the exhibit, singing Mexican folk songs as she played Xavier's guitar. Billie tried to sing along with her, making up his own words in Blackfoot as he went along, the two of them giggling like kids.

After, Curva stretched out next to him, her skirt rising

and exposing her bare legs. His fingertips floated over the scar on her thigh, left by a bullet fragment that entered there when Curva fought with Berumba's revolutionaries.

Did it hurt? he asked.

Curva shrugged. Not until I saw all the blood. That's when I knew I'd been shot and hollered for Xavier to help me.

Did he?

Sí, sí. He came running and made a sling so he and the other men could carry me to the doctor in town. It took forever to get there. I thought I would bleed to death first.

But you didn't.

Billie and Curva didn't talk about marriage; nor did they want to live together. Not only were they both uneasy about giving up their respective freedoms, but they also thought it would cause too many complications. Billie never forgot that his mother, a *ksikk*[4] person, had not been accepted on the rez. Though Curva wasn't *ksikk* exactly, she came from another country, and the Blackfoot still resisted strangers in their midst. Afraid of losing their culture, the resistance was protective.

The truth is, neither Billie nor Curva wanted to give up his or her way of life. Billie had his cabin and art studio; Curva her farm and greenhouse, and Sabina kept her busy, as did Victor at times. And while Billie wasn't drawn to other women, too shy to approach them, and Curva didn't see much of Henry anymore, she wanted the freedom to bed down with another man if she felt like it. She wasn't seeking someone to replace Billie. He was enough man for her. But she craved enhancing what she had if the urge struck her.

---

4 white

185

Of course, Suelita still tempted Curva to keep her hand in, so to speak, especially when a new man showed up in town, looking for work either on one of the farms or with the rebuilding following the tornado. Some were much younger than Curva. The young ones are the best, Suelita claimed. They're always ready. The old ones? Too unpredictable.

Curva listened. She didn't need much encouragement.

Suelita's comments stirred Curva's curiosity and her desire for adventure, currently limited to exploring new male bodies, always so different. And while in bed, she also quizzed these men about themselves, urging them to tell her their deepest secrets. Of course, her dandelion wine loosened their tongues, and it didn't take much for them to open up.

Billie looked the other way, just as Henry had done They recognized that for her sex was a lot like mothering—the fondling, the nurturing of something into existence. And it amazed her that two people, even strangers, could join their bodies together and play them like instruments, running up and down the scales of passion until they hit all the notes.

Meanwhile, Xavier continued to visit periodically, though she never knew when he might appear. One night, Curva awoke to find him sitting in a corner of Billie's tower, watching them sleep. Leaning forward, elbow propped on one knee, chin resting on his hand, he brooded over the couple.

When Curva whispered to Xavier *vayase*, he stood up and walked through the wall, disappearing into *la noche*. Some nearby coyotes gave a spine-tingling howl, waking Billie. He said, The boys are restless tonight.

She just nodded, and he slipped into sleep again. Curva kept watch the rest of the night, half expecting Xavier to reappear. He didn't, though the coyotes howled and barked

186

intermittently until dawn, unsettled by something wandering in their midst.

Usually, though, Xavier's visits had a much different flavor. He wanted to talk and sing and—of course—eat. Always, he needed food, *mucho alimentos*. At least lust didn't drive Xavier any longer as it had in life. Something else was propelling him. Many times he said, I need you close to me, *mi hermana*, like when we were children. It makes me feel alive!

Curva never knew what guise Xavier might appear in. He didn't repeat the zoot-suit outfit, though he did show up once as a sultan. During another visit, he dressed as a Russian Cossack, baggy trousers tucked into knee-high black boots. It was January then, the worst part of winter. He wore a fur hat that covered his ears and did a Russian dance for her, arms crossed, kicking his legs straight out from a squatting position.

Laughing, she asked, Where did you learn this dance and get the outfit?

He stood up, hat askew. Where do you think? Hades has many nationalities.

You make it sound like a vacation spot.

Yes, many take extended vacations there.

She'd laughed, but she also felt a chill at his words. Such visits renewed her desire to discover the one concoction that could grant the drinker eternal life. The dandelion wine was a good tonic, but it wasn't powerful enough. She had tried mixing it with various herbs she grew in her greenhouse and minerals she discovered inside rocks from the prairies: hematite and cinnabar. At a Calgary pharmacy, she'd bought some of the things Ernesto Valenzuela Pacheco kept in his lab: baking soda, bleach, potassium, alcohol, hydrogen peroxide, quinine, hydrochloric acid, and sulfuric acid. Some she mixed into her solution and drank. But all it did was make her sick for days. She tried combining these items in other ways, and that led to a minor explosion on her stove. It rattled all the dishes in her cupboards and gave her a good jolt.

She realized the remedy might be in the greenhouse. The hydras and planarians' agelessness, as well as their ability to recreate themselves, intrigued her. In her free time, she studied them intensely, as she did the other things growing under her care. She felt reassured when new flores appeared where she'd clipped off the dead blooms. The leaves visibly trembled from the energy that surged through them, the flores' death nourishing the host. Her *jardin* seemed to be communicating with her during these times, showing nature's power and how much it could teach those who watched and listened. If it could renew itself endlessly, die and be reborn, surely humans could too.

Shirley

Since Shirley's appearance in his airplane, Curva had found herself falling into occasional reveries about him. Compared to other men she'd known, he dressed in stylish clothes and was more conscious of his image, making him stand out from the crowd. So did his metal bird, something she wanted for herself. Then she could fly wherever she wanted, covering great distances in a short time. It had taken her years to travel from Berumba to Alberta on a horse. He could do it in a few days.

Curva imagined them flying off together, exploring new places. They could even go to Mexico. Of course, she didn't have any major reason to return to her homeland. But she did miss hearing others chatter in Spanish as well as her country's folk music. Memories of *fiestas* and promenading in town squares after dinner also filled her with longing.

But Shirley's plane wasn't the only thing that intrigued her. She hated to admit it, but thinking of him sent shivers of excitement through her, similar to how she felt the first time she held a gun. Like a gun, he fascinated her, just as snakes did: slick, elegant, but potentially deadly. D-A-N-G-E-R flashed in front of her eyes. She could lose herself and everything she stood for if she got swept up in his way of life. He didn't give a damn about any of the things she loved, and the intense attraction made her feel like the type of woman she never wanted to be: incomplete without a man to cling to.

So the buzz she felt over Shirley wasn't necessarily pleasant. Yet she couldn't understand this reaction when she really didn't care for the man. His intentions were clear—land and oil. Shirley had told her he'd worked on a few oil rigs himself in Montana and knew something about oil fields, having been a roughneck long enough to learn the ropes. Now he had hired Texas oil company executives who were also lured by black gold. Shirley hoped to purchase oil rights for the Texas company and also buy up some land in Alberta for himself, expecting to get in on the ground floor of a boom.

Curva's stomach churned when she thought of the development an oil boom would bring to the area. Buying up land was one thing, but drilling a bunch of oil wells would change the area completely with an influx of giant *insectos* taking over the prairies, as well as scores of workers. She felt protective of the town, wanting to keep it as was, having witnessed the changes Berumba went through when capitalism and greed took over the residents, who

189

no longer were in control of their lives. It wasn't that she disapproved of growth and change. Watching her plants and animals thrive and evolve taught her how positive it could be. But when expansion and money grubbing were embraced, something dark and sinister seemed to dominate.

Shirley, of course, knew nothing of Curva's concerns. Nor would he have cared, though Curva had knowledge that he wanted. Some Weedites had mentioned in passing her mysterious abilities—so she might be useful to him in more ways than one. Besides land and oil, he wanted to find out more about the Old North Trail; a few old-timers who lived near Sweetgrass had told him she was one of a handful of people in recent years that had actually traversed it.

Shirley had development ideas that would bring visitors to the trail—and their money.

He wanted to open up the ancient route and turn it into a gold mine. He pictured hotels at various points and sporting goods stores. Sightseers would be intrigued to know the trail had been an Indian thoroughfare at one time, making them more eager to explore it. He might even give Curva a job on the ranch he planned to buy in Alberta. She could care for his horses and take sightseers on trail rides. The greenhouse, too, could be a big draw. Something new: That's what people wanted. Shirley was eager to fulfill their desires.

There was one flaw in Shirley's plans. He hadn't been fully honest with himself about Curva. She intrigued him. Her reputation as someone not to tangle with attracted Shirley as much as her mysterious greenhouse. The more she refused to let him see inside the structure, the more certain Shirley felt she was hiding something from him. While he wanted to tame Curva, he also wanted to monitor what happened to the oil and gas rights. The more land he could buy, the better chance he had of making a killing.

Curva on the Old North Trail

Hola, mi estimado Xavier,

I watch wildflowers open in the morning. Dew hangs like jewels from their leaves and petals. They close at night and sleep. They nod their heads and shut their eyes and blink at me. I say to them, *Buenas tardes*, and Manuel and Pedro mimic me. I say, Shush, but that only makes them talk more. Shush, they say. *Buenas tardes.*

Sometimes I don't know if it's the flowers answering me or the parrots talking. They keep it up until I cover their cage. That quiets them.

Everything out here speaks in some way. The wind nudges the trees. They sway from the movement and creak and groan. I laugh when I hear this sound. Old women, I think. Some of the pine trees look like women wearing skirts.

The woods are noisy with animals scurrying around under the dry brush and busy, busy insects flitting back and forth. Bees buzz. Flies hum. Grasshoppers and crickets chirp. Dragonflies whirr. Mosquitoes whine. Birds twitter and trill. And those great golden eagles swish, swish through the air when they pass over.

I have my own mariachi band.

It's spring again and I watch things grow. In the fall I watch them die and send their seeds into the ground for a long hibernation. It's something I can depend on. This death and rebirth. Everything else is unpredictable. I don't know from day to day where I'll be or even who I am. I too change like the seasons. Every new experience I have on or off the trail alters me.

But I know the grass will poke through the soil in the spring and retreat in the winter. I know the sun will rise in the morning and its rays will make everything grow, filling me with warmth. I know it will set at night and the moon will take over. I know the moon will go through many stages in a month and so will the stars. I know how tree leaves glow when the sun slants off them and the musky smell the earth gives off at dawn. And I know the sound that songbirds make when calling to each other. I notice all of this on the trail. When I'm here, it's hard to think of myself as separate from my surroundings.

None of these things think about time. But I can see the results of its passing on my skin and in my body. I'm getting older, *mi hermano*. When I look in a mirror, I see lines starting to appear on my face. Dios is aging, too. More than me. He's slowing down, and I have to let him ride on the travois part of the time because he has trouble keeping up.

Dios is as important to me in some ways as a man. He licks my face with his rough, warm tongue and pokes his nose into my crotch, making me hot the way you used to. I finish the job with my fingers and one of Dios's bones. He yelps with me when I let out my own howl. Manuel and Pedro mimic my cry.

Suelita would laugh if she knew.

I saw her yesterday hanging around the edge of our campsite and talking like mad to a tree. She would go crazy without someone to talk to. I thought I saw Don Quixote too passing through the woods on his poor old horse. I called out to him, but he and his horse ran off. I must have scared him away.

Tonight I'm smoking some weed from my stash. The world loses its hard edges. Things blur together and time stops. It gives me a floaty feeling, and even the saddest things seem hilarious. Sometimes I find myself laughing and crying at once.

When I'm smoking, I don't feel alone anymore, and it makes me have colorful dreams. They fill up my nights. My own private theatre. Something to look forward to.

Sometimes I wonder if I'll ever reach my destination. Then I count the days passing so I have some idea of where I am and how long I've been traveling. But I lose myself for a while in each day and try not to think about where I'm going. That way I don't get trapped in being disappointed if things don't turn out the way I want.

In the towns or cities it's different. I become different. I forget this rougher, simpler life close to nature and enjoy taking warm baths and feeling like a normal woman again. I talk to strangers in bars, in cafes, in stores, practicing my *Inglés*. They want to hear about my travels and I have many stories to tell. Sometimes I make them up. You know me, Xavier. I have always liked a good tale.

You won't want to hear this, *mi hermano*, but I also enjoy a night or more with some nice men I meet in these places. Sometimes, they want to join me when I hit the road again. But I tell them you're my only travel companion. And it's true. You and the animals.

The Berumba Delegation

The morning when Ernesto Valenzuela Pacheco turned up in Curva's kitchen for the first time, Kadeem, the wizard, came tagging behind, heavy lidded and yawning. His broad-brimmed hat teetered on his head, and he gripped a rolled-up parchment, not looking a day older than when Curva had seen him last on the trail. Each man appeared

193

strong as a donkey.

So involved in transforming ordinary food into something heavenly, at first Curva didn't notice her visitors. She stood at the stove, singing and stirring, stray cats chasing each other around her legs. She dipped a spoon into the tortilla soup she was making and tasted it. *Más sal*, she said to the cats and generously shook the saltshaker over the pot. They meowed, ears perked up, waiting for her to drop some scraps. Manuel and Pedro meowed back.

On another burner, Curva was brewing dandelion flowers with raisins, water, sugar, lemon and orange peels in preparation for another batch of *vino*. Eyes closed, she sniffed each container, inhaling deeply, vapor steaming up the windows. *Bueno, bueno*, she said.

Bueno, bueno, a male voice chimed in.

It wasn't Manuel or Pedro.

It wasn't Xavier.

Startled, Curva jumped, simultaneously spinning around and reaching for her .38, tucked into the pocket of her peasant skirt where she'd put it after target practice that morning.

You don't need your weapon, *señora*. It's your old friends visiting again from Berumba. And they opened their arms in welcome.

Curva wasn't sure how to respond. Though her former employer and his sidekick were acting as if they were old friends of hers, when she lived at Ernesto Valenzuela Pacheco's house, Curva had been outside of the men's intimate circle. An employee as far as the master of the house was concerned, she knew her place.

Putting convention first, Curva ignored their outstretched arms, inviting them to sit at the kitchen table. *Aquí*, *Señor* Pacheco. *Aquí*, *Señor* Kadeem. Sit down. Sit down. And she

194

pointed to the scarred wooden chairs. Remembering how Xavier always seemed famished when he turned up, she assumed these guests from far off would also be hungry and offered them some *sopa*. My own recipe, she said.

Sí, sí, sopa. Muy buena!

Curva filled two bowls with soup and placed them on the table before her guests. She served herself one as well, crushing some tortilla chips into the broth, topping it with grated cheese she'd made from her goats' milk as well as the avocado she grew in the greenhouse, chopped into tiny pieces.

You have everything here, *señora*, Ernesto Valenzuela Pacheco said. He spread his hands wide: Everything! Big sky. Big country. We like. Don't we, Kadeem? He nudged his friend, who was dozing over the soup, the edge of his hat brim skimming its surface. He jerked awake, startled. No, no, he said. I will tell you everything.

Everything, Manuel and Pedro echoed.

Ernesto Valenzuela Pacheco laughed. Everything? What do you mean, *mi amigo*, ev-er-y-thing? Should I get you a priest so you can confess?

Kadeem rubbed his eyes and looked around. You are not the *policía*, he said.

No *policía* here, Curva said. Just Mounties.

Ah, of course, it's Curva, Kadeem said. The pulsations of your greenhouse led us here. Look, we have this map for you. He unrolled the frayed scroll he'd been carrying under his arm and spread it out on the table.

For me? she asked.

Sí, for you. It's very old and very precious. The only one of its kind left in the world. During my travels to the pyramids in Egypt, I stumbled over an ancient pottery vessel in the

195

desert. This map was inside it.

Curva frowned and said, What would I want with this map? My traveling days are over. She glanced from one man to the other.

This involves a different kind of travel, *señora*. Ernesto Valenzuela Pacheco has told me of your interest in prolonging life. He waved his hand over the parchment. This may help you.

Curva carefully picked up the scroll and studied it. I don't understand, she said. There is no map here. It's blank!

Sí, señora. You must fill it in.

Curva glanced at her former employer. Is this a joke? she asked.

He shrugged his shoulders and picked up one of the cats. It settled onto his lap, and he scratched its ears. Purring filled the room, and steam rose from the dandelion mixture simmering on the stove, fogging up the windows.

Kadeem leaned closer to Curva and whispered: The ink is invisible. You must find a way to make it appear again in order to learn its secrets.

Curva threw back her head and laughed. The sound resembled a sonic boom. You bring me a map that isn't a map. You tell me I must find a way to make the ink visible again. I'm not a magician, *señor*. You're the one who knows all these tricks and spells. I just grow things and make dandelion wine. You want some?

Sí, some *vino* would warm the heart, Kadeem said. Ernesto Valenzuela Pacheco nodded in agreement and continued to stroke the cat, lost in a dreamy haze.

Curva got up and returned with three glasses and a jug of *vino*. She filled the clear tumblers with the pale yellow liquid. They all picked up their drinks and Curva said *salud*.

Sí, salud. We need good health, Kadeem said.

Mucho, said Ernesto Valenzuela Pacheco. He raised his glass to the light. Look, *mis amigos,* liquid gold. Curva has had the recipe for it all this time.

Kadeem held his glass to the light as well. *Sí,* it's true. All those years you wasted trying to turn base metal into gold, you could have been drinking this *vino* instead. Maybe it is the elixir of life.

Ernesto Valenzuela Pacheco drained his glass and smacked his lips. *Delicioso,* he said, and asked for a refill. Curva gave him one and poured more for herself as well.

Kadeem, you're falling behind, she said, and aimed the jug at his glass.

I want to savor this potion, *señora.* It should be inhaled, not guzzled. Did I give you the map?

Sí, it's right here.

Of course, I remember now. Did I give you the seeds also?

Seeds? What seeds?

The kind you plant in the earth. Kadeem poked Ernesto Valenzuela Pacheco and said, Where did I put them, *mi amigo?* My pockets are full of holes. He passed one closed hand over his friend's ear and when he opened it, four seeds were there, brown and shriveled. Ah, *sí,* there they are. I found them in the same container as the map. Plant them in your greenhouse, *señora.* Then we'll see what kind of a gardener you are. Can you give life to something so many years old?

Curva took the withered kernels and rolled them around the palm of her left hand. She thought she could feel them pulse and held them up to her ear. It sounds like a heart beating, she said. Listen! She handed them to Ernesto

Valenzuela Pacheco.

I'm afraid my hearing isn't so good anymore. I don't hear anything. He set them on the table. They rolled and then hopped a little on the plastic cover, making a soft clicking sound.

You've cast a spell on them, Kadeem, she said.

No, they're just eager for the earth. Give them a home, *señora*. That will settle them down. We all need a home.

Curva got up and carried the soup bowls to the sink, the cats following her. She sang *La cucaracha, la cucaracha / Ya no puede caminar / Porque no tiene, porque le falta / marijuana para fumar*.[5] The men's voices joined hers, as well as the parrots', and they all burst out laughing at the end of the chorus, the sound shaking the house and bouncing off the windows, causing them to rattle. The vibrations rolled across the prairies and into the surrounding homes, making everyone in the area smile.

But when Curva returned with more *vino*, her guests had departed, leaving only Kadeem's cape behind and the parchment. The seeds were still doing a sedate dance on the table, clicking together at times like castanets. Enlivened by her recent visitors, she sang *La Cucaracha*, threw the Trinidadian's cape around her shoulders, furled the paper before placing it in a drawer, slipped the kernels into her pocket, and danced all the way to the greenhouse—a combination rumba and cha cha cha. She planted the seeds in four separate pots, using the richest Canadian soil she had. She even sprinkled them with a few drops of dandelion wine to add a little acidity to the earth.

---

5 The cockroach, the cockroach/Can't walk anymore/Because it doesn't have, because it's lacking/marijuana to smoke.

Sabina

When their punishment period had ended, Victor asked Sabina if she wanted to go fishing after school.

Sabina said, I'm off to help Billie.

Victor said, You're turning into an injun.

She slapped his face and the impact of her fingers made red marks. Sabina didn't care. He had insulted her and her friend.

Guilt filled Sabina whenever she thought of what she and Victor had done. She would never forget the look of betrayal on Billie's face when he arrived home to find his art destroyed. So she became his helper, hoping to atone for her part in the wreckage. She cleaned his cabin and studio, handed him tools, and watched how he worked with wood and paints.

Billie painted her into the mural he was working on, capturing her flame-colored hair and sky blue eyes. He also gave Sabina her own project to shape, a small block of wood for a totem, and said, I learned to carve them when I lived with the Squamish Nation on the coast. Most coastal tribes make them.

Sitting on a bench in his workshop, Sabina asked, Why do they make totems?

Billie planted himself in front of the post he was working on, a lit cigarette dangling from his lips. Wood chips flew into the air as he cut into it. He paused and went on, The totem poles show our belief in being spiritually connected to animals. The images tell our story as individuals and a people. Now I'm teaching my tribe about them. They'll become part of our heritage, too.

Sabina stared at him, paying full attention.

Billie puffed on the cigarette and watched the smoke drift away, lost in thought. Then he tossed the stub into a nearby can of water where it sputtered. He said, We believe each person has a totem animal that guides us in our life, and handed Sabina a pencil and carving knife. He chuckled: You can get started finding yours.

Fingering the tool Billie had given her, Sabina didn't know where to begin—what to carve or draw. Billie told her not to think too much about it. Let the tools do the work, he said. You'll be surprised.

And she was. After working on it for a few weeks, the piece began to transform itself into something she hadn't expected. The image was crude, but there was no mistaking the animal she had called forth: an owl.

Billie nodded when he saw the results. That's your totem now, he said, patting her shoulder, your animal spirit. It'll bring you good medicine. Maybe even some wisdom.

Sabina liked the idea of having a totem animal that would bring her good luck—Billie's explanation of good medicine. She didn't know about the wisdom, though. She hadn't shown much when she encouraged Victor to destroy Billie's totems.

Whenever Sabina walked onto the reserve, it was like stepping into another universe. Time moved differently, sideways almost. Even in circles. People didn't rush to get places. They sat together, smoking and talking. The pace was much slower, as if there was an endless amount of time for everything. Even the speech seemed unhurried. It reminded her of Curva's stories about Berumba in its early days.

Though Curva didn't pay much attention to clocks and schedules, the rest of the town did, and that shaped Sabina's

200

sense of things. Late for her first day of school, Sabina soon learned to be on time. Otherwise, she received a detention.

During one of her visits to the reserve, she learned the Blackfoot believed humans don't have dominion over all in sight. Yet Ian had told her the Bible claimed they ruled the animal kingdom. Billie held that a person wasn't any more important than a rock or a tree; everything in creation was equal. Nor were the Blackfoot interested in upward mobility, a term she had learned in Social Studies. From what she could see, they didn't seem very competitive. Most appeared content to just hang out with one another, avoiding the outside world, though some were spending more time in town since the bones were discovered there, assisting Billie.

She asked Billie why they kept to themselves so much. When she asked the question, he was working on his mural and sucking on an unlit pipe. He kept on painting and didn't say anything for a while. Then he set down the pipe and wiped his face with a red-checkered bandanna.

The rez feels safer, he said. Most people in town don't really see us or get us. You know what I mean?

Sabina nodded, though she wasn't quite sure she understood.

He went on, They only see what we aren't: we aren't white. We don't share the same culture or history. So we're invisible to them. On the rez, we feel seen and valued. That's why it's easier to keep to ourselves.

Billie picked up his pipe, stuck it in his mouth again, and resumed painting. Sabina grabbed some used brushes and washed them in a bucket of clean water, puzzling over Billie's comments and things she'd heard the tribe's elders talking about. They believed the Industrial Age had done more damage than good, and that's why they resisted

201

getting caught up in modern life any more than they had to. They clung to a past that had defined them and gave them some stature.

These insights helped Sabina understand Billie's desire to build a museum that would preserve his people's history and give witness to a cultural past almost lost to them. He wanted to restore pride and dignity to the Blackfoot and offer the youth a renewed sense of belonging.

And what did Sabina want? She longed to be recognized as one of the *Ni-tsi-ta-pi-ksi*—the real people. Billie assured Sabina she was an honorary *Siksika,* a Blackfoot. But Sabina wanted to be more than honorary. She wanted to actually be one. She begged Billie to tell her stories about the tribe's origins and his own youth. He always got such a serious, faraway look on his face when he talked about the old times.

Billie said, Remember when I told you about my vision quest and the run-in I had with an angry beaver.

Sabina nodded and laughed.

Well, it reminds me of the Beaver Medicine Legend I heard about as a child. I identified with the younger orphan boy, Akaiyan, whose older brother had abandoned him on an island. But after my vision quest, the tale seemed part of my story too.

Billie dabbed some paint on the mural and continued: A little beaver had found Akaiyan, who was weeping, and invited him into the beaver lodge. The beaver family invited Akaiyan to spend the winter with them, and he learned many things about herbs and roots and tobacco, as well as their songs and prayers and mysteries. In the spring, he returned to his tribal camp, teaching his people the wisdom and power of the beaver. He also invited all of the prairie and mountain animals to add their power to the Beaver Medicine, which is why it is considered the most potent of the bundles.

Billie sighed and said, I hope some of the beaver wisdom has rubbed off on me and I can pass it on.

Sabina still visited Ian and Edna whenever she had a chance. On her twelfth birthday, Ian gave her a gift. When she opened the box, wrapped in newsprint and tied with twine, she whooped. My own gun!

Not quite, Ian said. It's a camera that looks like a gun, lass. My own invention. You just point, pull the trigger, and bam, you have a picture. What do you think?

Sabina loved it, slipping the pistol into a special holster Ian had made for it. Her other camera had been bulky and difficult to carry around. Now she always had one at the ready.

Later that day, she stumbled across a dead horse in a nearby field. Maggots had invaded its carcass, and the grayish-white, fleshy worms swarmed over what remained of the body. Sabina stood transfixed by this run-in with death. The stench from the decaying corpse finally drove her away, but she couldn't leave before taking a picture of flies buzzing around the animal's head and the flesh riddled with maggots. The image burned in her mind and would live in her memory. But she had to capture it on film as well.

It wasn't just Ian's storytelling and darkroom skills that drew Sabina. She also was fascinated with his magic tricks. He entertained her with bouquets of flowers that he plucked mysteriously from the sleeve of his jacket or hundreds of hankies that he pulled from his trouser cuff. And he had numerous card tricks as well. His fingers nimbly flexed the deck and produced impossible combinations of cards.

After, he sat in his chair in front of the living room window and whistled through the wide space in his upper teeth, tapping his fingers on the arm. During those times, he seemed lost to Sabina, inhabiting a fantasy world she couldn't enter except through the stories he told her.

He described a girl who had special powers. Whenever she raised a hand, she upset the natural order, causing mammals to fly—without magic carpets—and generally creating mayhem. The girl didn't seem aware of her unusual abilities, innocently making those around her do phenomenal things, from turtles turning into roadrunners to the elderly regaining their youth.

Sabina listened, her eyes on Ian the whole time, not wanting to miss a word that came from his mouth. It amazed her that he could know such things. Ian's fictions were as interesting to her as Billie's, yet the men's tales were no more compelling than Curva's stories about her travels, especially along the Old North Trail.

Curva on the Old North Trail

Hola, mi estimado Xavier,

You must be wondering what I've learned all these years on the trail? You won't be surprised to hear I can be a foolish woman and I hate being one. Foolish, I mean. Only a fool would think she could stay in the womb forever with her brother and that's what I believed before you died. Curva! Curva! Curva! I shout at myself sometimes. How could you have been so *estúpida*.

I wasn't the only foolish one. So were you. You really believed I could be *su mejor muchacha*. I believed it too. It seemed normal for us to love each other *totalmente*. It made me feel special when you stroked my hair and said no other *muchacha*

204

could measure up to me. I believed you.

Now, I don't know what to think. I look at myself in the mirror. *Ordinaria*, I think. Not special. Not beautiful. *Grande. Muy grande* for a woman. Not soft and cuddly like so many *muchachas*. So I wonder what you saw when you looked at me. It must have been yourself you were in love with.

I don't blame you. I fell for you, too. No. I didn't fall for you. I always loved you. As a *bebé*. As a *muchacho*. As an *adolescente*. As a *hombre*. We should have been conjoined twins. Then when you died, I would have too. You and I were that close.

Why tell myself these things? It's like putting salt on an open wound. It burns. And for what reason? To punish myself some more?

No. Thinking about you helps me to keep you alive .

Four

Bone Song

How hopeful a false
spring feels, the buds
bursting to bloom
but holding back,
the earth lessening
its grip on plants,
daring them
to expose themselves
too soon.

Black Gold

While Curva might stop clocks at times, she ultimately didn't control time, and it continued its inexorable march, and so did Shirley. He had become a frequent visitor to Weed, having leased mineral rights from many landowners surrounding the town, as well as from the nearby Blackfoot reservation. Executives from the organization he represented had started drilling wells on some parcels of land and found oil.

Shirley swept up Curva's neighbors with stories about the area's growth and subsequent stature on the prairies. He stood in front of a group at the Odd Fellow's Hall, his Stetson pushed back on his head, words slithering out of his mouth: You'll make a bundle when these wells start to produce. If you haven't signed up yet, I still can contract with you. I'll make sure you have real concrete sidewalks in this town—not just these rickety wooden ones whose boards are rotting—and good roads. This gravel surface wrecks our vehicles!

Some resisted, but those who sold out to him suffered brief tugs of remorse whenever their clocks slowed, reminding them of Curva and her warning. But these feelings weren't enough to prevent the oil boom.

Meanwhile, word had spread that Southern Alberta was experiencing a lot of expansion. Job hunters and entrepreneurs got wind of it and made their way to Weed. The rebuilding after the tornado had attracted newcomers to the area. Workers on the dusty plains were laying iron, adding railway lines to Weed, and reshaping everything. Nathan Smart added on to his general store so he could carry more supplies—doubling its original size and forcing his wife

Sophie to work there full time.

A Swiss gentleman from back east visited the town, liked the possibilities, and built a bank.

A Greek immigrant opened a café.

A Chinese woman started a clothing store.

Some Germans opened a laundry service and dry cleaners.

A French Canadian family built the Weed Hotel, its billiard and beer parlor attracting patrons from miles around; after a night of gaming, gambling, and drinking, many of them ended up in the hotel rooms, too far gone to navigate home.

The Odd Fellows enlarged their hall, used for many purposes, from church services to funeral services, from bake sales to meetings. The occasional Odd Fellow gathering took place there, too.

The resurrected Weed thrived after the post-tornado chaos, and the town still catered to the farmers and ranchers that surrounded it. But it had extended its boundaries, attracting those who were more interested in commerce than agriculture.

Whenever Curva visited, she walked the rapidly expanding streets and watched the workers hammering and sawing and pouring concrete. Not even the occasional streams or sinkholes that sprung up around her could halt the new construction. She stopped at times to chat with Catherine Hawkins, Sophie Smart, and other neighbors and friends, urging them not to give in to Shirley's attempts to buy their oil rights. He'll turn this into another American boomtown, she said. It will be filled with outsiders.

Nathan Smart, whose business was thriving, rolled his eyes. You've got to be kidding, he said. Why should we turn away newcomers? You were a newcomer once yourself.

Curva smiled, her gold tooth glinting in the sunlight, but she didn't like being put in the same box as these strangers. She hadn't come to the area to exploit its resources. Surely she had more to offer than these new arrivals did. But she didn't say what was on her mind.

On the way to her truck, she ran into Inez Wilson. Curva said, *Hola!* I miss seeing you and the others at my place.

Shuffling her feet, Inez studied the ground and said, Shirley's asking a lot of questions. He wants to know all about you.

Curva shivered and said, Shirley? What's he up to?

Inez shook her head: I don't know, but he's telling everyone you're illegal. My husband and some of the other men think we women should stay away from you. They say you could cause trouble.

Me cause trouble? Curva laughed: Shirley's the one causing *mucho problemas*. They should be watching him.

Inez nodded: I tried to tell my husband that, but he just threw his hands up in the air and said you had blinded me.

Curva patted Inez on the shoulder: Don't get into trouble on my account, *mi amiga*.

Turning away, Curva strode to her truck, not looking right or left, ignoring the rivulet that followed her. Once she reached her *casa*, she paced the rooms, brooding about the massive changes taking place and the way her friends now viewed her. Illegal! Furious, she grabbed her rifle and ran outside, shooting several bullets into the sky, releasing a little of the anger she was feeling and wishing Shirley were flying over just then.

Curva's subsequent visits into Weed grew more infrequent.

And Shirley? He found several sections of land for himself—not far from Curva's property—and held the mineral rights. He expected to be a wealthy man in no time—more wealthy, that is, than he already was. Yet he hadn't expected Curva's continued resistance to his presence there. He thought she should be delighted to have his company strike oil at her place, but she wouldn't have any of it, one of the few residents to refuse his offer.

One night, he stopped by unannounced. Sabina answered the door, and Shirley invited himself inside, plopping down on the lumpy sofa, kicking up a poof of dust. He planted his Stetson next to him. Your mother around? he asked.

Yeah, sure, Sabina said. She's in the barn.

Can you get her? I have some business we need to discuss.

Sabina skipped out the door. A few minutes later, Curva appeared, Sabina at her heels. She turned to her daughter and said, Can you finish feeding the animals. Glaring at Shirley, Curva said, I didn't invite you inside, *señor*. What do you want?

He chortled: I need a little of that dandelion wine I've heard so much about.

Turning away, she said, I only make it for my friends and myself.

You mean I'm not a friend?

Leaning against the sink, Curva eyed him suspiciously and fingered the pistol she had slipped into her pocket. She shook her head and said, No, *señor*, you're no one's friend.

He wagged his finger at her and flashed a wad of leases: You could be rich and fix up this house. Hell, build a new one! Buy new furniture. Put Sabina in college. Why are you so stubborn, woman?

Curva scowled. Why are you so blind, *señor?* You think

210

I came all this way just to watch Weed turn into another Berumba?

Berumba?

Yes, *señor*, Berumba.

Okay, *señora*, so what's the big deal about Be-rum-ba?

I learned many things there.

What "things"?

Curva scowled. I don't think you'd understand.

Try me!

She stared out the window a few minutes—envisioning the Berumba she loved—before answering. The place started out *muy tranquillo*, she said. People helped each other. They spent *mucho* time together when they weren't working—eating and drinking. Enjoying life. Satisfied. No one had much money, but it was okay. They got by. Everything was in harmony. The animals. The people. The land.

Shirley lit a cigarette, sucked deeply on it, and flicked the used match onto the floor. He said, You make it sound like some paradise.

It was *paraíso* before *hombres* like you showed up. The Banana Company people came to town and took over. They didn't give a damn about us. Made *mucho dinero* and then left. We were never the same after that. That will happen here.

Shirley waved off her words. He said, You're making a mountain out of a molehill.

Shrugging, Curva wiped the counter with a dishcloth. No, I'm not, she said. You're out for all you can get. You'll tramp on anyone in your way. Including me. I heard you're telling everyone I'm here illegally.

You got papers saying you're legal?

I've got papers saying I own this place. You think I'm illegal just because I'm from Me-he-co. You're an *americano*.

Are you legal?

She threw the dishrag into the sink and wiped her hands on her skirt. She hated everything about Shirley and what he represented. She also hated the attraction she had felt whenever she saw him. This time she was grateful to only feel disgust.

Shirley startled her when he got up and stubbed out his half-finished cigarette on a nearby plate that held the remains of Sabina's dinner. He said, You make it sound like I'm ruining your nice little nest here. Birds can't stay in their nest forever, you know. They need to get out and find food. Fly. You can't protect this town, Curva. It's taking off without you. He made a flying motion with his right hand.

Curva heard Billie's truck pull up outside. He appeared on her doorstep minutes later, giving a light knock before entering. Shirley shook his hand: Hey, Billie, good to see you. Did you bring the signed leases?

Didn't know you'd be here, Billie said, or I would have. Stop by tomorrow and I'll give them to you.

Leases? Curva said.

Billie pulled up a kitchen chair and straddled it. Yeah, Billie, said, they're gonna drill on the rez.

The rez?

Sure, Shirley said. The surveys show Billie and his people are sitting on oodles of black gold.

Curva looked dismayed and said, Bee-lee, you're not going to let this *gringo* take over your land?

Shirley shoved his Stetson on his head and headed for the door. I'll see you tomorrow, Bee-lee. Let me know when you want another ride in my plane, *señora*. You'll see things differently from up there. He winked and walked out, the screen door slamming behind him.

Billie leaned back on the chair, watching Curva carry dishes from the table to the dishpan, her hips swiveling under the thin fabric of her skirt. She poured water into the pan and a little soap. He missed hearing her usual laughter and chatter.

He asked, What's on your mind?

She swung around. I can't believe you of all people would give the *gringo* your mineral rights.

Billie spit out, You think I'm some noble savage? You expect us to stand by and let everyone else get rich? Doesn't matter if we're dirt poor as long as we're true to our ideals?

I thought you cared about nature. Being one with the land.

Billie hit the table with his hand. We do. Oil is part of nature!

Curva slammed a pot on the counter, punctuating her words: Oil is black and slimy and evil. You'll see, Bee-lee. It will rule. Ugly oil wells will be everywhere.

Billie pulled a tobacco pouch from his pocket, took a cigarette paper from inside it, dropped some tobacco onto the tissue, and rolled it with one hand, licking and pressing the paper together. He popped the smoke into his mouth, struck a wooden match against the bottom of the chair, and lit it, puffing greedily, spurts of smoke mingling with the words that left his mouth: You know what kind of land we have on the rez. It doesn't grow much. Never has. This is a chance to make something useful from it. There'll be enough money in our tribal fund to build my museum and more. I thought you were all for that.

Curva walked to the screen door and looked out into the night before answering, afraid Shirley might be there, listening in on their conversation. She noticed the light was on

213

in the greenhouse and pictured Sabina watching the butterflies mate, one of her favorite things. It touched her to think of her daughter in that way, so involved with these incredible creatures. Then she remembered that Billie was waiting for her response.

She said, I'm all for you building a museum. I just don't like financing it this way. This guy is bad news with his airplane and beeg talk. You'll see. Once the oil is all gone, Weed will be a ghost town.

But I'll have my museum! And the Blackfoot will have some money. We can be self-supporting. Not children waiting for handouts. You can afford to be honorable. You've got an income, some savings. You own this place. We can't ever own our land, but we can hold the mineral rights.

Curva wasn't listening to Billie. She was sure she heard Shirley's plane buzzing overhead, circling her place. Suelita Flores stood next to her, whispering in her ear *Sí, sí, mi amiga, él es muy atractivo, es hora de volar,*[6] and she laughed heartily, making Curva laugh, too, the sound disturbing the air above them, causing *mucho turbulenci*a in the sky for Shirley.

Oil Fever

The next few months flew by in a flurry of activity in and around Weed. New people arrived every day. Oil wells sprouted on the land like giant erector sets. Everything shifted into high gear. The high level of excitement made residents feel they were gripped by something uncontrollable.

Catherine Hawkins found herself eyeing the guys who flooded the place to work on oilrigs. Curva's words still rang in her ears that a young man was in her future. The future

_____

6 Yes, yes, my friend. He's very sexy. It's time to fly.

was now, and Catherine was ready. She didn't want to run out on her husband and kids, but she did long for some diversion. Caught up in the heady atmosphere, she fussed with her hair and applied lipstick and rouge before prancing downtown in a pair of new spike heels that showed off her shapely legs. Passing a group of oilrig workers, she got some whistles, which created flutters in the pit of her stomach. It added flavor to her life just to know other men still found her attractive.

Catherine wasn't the only one feeling the effect of rapid changes. No longer able to linger in her garden or meet with the Ladies Aid Society at the Odd fellow's Hall, Sophie Smart had to help out at their store. She missed gossiping with the women and working on their many sewing projects for poor children in other lands—quilts, coats, dresses, shirts. But Sophie also liked the extra money she had in her bank account and the new places to spend it that were sprouting around her. Between customers, Sophie leaned dreamily on the counter and thought about all the things she would buy with the money she and Nathan were making—an electric toaster, a new washing machine, a poppy red dress she fell for in the nearby ladies ready-to-wear store. She spent hours fantasizing about these new purchases and the way they would enliven her days.

The frenzied construction and all the oilfield activity made everyone move at a heightened pace. Many felt as if another tornado had hit, except this one built up the town instead of tearing it down. The residents barely had time to catch their breath before another house mushroomed on the prairies or an additional oil well came in. While Curva had stirred things up when she first arrived in the area, it was nothing compared to what Shirley had turned loose.

The tornado and its aftermath had revealed one force of nature. Oil was another, and oil fever gripped Weed. The thick black goo could hardly be contained, threatening to overflow and flood the surroundings. But the townsfolk only thought of all the money it would bring in. They pictured themselves awash in riches.

A few of the women still occasionally hightailed it to Curva's *casa* for wine or brownies, an island of calm amid this flurry of action. Time stood still there, offering respite from the accelerated tempo that had gripped the townspeople. The geyser at the center of Curva's greenhouse gurgled and murmured, its refreshing spray cascading twenty-four hours a day. The sound soothed those within earshot and slowed them down. But oil's seductive power had more influence over them than she once did. Most neighbors resented her attempts to stop the frenzy that had taken hold of them, and Curva's so-called supernatural abilities and magical presence receded. Shirley's world had firmly established itself.

Curva tried to ignore the mania that clutched her neighbors. It saddened her to see everyone so tightly wound. When she went to town, she hardly recognized the place any longer. New shops and houses had sprung up everywhere she looked—bakery, clothing, and shoe stores; banks; a movie house.

The excitement also impacted Ian and Edna. Ian wrote ten children's books in less than a year and found a publisher for them all, leaving him no time for the darkroom or Sabina. Edna built and opened a new school and became the principal.

But Edna had other things on her mind than teaching. She struggled with her highly sexual nature that Curva

216

had pointed out in her palm reading. Edna's sexual urges themselves, never easy to keep under control, were worse now that someone had recognized and validated them. After Curva's comments about Edna's big Mount of Venus, her daily contact with sexually active teenagers made her more conscious of her own desire. So did being around the strangers in town, drawn by the boom. Handsome lads, they aroused Edna's fantasies of slipping away into the fields with one of them on a warm moonlit night. But then she caught herself. What was she thinking? She was the school principal, though she wouldn't be for long if she followed her urges. That Curva! She'd started all of this.

To say that life had become more complicated for Weedites would be an understatement. None of these things were bad, *per se*. Who would argue that creativity and progress and new schools aren't important? But few had extra time anymore to just hang out with one another. The focus was mainly on development, making money, and finding ways to spend it.

Even the Saturday barn dances ceased. Residents were so possessed that they couldn't unwind. They resembled Mexican jumping beans, moving erratically, or tops, spinning crazily, toppling over if they slowed down for even a minute. By the weekend, they were so exhausted that playing music and dancing didn't attract them.

In the midst of all these changes, Curva continued her daily routine. But she also regularly took the area's pulse. Don Quixote had taught her that things aren't always as they appear on the surface, so she studied what was happening around her for its hidden meaning, trying to discern the message it carried.

She didn't feel it was an accident when she came across a snake in the road or a dead animal in the fields. Each was trying to speak to her through its image and carried multiple meanings, as did the constantly changing pictures in the clouds. The snake alerted her to be on the lookout for someone underhanded, and, sure enough, Shirley had appeared at her place soon after. And the animal carcass communicated that something was dying, which coincided with the death of the Weed she had known and loved.

Curva now also made wine from the fruits, flowers, and vegetables she grew, expanding her range, amazed at the process they went through to become spirits. Metamorphosis happened constantly. One thing changed into another form, like the clouds' transmutations, the graceful way they shifted shape. Death appeared to be just another stage in an ongoing process, and she tried to understand the oil boom in that light. Yet it was difficult to believe Weed's transformation was ultimately positive when her friends and neighbors struggled to keep up with all the upheaval.

And Billie? He sent fat checks to all the tribal members—their share of the profits. The rest went into a trust managed by Billie's assistants, Robin and Joe. The band now could afford to develop its community, and there was plenty of money left for the museum Billie had envisioned.

An architect from the Cree Nation designed a structure that exactly fit Billie's vision for the place. Located on the burial ground and called Ni-tsi-ta-pi-ksi Cultural Center, it resembled a giant teepee hovering over the land like a hydroplane, its profile visible for miles around. Totem poles Billie had taught other Blackfoot to carve guarded the periphery. The museum also honored the fossils found in the area, featuring them in glass cases, and there were many displays of indigenous life, past and present. A constant reminder to locals of the Blackfoot, the museum was lit up at night and glowed like a flaming arrow on the plains.

The Weedites may not have liked the way this structure stood out, but they didn't have any say in its construction. They had to put up with it. Still, the place did attract visitors. That meant more money for the shopkeepers and restaurant owners. And the townspeople themselves were drawn to it. By pressing a button in the Vision Quest Theater, they could begin a mini-quest that would mimic a real one. Billie hoped it would inspire others to undertake their own adventures. They also visited the Old North Trail exhibit. After leaving Ni-tsi-ta-pi-ksi Cultural Center, they felt they had made a journey to another time and place, not just to view a collection of dinosaur fossils and Indian artifacts that Billie's people had collected from all over the province and beyond.

At Curva's urging, Catherine Hawkins talked her husband into exploring the place. So did Inez, Sophie, and Curva's other friends. They all met at the museum one Sunday and bought tickets from a tribal woman who wore her traditional dress. They muttered to one another about the high cost of entry as they shuffled inside. Light from a round skylight at the massive teepee's top flooded a slightly raised circular platform. At the platform's center stood a carved wooden sculpture of a Blackfoot warrior aiming his arrow at the sky.

Sophie was the first to speak: Holy cow, this place is amazing. Look at the stairs! They circle the interior.

In a daze of light and skyward movement, they climbed past glass display cases of female and male headdresses;

glowering animal masks; intricately beaded ceremonial costumes; horned buffalo war bonnets; beaded leather moccasins; powwow dancers' porcupine headbands; warbonnets; and more. Catherine gasped at the exhibit of a white woman in a nun's garment. The nun stood behind a desk and glowered at students lined up in front of her. When Catherine pressed a button, a voice described the Christian boarding schools many tribal children had to attend that caused them to reject themselves and their communities. Catherine shook her head and said, I didn't know this happened. She looked around at her friends to see how they were responding, and they, too, had shocked looks on their faces.

The group continued past exhibits that included hunting and gathering tools, weapons, photos of early reservation life, as well as teepee replicas and their contents. Inez blurted out, Billie oversaw all of this, you know. The women nodded at each other, impressed that he could recreate such realistic settings and inhabit them with equally realistic-looking replicas of tribal people. It made Billie a kind of magician.

Images the Weedites saw at the cultural center haunted them for days, even turning up in their dreams. The Blackfoot history had also partly become theirs. Though they hated to admit it, the museum now was an integral part of everyone's consciousness. It also drew as much attention as Curva's greenhouse, resembling something from outer space suspended over the earth.

The Blackfoot's development plans didn't stop with the Ni-tsi-ta-pi-ksi Cultural Center. They also wanted their own university. Faculty would teach their language and other subjects not normally found in publicly funded colleges: indigenous food and cooking; tribal music and dancing; totems and carving; history and rituals. Math and science, incorporated into the other classes, would be hands-on subjects.

The Weedites could no longer ignore the Blackfoot. They weren't just "injuns" on the reservation. Their money was as good as anyone's. No longer poor outcasts, they too were becoming movers and shakers.

Curva on the Old North Trail

Hola, mi estimado Xavier,

The wild animals I've met on the trail have taught me mucho. I watch them interact with each other. No one is telling them what to do or how to do it. They follow their noses. And what noses they have! They know everything about me before they even see me just by sniffing the air.

I've been trying to train my nose to be more like theirs. Now when I'm in town I push away any thoughts I have and just smell people. Some reek of goodness; they know what's right for everybody. Others give off a dusty odor; they're already in the grave. My nose tells me many things.

I think dreams are noses. They sniff out things I wouldn't know any other way.

One day a woman at a rooming house in Elko, Nevada, started talking to me. She seemed very friendly and wanted to know all about my travels. We sat on the porch at night and talked and smoked and drank *vino*. You know how I am after a little *vino*. I blabbed about things I wouldn't have told other strangers. I talked about my time in Berumba. I told her of *hombres* I've met on the rodeo circuit. Bone-hard *hombres* who don't know how to make love. She nodded her head and seemed to understand what I was saying. I told her of times I stole food from stores because I didn't have any *dinero* and almost got thrown in jail.

I even told her about the *hombre* I lived with for a while

221

in Wyoming. I met this guy at the rodeo they held once a year. He was the clown and protected us riders once we got thrown. He ran around the ring in his baggy clown clothes and big red nose, waving off the horses and bulls. *Muy peligroso.*

I ended up saving him from a bull that chased him all over the ring. I kicked the horse I was riding with my boots, and we cut in front of the bull. The clown had time to duck into a chute. His name was Mike and he'd grown up on a nearby ranch. Such an ordinary name and an ordinary man. But we had many laughs together, especially when he found out I was a woman. He helped me become human again, and he didn't tell my secret. I'd become like an animal myself after spending so much time with them. I hardly knew how to act with people.

Yet I finally had to leave him. You and the trail called to me, and Mike didn't want any part of it. He wanted kids. That's all he could talk about. Getting married and having *niños.* Being tied down by a *familia* wasn't what I wanted. So I said *adios* to him. He wasn't in the cards for me.

A woman needs other women to talk to sometimes. It's too much to carry these things all by ourselves. You're not a woman but it's why I scribble all over these pages to you. I feel someone is listening to me, and I can read these pieces of paper when I get lonely. Being on the road so much makes it hard to make *amigas.*

But this time I had said too much. The woman at the rooming house wasn't an *amiga.* My dream nose showed me why.

I dreamed she was standing on a stage in the town square and telling *mucha* people all the stories I told her. The dream turned out to be true. She was a bartender and my stories soon came back to me from people she served drinks to. Yak yak yak. That's all she did. She was not *mi amiga*. Foolish Curva. I trusted her but she was just a gossip and needed some fuel for the fires she starts.

I got out of that town fast.

The Magician

Curva was sitting at the kitchen table, studying the blank parchment Kadeem had left her, when Xavier strode into the room, wearing a magician's hat and a black cape that swirled around his legs. He stood in the doorway, silhouetted by the sunlight, resembling a dark keyhole.

She glanced up when his shadow fell across the table. *Mi hermano!* Why are you wearing that crazy outfit? She gestured towards a chair: Sit down, sit down. Maybe you can help me with this map.

Xavier flung the cape back over his shoulders, revealing the scarlet lining, and leaned over the table. Map? I see no map. Maybe my eyesight is going. Is that why I can't see Sabina? Where is she?

No, no, there's nothing wrong with your eyes. Sabina is helping *mi amigo* Bee-lee at the Center. Look, Xavier, Kadeem gave me this paper. You know what crazy ideas he has. He said I must make the ink visible if I want the secret to immortality. Any tips?

Xavier laughed and said, Why not sprinkle a little of your *vino* on the page?

Bueno, bueno, idea magnífica. I like, Curva said. She jumped up and descended into the cellar, returning with a jug of *vino*. You want some, *mi hermano?*

Sí, I could use something to warm this heart of mine. It's gotten too cold.

Curva poured two glasses and handed one to him. *Salud,* she said.

Gracias, señora.

So formal?

So proper, *mi hermana.* You should be treated with respect, he said, standing up and bowing.

Curva studied Xavier, not sure if he were serious. The tall magician's hat he was wearing seemed a little large on him and covered his ears. She smothered a laugh, reminded of when he was a boy and would wear his father's sombrero, the brim nearly touching his shoulders.

Where did you get that outfit? Curva asked.

He smiled. I can't tell you all of my secrets. I get around, you know.

I can see that.

Xavier offered a chair to Curva. At your service, *señora.* She gave a mock curtsey and sat down. He joined her. They sipped their *vino,* relishing just being together again. Curva filled the silence with a torrent of words, describing all the growth she was witnessing in her greenhouse, except for the four pots that held the kernels Kadeem had given her. Nothing's happened yet, she said. I guess they don't want to be reborn. But my butterflies: *Olé!* They've left their cocoons and some are on their way to Mexico. Very exciting!

New life? Sounds good. But immortality? He swilled his glass of *vino* and held it out for a refill. Very tasty, he said. Not like death. People have to accept death, *mi hermana,* before they're ready for immortality. You should know that!

Curva poured him more *vino* and topped hers off. I don't agree, she said. Immortality beats death.

Xavier shook his head. You've paid too much attention to Ernesto Valenzuela Pacheco. I remember him spending hours seeking something to extend life. But death got him first. It's still the gateway.

Xavier got up, walked over to the fridge, and opened the door, sniffing at its contents like a dog. Are you saving these leftovers for anyone?

Sí, for you. I knew you'd be back.

Xavier grabbed a bowl of tortilla soup and carried it to the table. Curva watched the cape sway as he crossed the room, mesmerized by the movement. You still haven't told me why you're wearing that getup, she said.

He shrugged: You know me. I've always loved magic. Death is all about sleight of hand. Making things disappear. You're a magician too!

Not funny, Xavier.

It's true, don't you think? Death is a magician. Now you see someone; now you don't. Here today, gone tomorrow. You've heard all the clichés.

Curva pointed at the stove. Don't you want to heat the soup?

Xavier shook his head. Not necessary, he said. I've grown to like cold things.

That's not funny either, Xavier. Don't magicians make things reappear too? Can you do that? Can Death?

Look at me. I've reappeared, he said. He lifted the bowl to his lips and guzzled its contents. Then he set it on the table, wiping his mouth with his sleeve.

Does that mean I'll also come back when I die?

I can't tell you everything, *mi hermana*. I've sworn to be silent about these matters. It's the condition for me making these visits. There need to be some mysteries, don't you think?

Well, here's a mystery for you, Curva said. Help me with

this map.

Xavier picked up his glass of *vino* and used it to wash down the soup. *Muy bueno,* he said. *Más.*

Curva gripped the jug and refilled both of their glasses. A few drops fell on the parchment.

Look! Xavier said. He pointed at a spidery brown line that had surfaced there. I was right.

They both bent over the table and watched the damp area begin to talk to them visually. Fragments of words appeared. Xavier dipped his fingers in the *vino* and flicked more of it onto the paper. Additional letters crept across it.

Can you understand what they say? Curva asked.

Nada. It's all Greek to me.

Maybe it is Greek, Curva said. That would make sense, wouldn't it? A scroll appearing in an old pottery container on the desert? Ancient Greeks could have left it there.

If you mix a Greek and a Mexican, what do you get?

A mutt, Curva said.

Or else Kadeem.

Curva laughed. He's a Trinidadian.

The same thing, he said. Xavier was studying the letters. Do you know anyone who speaks Greek?

Kadeem does. The fox. He must have known all along I would need him to interpret.

The gravel scattered in the driveway, and Curva heard a vehicle come to a stop.

Xavier looked startled. Company?

Curva glanced out the window. It's Bee-lee. He must've brought Sabina home. I'd like them to meet you.

When she turned around, the room was empty. But she could still feel his presence, lurking, watching, and she was sure she could smell his spicy shaving lotion, a brand he loved. She'd forgotten how shy he could be with strangers.

Accompanied by a gust of freezing air, her face flushed, Sabina pushed open the screen door and burst inside, waving her camera at Curva. I took pictures of everything! she said. We're going to use them to advertise the Center. And I helped Billie set up more exhibits. He even let me include the totem poles I made.

Fabuloso! Now you can help me cook dinner.

Sabina groaned. Couldn't Billie help you? I need to check on the butterflies.

Billie stood inside the doorway, shuffling his feet. I've gotta meet someone in town, he said. Maybe I'll stop by later. After dinner.

Curva asked, Who's the hot date?

His face flushed. Shirley. We need to talk business. What's that strange smell?

Curva laughed. My new perfume. You like, Bee-lee? She was sure she heard Xavier laughing, too. She said, Are you trying to change the subject?

Billie raised his arms as if in surrender. Me? No. What's the subject?

You said you were meeting Shirley. What's that *bandito* up to now?

He has some ideas for promoting the Center.

Ah, just what we need, no? More development. More people. More money. More of his oil wells.

Sabina had heard her mother's rant about Shirley enough times. She slipped past Billie and out the kitchen door, heading for the greenhouse. From her current height of five foot, it was clear she wasn't going to take after Curva physically.

Billie shoved his hands in his pockets and turned to leave.

The way you talk, he said, the rez was a kind of Eden before we got rich. You forget what it was like for us. No money. Trapped by poverty. You don't know about the complex Indian Act. It says how bands can operate and sets out rules for governing our reserves. It's been used to control us since the late 1800s. We can now leave the rez, but the Act made it much harder in the past. Now most of us stay because we feel safer there. You have some noble idea that being poor and free of "progress" means everyone's better off. You need to come down to earth. Get real, *señora*.

Curva had never heard so many words come out of Billie's mouth at one time—a veritable flood. And for once she was speechless as she watched her friend and lover slam the screen door and stride across the driveway to his truck.

Xavier's laugh caught her off guard and made her jump. So that's Bee-lee, he said, standing at her side, resting a hand on her shoulder. She nodded, *Sí*.

He stood next to her, and the two of them stared out the window, watching the dust rise from the dirt road. It picked up intensity as the truck gained speed, sending up puffs that resembled inscrutable smoke signals.

The Gringo

Snowdrifts piled up in the yard, creating a sea of white, occasionally broken by the tops of fence posts. Curva sat at the kitchen table, nursing a cup of coffee and staring at the map Kadeem had left, trying to make sense of the marks that had appeared there. Snow and freezing temperatures made it more difficult to do anything other than hibernate. Her wreck of a car seized up during the severe cold spells, and its heater barely worked. She became dependent on friends and neighbors to give her lifts into town when it was too cold to ride one of her horses. The frigid weather made her seize up as well.

Her concentration scattered when she heard a vehicle's wheels crunch on packed snow in her driveway. Her dog growled, part of a litter Dios produced with Diosa before he died. He looked so much like his sire that Curva ended up calling him the same name. Diosa was so heartbroken about her companion's death that she had wandered off and is still looking for him.

Curva glanced up, expecting to see Billie's truck. He often stopped by on the way to the Center to have coffee with her—or to climb between the covers and play, especially on a cold day like this. But it was Shirley striding across the yard. He wore a green ski jacket and jeans, his Stetson planted squarely on his head. Dios growled menacingly at him. Curva felt like doing the same.

Hey Curva, he yelled, Call off your mutt.

Curva turned the map face down and opened the door. A rush of cold air blew past her.

She yelled Dios, *venido aquí.* The dog understood her better in Spanish than in English. He loped towards Curva but lost his footing on ice that gripped the doorstep, sliding off. She bent over and wrapped her arms around him. Oh, you crazy animal, she said, imitating the way the dog stuck out his tongue and panted, barking a little herself.

Then she remembered her guest and jumped up. Shivering in her caftan, she said, What are you doing here, *señor?* Shouldn't you be checking out all your oil wells? There's no money to be made here.

You have me all wrong, Curva. I have more interests than money. Your greenhouse, for instance. You've never given me a tour, but I've heard lots about it and your hospitality. Aren't you going to invite me inside? It's freezing out here!

Frowning, she gestured for Shirley to follow her into the warm interior, her flowery dress billowing behind.

Tossing his hat onto a nearby chair, he strode over to the wood-burning stove at the center of the room and held his hands near the heat, turning them until the chill melted.

Gliding to the table, she rolled up Kadeem's map and slipped it into a nearby drawer.

My greenhouse isn't for *turistas, señor*. Anyway, there's nothing to see. Just some plants and birds and butterflies. Nothing *especial*. Only of interest to me, I'm afraid. She crossed to the stove and added a log, adjusting the door afterward, brushing away some ashes.

Why does everyone talk about it then?

She approached one of the windows and stared at the snow, but the barren landscape depressed her—white everywhere, everything in stasis. She needed to view growing things to feel alive herself. That's why the greenhouse was so essential to her. And it's why she wouldn't allow Shirley to exploit it.

You're not answering my question, Curva.

She let out a big sigh: Don't you wish snow came in different colors? I'm going to paint a rainbow on all of my windows so when I look outside I'll see something besides white and grey.

I've heard of looking at the world through rose-colored glasses, *señora*, but not a rainbow. You're a strange woman. He shrugged off his jacket and hung it on the same chair that held his hat.

Curva bristled: What do you want from me, *señor?* I didn't invite you to stay.

230

He got a bemused look on his face and said, You remind me of alligators I used to wrestle in Florida. I got kind of attached to them. They can be quiet for a while, and you think you're safe around them. Then suddenly they strike.

Curva howled, the sound rattling the dishes in the sink. You, an alligator wrestler? You *do* have other interests. But alligators—they can be deadly. Why're you here if you think I'm dangerous?

I like danger.

But you think I look like an alligator? That's not flattering.

You don't *look* like an alligator, but I wouldn't turn my back on you.

Nor I on you, *señor*. What is it about danger you like?

Challenges make life more interesting. You know that, señora. They test you. That's why I fly a plane. I never know what I'll run into up there. Bad weather. Winds. The unexpected.

Curva picked up another log, opened the door on the woodstove, and tossed it inside, sending sparks into the air. She went over to the counter and leaned on it: You weren't wrestling alligators just for the fun of it.

Shirley laughed: True. I made good money doing it. I also worked a few air shows. Parachuting and landing on selected targets. That paid pretty well, too.

Am I just another target you're trying to land on?

Outside Dios growled and then barked. Curva went to the door and opened it, relieved to see Billie park his truck next to Shirley's. Dios ran over to greet Billie, jumping up and licking his face. She felt like doing the same.

Curva didn't want to acknowledge that perhaps likes attracted—to admit she resembled Shirley in any way. Yes, she also was an adventurer. Still, her arrival in Weed had been very different from Shirley's. She didn't drop out of the sky in a fancy plane, looking to buy up a lot of land and mineral rights and then lord her power over everyone. Yet Curva would have been astonished if anyone suggested she also had changed the community and at a more profound level than Shirley did.

But at the moment, Billie had never looked so good to her. He waved, slogging through the snow to her door. Time to get out the snow shovel, he said and stepped inside, kicking off his boots and lining them up on a mat next to hers.

Sí, Bee-lee, I know. Shirley is just leaving. He's on his way to check on his wells. Curva embraced Billie. He smelled like the woods and looked a little like a friendly pirate with his black eye patch. He wore a red plaid logger's jacket and brown cords, and his long hair hung loose today. She looked forward to playing with it after Shirley left, braiding it, even intertwining it with her own.

Shirley shook Billie's hand and picked up his jacket and hat. Damn cold, he said, setting his hat squarely on his head and slipping into his coat.

Looks like a Chinook is on its way, Billie said. That should warm things up for a few days.

Shirley nodded: Can't get used to them. Strange to see the land stripped naked after being covered with heaps of snow. See you around, Billie. And he stomped down the wooden steps, barely missing the ice patches. Dios nipped at Shirley's heels all the way to the truck.

Curva on the Old North Trail

Hola, mi estimado Xavier,

A moose came crashing into our camp two days ago. It would have trampled both Dios and me if I hadn't aimed

232

and shot right away. I had to shoot to kill. Between the eyes. If I hadn't, I wouldn't be here to write about it.

I spent the rest of the day skinning the animal and up to my shoulders in blood. I dry-cured some of the meat and saved a big hunk to roast over the fire that night. I still had a few potatoes left and roasted one in the embers with the meat. A salad of miner's lettuce and berries. *Delicioso.*

The smell attracted lots of curious neighbors. The squirrels stayed up in the trees far away from the foxes. I placed the leftovers on the edge of our camp for our friends to feast on. It was nice to have the company and it turned out to be a real party.

I played for them and sang:

La cucaracha, la cucaracha
Ya no puede caminar
Porque no tiene, porque le falta
Marihuana que fumar.

Even the deer, raccoons, opossums, and rabbits got into the music, bobbing their heads and tapping their feet. Who said animals don't have rhythm? Soon the whole clearing was filled with a bunch of crazy fools dancing and singing and carrying on, and it wasn't just the critters.

Remember that mad Trinidadian Kadeem? He and his band turned up in wooden caravans pulled by horses. They're painted all sorts of colors. Red. Blue. Green. Yellow. Purple. I like all the curly designs on them. I looked inside. So cozy! Cushions to sleep on. Built-in cupboards. Chairs. They're more comfortable than a tent, and they don't have to be set up every night. A real *casa.*

I wish I'd known about them before I started this trip. It would have been much easier on me.

I was so excited to see other humans on the trail I almost

crushed them with my bear hugs. I learned the Trinidadians had traveled the trail for years before they found Berumba. They know it better than I do and have given me tips that will help me reach the Calgary Stampede.

Today one of them walked alongside the wagons and played drums that hung from his neck. *Boom boom. Boom boom.*

It sounded like the mountains were talking in a big booming voice. Enough to wake the dead. I heard the bones of former travelers now clicking underground in time to the drums, and I kept waiting for you to appear.

Another visitor played a violin. The sounds were *triste* and made me cry buckets. It was like a human voice lamenting over many sorrows. The tears slithered along the ground down to the river and made it rise. Flowers have started to grow in their wake. I haven't cried like that since you died. I don't understand where all those tears come from. This body can't hold so many.

I won't be listening to violins again anytime soon.

The caravans overflowed with families and the things they were selling. Pots, knives, forks, and spoons they've made. Dishes with pretty pictures on them. Embroidered pillowcases and tablecloths and doilies—things I don't care much about. Nails. Hammers. Saws. Rugs piled on top of the caravans. Even eggs. One cart housed a bunch of chickens. I could hear their screeching for miles. Their voices wondrously scattered chicken feed all over the ground wherever I looked. Chicken feed like snow.

A couple of belly dancers moved to the music, one on each side of Kadeem. The women rotated their hips and shook their bare bellies. They left a trail behind them of purple silk. It was wound around their ankles and unraveled with every step they took. An endless stream of ribbon and a great trail marker.

I want to do that dance more and show off my belly. It's the best part of my body. A pillow for a man's head and a little cave inside.

Of course, Suelita refused to be left out of the party and also turned up. She showed the belly dancers a thing or two with her own bumps and grinds.

I wanted to hear all the news from Berumba and she gave me an earful. *Mi amiga*, she said. You aren't missing much. The town hasn't been the same since you left. You've inspired some Berumbians to also explore the world, hoping to create their own Berumba elsewhere. Many have followed you north, you know. They keep hearing your music and can't resist chasing it like a dog after bones.

She roared and said, Oh no! Did you hear that? I can't get bones off my mind. She patted Dios on the head. You know what I mean, don't you, old fellow. Those bones are good even when they don't have any meat on them. And she ran her hand over Kadeem's paunch. He has a good one, you know. Hey, *mi amigo*. I'm talking about you.

I never expected to see Kadeem look at a loss for words, but he was. He even got red in the face. But Suelita didn't stop. She pushed herself between him and one of the belly dancers and took his arm. Kadeem and I are *viejos amigos*, Suelita said. We go back a long way.

He stubbed his toe on some rocks and stumbled. Suelita caught him before he fell. See, he's falling for me again! Hey Kadeem, don't worry. I won't leave you.

I passed around the smokes and they all shouted *Olé* and puffed away. The vapors and laughter swirled around us like fog; the campfire made everyone's eyes glow in the dark.

I plunked and sang and they all joined in. Later I started

235

a line dance that circled the clearing and everyone followed. They kicked out their feet and shook their bottoms. Even the animals got into it. It was hard at times to know the difference between animals and humans.

I wished you were here. You always liked to dance.

When I woke this morning, everyone had vamoosed, leaving only cold ash from the campfire and a few chickens that had wandered away. But the Trinidadian's warmth has filled my bones and will keep me going.

The Greenhouse

Another batch of Monarch butterflies had hatched from the milkweed Curva kept inside their cage. When she opened the enclosure, they flooded the greenhouse, hovering over flowers, trying out their wings, exploring.

It was a miracle.

She watched them float through the air. Their orange wings, trimmed with black, resembled cathedral windows. The empty casings—soft green with gold spots—carpeted the cage. Curva gathered them into a paper bag, planning to toss them in the compost later, and rotated her hips, practicing belly dancing moves she'd learned years earlier from Kadeem's women.

She also was keeping an eye on the four seeds she'd planted that Kadeem had given her. She checked the clay pots every day for signs of life and watered them regularly. So far nothing had turned up, though she sang all her favorite songs to them and moved the containers around the greenhouse, seeking the best possible light.

She continued to mix a little dandelion wine into the soil now and then, hoping it would encourage growth and inspire the kernels, though seeds so old would not produce overnight. Dormant too long, they might not produce at all. Still, she remembered how lively they were when Kadeem had left them with her. That possibility gave her hope. As she stood there musing over the pots, it occurred to her the translucent chrysalis shells might promote development—a kind of fertilizer. Curva retrieved the shells from the bag and crushed them between her fingers, sprinkling them over the soil. Then she sang to the seeds again, a lullaby her mother crooned when Curva was a toddler:

Mira la luna
Comiendo su tuna;
Echando las cáscaras
En la laguna.

Aquel caraco
que va por el sol
en cada ramita
llevaba una flor
que viva la gala
que viva el amor
que viva la concha
de aquel caracol.[7]

It makes me very sad to hear you sing that song, *mi hermana.*

Curva jumped when she heard Xavier's voice and then laughed. She said, You remember, *sí?*

Xavier was wearing his white zoot suit again, his hair swept back into a ducktail. He said, *Sí.* We never squashed snails again.

---

7 It looks at the moon, eating his prickly pear; throwing the rinds in the lagoon. That snail that goes for the sun in every stick, it was taking a flower through that the gala lives, through that the love lives, through that the conch lives of that snail.

Maybe you didn't. I do. They try to eat my *bebés. Muerte!* No more snails. Our *madre* didn't like it when anything happened to her plants and flowers. She would forgive me.

A bevy of butterflies fluttered around Xavier, and one landed on his head. They must think they've landed in Mexico, he said, gently brushing them away. Chain-smoking, he dropped a lit cigarette on the ground.

Hey, Curva said, her face burning. You think all I have to do is pick up after you, *señor?* Her parrot repeated the word *señor* over and over, looking at Xavier from first one eye and then the other.

Xavier shrugged and did a sophisticated soft shoe on a slab of concrete, making a sweeping bow at the end.

Curva applauded: You look like an escaped ghost in that white outfit.

Hah, you forget! I am a ghost.

She shook a finger at him: Have you returned to haunt me?

He twirled the gold chain that was attached to his waistband and said, You know me. I'm not like that.

I'm not so sure I know you at all. My Xavier would never wear *extraño* clothes. He wasn't that kind of *hombre.*

He got down on his knees in front of Curva and pressed his hands together as if in prayer. Forgive me, *mi hermana.* What can I do to redeem myself?

She looked at him intently and said, Give me Xavier back.

He stood up and bowed at the waist. At your service, *señora.* Xavier is back.

Not the Xavier I remember.

People change. I need to try new things. Be open. You aren't the Curva I remember, but I don't complain.

She grabbed the hose, turned on the water, and sprayed

the pots containing Kadeem's seeds. Then she flicked the nozzle and gave Xavier a little shower.

Help! he called out, extending his hands to the heavens. She's trying to drown me. Then he turned to Curva: Don't you want me to visit any more?

Laughing, Curva turned off the water and took a bag of fertilizer from a shelf. I'm always happy to see you, *mi hermano*, but I never know when you'll turn up.

He shook the water off himself, threw his arms wide, and sang,

I'm just a poor wayfaring stranger
A travel'n through this world of woe.
But there's no sickness, no toil nor danger
In that bright world to which I go.

Curva clapped. Bravo! I did you a favor then. You got a head start on the bright world. You're the one who should pity me. I'm still in this world of woe.

A pair of green finches twittered and trilled, swooping low to the ground and then soaring, joining in the chorus of other birds aroused by Xavier's presence. Curva grabbed a handful of grain from her pocket and threw it in the air. The birds dove for each speck that hit the ground.

Xavier said, I'm a world traveler. I go anywhere I choose. I'm off to Hong Kong tomorrow.

Curva frowned: Hong Kong?

I saw the movie King Kong and I want to see where he's from.

You're playing with words again, Curva said, laughing. Here's some fertilizer. You could become another King Kong.

He said, You know I don't need anything to make me grow, and he motioned to his zipper.

She turned away: *Lascivo*.

You didn't used to mind it.

I don't mind it. The voice startled both Curva and Xavier. It came from Suelita Flores. She was sitting on Curva's workbench, wearing a crimson dress. Her full breasts pressed against the thin fabric, and she spread her legs wide, the dress hiked up to her hips.

Hey, Xavier, Suelita said, you remember me? Your first love? And she winked at him.

Xavier blushed, the color starting at his black collar and flooding his face.

Your first love? Curva said, surprised she felt a sharp pang of jealousy. I thought I was your first and only love. Then she turned the hose on Xavier full force. Slicked-back hair dripping wet and hanging over his face, and his suit sopping, he raised his hands in surrender: It was all in the family. She was like an older sister to us both.

Or a *madre*, Curva said.

Suelita looked at them in astonishment: A *madre?* No, no. I'm no *madre* to you. A sister maybe. Not a *madre*. Suelita wrinkled her nose, pursed her lips, and tugged at the hem of her dress, trying to cover her knees. *Madres* don't have sex with their sons, Suelita said primly and brushed away a family of ants that was marching up her leg.

Curva had never been possessive of her lovers or felt much jealousy if they got involved with other women. She believed in sharing—on all levels. Suelita's ideas about walking marriages had strongly resonated with Curva. She liked the freedom a walking marriage gave her. She liked spreading the wealth. And she also liked variety in her men. So Curva was amazed by her own response.

Her beloved *hermano* had betrayed her, along with Suel-

240

ita, Curva's *el mejor amiga* and *confidente* all these years. Not only that, but they had enacted their disloyalty with each other.

Still, Curva's early intimacy with Xavier now seemed foolish. They had been naive to fall into such a thing. What were they thinking? Or were they thinking? If neighbors in their parents' village had found out, brother and sister would have been banished.

Xavier took off his drenched suit and hung it to dry on the abandoned caterpillar cage. His boxer shorts, a brilliant orange, and a matching undershirt clung to his thin frame, his bare flesh gray.

Seeing him so exposed pierced Curva's heart and made her want to protect him. Any anger she had felt soon dissolved. He was dead; she wasn't. She grabbed a wool Hudson's Bay blanket she kept in the hothouse for her trysts with Billie and threw it over Xavier. Shivering, he wrapped it around himself.

You look like a Cuban cigar, Curva said, breaking the silence.

He sniffled. I've never been to Cuba, he said.

I have, Suelita said. Fidel was a good customer.

A Cuban? Curva asked.

Sí, a *grande* man in Cuba.

Maybe I'll go to Cuba and meet him, Xavier said. I could use the help of a big man.

I thought you were going to Hong Kong, Curva said.

I have *mucho tiempo. Mucho!* Hong Kong! Cuba! What does it matter? Xavier yawned and headed towards some bales of hay.

I'll go with you, Suelita said. I have *mucho tempo, también.* You want to meet Fidel?

241

Curva flung the hose aside and put the bag of fertilizer back on its shelf. She said, And I have *mucho* work to do while you two flit around like butterflies.

Suelita pointed at Curva. I think she's jealous.

Xavier's head was nodding; his eyelids lowered until a few snores came from him. Curled up on a bale of hay, he had finally stopped shivering.

Shhhhh, Curva said. Our *muchacho* needs his beauty sleep.

Sí, sí, Suelita said. He still is a beautiful boy. He needs someone to care for him. And she stroked his damp hair.

Xavier croaked, You didn't return my gold chain with the keys on the end, *mi hermana.*

Curva jumped. I thought you were asleep.

The dead don't sleep.

Curva frowned: You don't dream either?

Xavier fingered the fringe on the blanket's edge: My days and nights are a constant dream.

Suelita lit a cigarette and blew large smoke rings into the air. The birds took turns diving though them. She asked, Anyone want a smoke?

You don't have the right kind of tobacco, Curva said. I grow my own. See? And she pointed to the *Cannabis* budding under a bank of lights.

Ah, Suelita said. The kind that makes you dreamy.

I'll have some of that, Xavier said.

You might never make it to Hong Kong if you smoke it, Curva said. You won't want to leave here.

How can I leave? You still have my keys.

I thought you wanted me to have the gold chain. What do you need keys for?

They're the keys to my future, and I'm the keyhole to yours.

242

I don't get it, Curva said. What future do you have? Isn't wandering between life and death your destiny?

Maybe it's yours as well. We can travel the universe with Suelita and all those other characters from Luis Cardona's novel.

Ah, that's what's in store for me then.

Curva noticed butterflies fluttering over the flowerpots containing the ancient seeds. She walked over to inspect the pots. The butterflies hovered, some landing on Curva's head and shoulders. Then they took flight again. The soil in one of the containers appeared to move slightly, as if something were about to poke through. Curva watched intently, her breath quickening, hoping to catch this new life in action. Excited, she said, Come and see, Xavier. You like watching births.

But Xavier and Suelita were no longer there, and the blanket Curva had wrapped around Xavier lay on the floor in a heap, a shed chrysalis.

The butterflies swirled around her and followed Curva out the door. A blizzard of monarchs flooded the sky, heading south.

Sabina and Ian

Sabina hadn't visited Ian or Edna since Billie's project had absorbed her. So she was surprised when Ian stopped by the Center one day and waved at her through the glass wall where she was helping to catalogue items. For a visitor, it was like looking into a hospital nursery, but instead of squalling babies, their red fists flailing the air, there were row after row of bones and other artifacts protected by white foam sheets that Sabina hovered over.

Working with these relics, along with the paleontologist Billie had hired from the Tsuu T'ina tribe, filled Sabina with awe. The bones themselves were porous and chalky, the earth still clinging to them in places. Hip sockets. Parts of skulls. Jaws still filled with teeth. Fragments of former lives.

Excited to show her friend around, Sabina ran out and gave a "Yah-hoo," her large, signature sombrero flopping on her head. Chattering non-stop, she led Ian past display cases that held intricately beaded Blackfoot costumes and the tribal women's weaving. They stopped in a large room where dinosaur skeletons were being reassembled.

Look, Ian, that's a *Tyrannosaurus*. Next to it is an *Albertosaurus*—after our province! It means Alberta lizard. And the one in the corner is a *Centrosaurus*.

Ian patted her on the back: Amazing, lass. How did you learn all those names?

Ben, the paleontologist, is teaching me. We still have oodles more dinosaurs to put together. Sabina waved at the workers and turned to Ian, saying, Can you believe all these bones came from right here, under our feet?

Aye, it's amazing, lass. That camera I gave you must be working overtime.

Sabina laughed. I have my own darkroom here. Want to see it?

He looked surprised, his bushy eyebrows raised in a "v," and said, Ah, that's why you haven't been by. You have been shooting up a storm.

Sabina responded, And going to school. And helping Curva care for the greenhouse and animals. And working here. And, and, and.... She threw her hands up in the air as if exasperated by it all, but the truth was, she loved being so active.

He nodded: Busy young lass.

Aye, she said and giggled, patting Ian on the arm. I sound like you.

Aye. I get it, Ian said. He picked up an ancient bone and studied it, turning it over and over in his hand.

Millions of years old, Sabina said. Where were we then? We weren't!

She threw her hands into the air: I can't believe it. No humans? Who wrote the books?

He shook his head: No books. Just bones. A different language, lass. One we don't understand.

Well, I understand your language. I've read all the books you've written. I love the main character in them. She seems so real. Actually alive.

They passed some visitors who were studying the replicated interior of a teepee. It held a family of four that sat around a fire. Sabina stopped. Look, she said. Billie carved those figures from wood. Aren't they good?

Ian flicked some imaginary dust off his jacket and said, Does she seem familiar?

Sabina frowned and said, Familiar? Who?

The girl in my books.

Sabina planted herself directly in front of Ian and put her hands on her hips: You mean she's someone I know?

He looked away: I just wondered if she reminded you of anyone.

Sabina twirled a couple of times on one foot before responding. I guess she does things I want to do one day. Travel. See the world. Have major adventures.

She does indeed, Ian said. I can hardly keep up with her!

But you created her.

Aye, I suppose you could say that. I sometimes think it's more the other way around. She has me reeling at times.

Really?

Ian hooted: Ah, you've got a feeling for language, lass. You picked up on reeling and really, didn't you? Show me that darkroom of yours.

Sabina led the way to the basement and stopped at a door marked TOP SECRET. KEEP OUT. He pointed at the sign and laughed. What skeletons are you hiding in this closet?

She said, No skeletons. I have to keep out the dust. You know that! And I don't want anyone messing with my pictures.

She selected a key from several dangling on a band around her wrist, unlocked the door, and pushed it open. The vinegary smell of chemicals assailed them. Hanging from the ceiling was a string attached to a light bulb. She pulled it, and a red light cast an eerie glow over the black walls. A small room, not much more than a large closet, about eight by eight feet, it seemed bigger than it actually was because of the colored light. The possibility of more space beckoned beyond the shadows.

She returned to the hallway, took the camera gun from its holster, and aimed it at his head. Don't move, she said.

He raised his hands in surrender and said, I give up! Don't shoot. He froze and Sabina pulled the trigger. Great, she said. Your picture finishes up the roll. Wanna help me develop it?

At your service.

They both entered the tiny room. A faucet and a sink were at one end. Three trays sat on an adjacent workbench. Shelves above and below the workbench held paper, scissors, buckets, and more. At the other end was a worktable. An enlarger, timer, paper, and a stack of negatives took up that space. Clothespins attached negatives to a clothesline that circled the top part of the room. The images were difficult to make out.

Ian poked and prodded, studying the negatives, inspecting everything, exclaiming, You have been busy, my girl. Quite a setup. Better than mine.

Sabina bowed: I just do everything you taught me. I take pictures of the artifacts and develop them here. Billie wants them all recorded in case something happens to the place.

Smart move, he said, bowing. You're worth your weight in gold to him.

She is.

Billie appeared in the doorway, the red light burnishing his darker skin. We've never met formally, Billie said, holding out his hand. Sabina has talked about you a lot.

Ian shoved his hands into his pockets. The light turned his white beard pink and made his bald head gleam. He cleared his throat: Aye, she talks about you, too. Well, here we are. He stared at the negatives on the line as if studying them.

Billie shrugged and patted Sabina's arm. Great job, he said. Don't forget your homework. I don't want Curva raising hell with me. Billie strode off, not bothering to say goodbye.

Sabina groaned and hung her head: Homework. Blah! Her sombrero's brim flapped low, hiding her face.

Your friend is right, lass. School comes first.

Sabina shoved the hat to the back of her head and glared at Ian. Even in that dim light her intense blue eyes glinted like steel: Why didn't you shake Billie's hand?

He shrugged: I thought you wanted help with this new film.

She turned away and said, I don't need your help.

247

Aye, well, then I should be heading home. Ian brushed past Sabina and headed for the stairs, his back slightly bent, his gait a little unsteady.

She watched him go. He's an old man, she thought, the realization hitting her for the first time. Though she dealt daily with prehistoric bones, she hadn't made the connection between them and aging. Soon Ian's bones would join the others underground, and he would just be a memory. Something fleeting.

She also hadn't thought much about death before, except when she'd had that brief brush with it in the quicksand. Now she realized everything dies in stages. The aging process itself reflects death's relationship to the body. Some parts die before others—knees, hips, the brain. Senility sets in. Or worse.

Sabina didn't want to lose Ian or his world. It was familiar and comfortable. He had introduced her to books, a porthole into lives she wouldn't have known about otherwise, awakening in Sabina a hunger for knowledge that was different from Curva's.

She almost called out for him to stay.

But then she remembered Billie and how stricken she had felt when Ian wouldn't take his hand. She pushed away any sympathy welling up inside her. Ian had hurt her friend and wounded Sabina as well. She wouldn't forget the slight so quickly.

She went back into the darkroom and shut the door, hanging her hat on a hook. It didn't take long to process the film. The familiar motions of mixing developer with hot or cold water until it reached the right temperature helped her to put aside the unpleasant scene with Ian and Billie. While she waited for images to emerge from the film in the developing tank, she checked out the negatives clipped to the clothesline. They reminded her of X-rays, their penetrating eye exposing the inner core of the bones and other artifacts she'd photographed.

Sabina recalled a story Curva had told her about the glass bowl she and Xavier had looked into when they were younger. The whole world was in there, Curva had said. The negatives gave Sabina a similar feeling. The remains became windows into other lives—other times. Handling the bones when she photographed and numbered them for the paleontologist made her shiver because they seemed to vibrate: some vital force appeared to be contained there. A link to the past, the bones had witnessed a lot over the years, before and after they were buried. Eons had flashed by. Wouldn't all of that be imprinted somewhere inside them? A record of some kind?

It made Sabina look at humans differently: they were just skeletons with a little flesh covering them. It was the frame that endured, not the flesh. The bones lived on to tell their story, and something in the earth contributed to their longevity. Sabina concluded that just as she couldn't develop film without a darkroom, so too bones couldn't endure without going underground first. Something mysterious happened to them there.

She hoped her pictures would reveal this secret.

Then she remembered photographs she'd taken when the bones were first uncovered and Billie's comments about them. He'd said, You've caught them in time; they don't usually live in time. You've trapped the spirit bodies that are still clinging to the bones. Look, you're showing here what our eyes can't normally see.

Sabina looked again at her negatives, trying to see those

spirit bodies. It was like gazing into the glass bowl Curva had described, the bones speaking to Sabina through images. No books, Ian had just said. Just bones. But he was wrong. They weren't just bones. They formed pictures in the mind, the first language. Words weren't the only way to tell a story. These images also created fictions—other worlds. And Sabina was a kind of author. She had given these visions life.

Whenever Sabina entered her darkroom, it was like going underground into a primitive cave. After dipping the negatives into chemicals, she marveled at what surfaced on the film. The trapped contents seemed to be speaking from some distant place, like pictographs discovered on cavern walls created by ancient people. It always gave her a thrill to watch first the outlines and then the complete image take shape, as if she were present at the beginning of creation, privy to how life came into existence.

Over the years, Sabina had helped Curva when she was called on to be a midwife. Now she was doing something similar with the pictures, assisting at the birth of these images. She hated to leave the darkroom and return to the world of light. It seemed so limited somehow, so lacking in depth, everything clearly identifiable, leaving little to the imagination.

Curva on the Old North Trail

Hola, mi estimado Xavier,

I'm back on the trail again. In the last town we visited, Dios found a friend that's joined us. I've never seen him so devoted to another dog. Her fur is all white, and I can see why he likes her. She's *magnifico* and *elegante*. I call her Diosa.

I hope she'll have his *perritos*. I want something of Dios to continue after he's gone. He's been with me so long. Almost twenty years.

I keep hoping Kadeem and his band will show up again. I'm sure they aren't far away. I'm always running into people from Berumba who've strayed.

There are also lost souls who wander into the bush and can't handle the loneliness. They haven't brought any supplies with them and don't know how to forage for food or shoot a gun or find their way out. I've spent many a day showing them how to survive out here before sending them on their way again.

That happened recently. The sun doesn't set till late in the summer. I already had eaten dinner and was passing time smoking and reading and singing to the animals before going to sleep. The dogs let out a low growl and then started barking. The parrots screeched and squawked. I grabbed my rifle just in case there might be trouble and cocked it.

A dark bay horse stumbled into the clearing. It had a problem walking on all the branches that littered the ground, and they made a loud cracking noise when they broke. Someone was slumped over in the saddle and looked half asleep or half dead. I thought it might be Don Quixote.

Lost, I thought.

Then an old woman raised her head, and I wondered if Don Quixote was wearing one of his disguises. A tangled mess of graying red hair hid most of her face and looked like a bird's nest. She brushed it aside and two blue eyes the color of robin's eggs stared at me.

I stared back.

She seemed surprised to find another woman in the wilds. I had been sitting in front of a fire, playing the guitar and singing. I guess my voice drew her to my camp—that, and the smell of food cooking. I'd caught trout in a stream earlier that day and had just finished frying them. They tasted good with miner's lettuce and the flat bread I'd made. The bears left me some berries for dessert. Since I hadn't fed the dogs the leftovers yet, they had to share them that night with this woman.

I set down my gun and helped her dismount. She was weak as a newborn and could barely walk, even with my help. I placed her by the fire and served the food on a tin plate. She didn't say a word. Just grunted and ate with her fingers. I worried she might end up eating them too.

She fell asleep slumped over the plate in her lap. I took it away and she sprawled out. A little spittle dribbled from the corners of her mouth. She twitched and muttered in her sleep. Let out a shriek that scared the animals and me. She must've had a lot to dream about.

I unsaddled her horse and put the horse blanket over the woman. It couldn't have stunk any more than she did and would at least keep her warm in the cool night. I curled up next to her. It was so silent I could hear her heart beating.

The next day she seemed *más vivo* and we talked for a long time. I liked having a woman around again. Her name was Ann, and she was looking for the Blackfoot reservation where she once lived. She wanted to see her *niños* again. They'd been really young when she'd left years earlier.

The stories about her children made me think she might be *loca*, but it was nice to yak with another person so I went along with her. I told her she didn't look Indian to me and she said she wasn't. Her husband was. Except they weren't really married. Not legally.

I said I didn't think her kids would still be hanging around waiting for their mother to return. She couldn't get it through her head they would be grown now with kids of their own.

I realized I couldn't change her mind. She was sure they were still *bambinos* and they needed their mother. I said I had to *vayase* and gave her directions to a nearby town and some food to take with her.

I've often wondered what happened to that woman with the sky in her eyes. Maybe she ran into Kadeem's group and joined them. I think I hear their drums in the distance now or maybe it's thunder. It doesn't matter. I just tell myself it's Kadeem and I believe it.

Something I can't believe. I've been tracking how far I've traveled every time I stop at a town. If my estimates are right, I'm almost at the end of this long trail. I should be in Calgary in time for the big rodeo there. Another month. I'm ready to win some cash and settle down. I'm getting too old to continue this wandering life.

In thinking back, I realize I've done the safe thing. I've taken a *ruta* others could have found if they wanted to. Not many wanted to. Still the trail's not new. I had some idea I'd feel closer to you since we both started out on it. I owed it to you to stay with it and finish what we began together.

What awaits me in Canada? I've been asking this question of the medicine bundle the old Indian gave me in Indian Springs. I wear it around my neck and keep it close to my skin. The fur reminds me I'm an animal too and makes me not want to be tamed. Sometimes it talks to me. Many voices come from inside it. The wind. The sun. The moon. The earth. They speak all at once, so I have trouble making out what they're saying, but just the sound is comforting. The meaning will become clear in time.

Five

Bone Song

Under a full moon
the snow's glare
reflects a ghostly
landscape.

Light transforms
everything
in its wake.

Queen Bee

At times, Curva didn't know what to make of Sabina. The girl baffled her. In some ways she lived in another world. Unlike Curva, Sabina was orderly, super-organized, and knew from birth what she wanted.

Every morning Sabina packed a lunch for herself to take to school, as well as snacks for later, leaving for the Center right from classes. Most days she arrived home sometime in the evening and zipped through her chores, hardly needing a parent.

Unlike Sabina, Curva felt she needed a *madre* at times. She could lose herself for hours in listening to her fountain's fluctuating rhythms, watching the butterflies mate, observing the bees in their hive, studying the hydras and planarians for clues to immortality, or fussing over her plants—unaware of time passing. A glass of dandelion wine or inhaling some weed compelled her to linger and enjoy, to immerse herself in the moment. Cleaning the house, washing dishes, or doing laundry—things she hated—didn't intrude on her much. She didn't feel impelled to be a great housekeeper when so much else called for her attention.

She also could practice shooting for hours, sharpening her skills, living on the bullet's edge, feeling the power of its propellant. When shooting a gun, she became one with the ammunition, seeking to penetrate beyond what normally is visible—into the heart of things. She didn't know why firing a weapon affected her in this way. But it had become an intimate part of her being, satisfying her desire to pierce life in as many ways as possible. When she was shooting, she seemed capable of blasting through time and into some timeless space.

On the trail, time had seemed circular, not linear. Curva had lived by the sun's rising and setting, not a clock or a calendar, and animals had no conscious sense of time passing. She'd learned from them. But living among other people interfered with Curva fully feeling that eternal present. Having Sabina around also made it harder. The girl seemed to rush headlong into the future, eager to discover what it held.

These differences between mother and daughter caused Curva to wonder at times just what she'd produced and to puzzle over the girl's *padre*. Who was he? Something had happened in her outhouse during the tornado that had made her pregnant. The bone she had found there still visited in dreams, causing many a delight-filled night. It had such a profound impact that even now, years later, she could get aroused just thinking about it.

As a result, here she was with an *hija* whose origins were mysterious. Curva had provided the womb, but Sabina didn't seem to need much else from her *madre*. Nor did the girl resemble her mother physically. Red hair? Where did that come from? Blue eyes? And her infatuation with cameras and taking pictures? *Loca!* Curva thought, at the same time feeling maternal pride in this unusual child.

At times, Curva wondered if she had given birth to a human mole. She didn't understand how Sabina could remain underground for hours in that darkroom at the Center. But Sabina's interest in human and prehistoric animal remains did make sense. Curva had a bizarre relationship with bones as well, including the ones at the burial ground. Both mother and daughter had an interest in death's many manifestations. Something might appear lifeless on the surface, like the prairie plants that died each winter, or the butterflies in their cocoons, but they miraculously blossomed later. Death was a tricky fellow, changing constantly, at one moment resembling Xavier in his multiple wardrobes, and at another being totally opaque.

It hadn't occurred to Curva that Sabina also had a passion for transformations. Her time developing photographs allowed the girl to pursue such investigations. Yet Sabina's pictures left Curva puzzled. She understood her interest in bones. But the photos? And so many? It seemed unhealthy for a teenage girl to spend hours in the darkroom, studying them. Shouldn't she be outside more, riding her horse or even fishing with Victor?

Curva fully supported Billie's project. But at times she disliked the way it absorbed Sabina, who seemed more attached to Billie than to Curva. Sabina had never called Curva *madre,* and Curva had never encouraged it. Though she may have resisted being called *madre*, she still took great pride in her captivating daughter. A curiosity, Sabina never failed to surprise Curva. She dressed as she pleased, not following any particular style or wearing what the other kids did. Clearly, something of Curva had rubbed off on the child as she passed though her. Curva wasn't exactly your typical female, and Sabina had picked up Curva's unwillingness to follow the herd.

One spring afternoon, wearing a protective hood, leather gloves, and outer garments, Curva was tending her beehive, watching the female worker bees gathering honey and laying eggs, reminding Curva of herself in some ways. The male drones walked on the combs, begging for food and grooming themselves when they weren't just roosting and waiting to impregnate the queen. The activity inside the hive never seemed to stop. Bees swarmed over the womb-like honeycomb and huddled together as if in communal prayer. She liked the idea that female honeybees ran everything. The male drones were only useful for mating with the queen, who killed any contenders for the throne. One stab of her stinger and it was all over.

Carrying the honey she'd collected, Curva retreated to the house and changed into black gauchos and a white shirt with billowing sleeves. Before slipping on her riding boots, she thrust out her stomach and swiveled her hips, practicing some belly dancing moves. Then, off to Billie's cultural center, she threw a wool poncho over her shoulders and strode out to the barn, Dios following. Her horse Pavel stood waiting in its stall for her to ride him and nuzzled her hand, looking for a carrot. She pulled one out of a pocket, and it grasped the whole thing between its teeth, throwing back its head and shaking its mane. Dios followed her around, barking and darting back and forth. Once Curva had saddled Pavel, she led it into the yard, mounted, and took off. The dog pursued horse and mistress as they sped over the road, heading to town.

The land hadn't fully returned to life yet. Another snow had fallen just the previous week. While much of it had melted, some still clung to hollows and ditches as if unwilling to give up its relationship with the earth, pressed up against it like a lover. Curva wondered if the snow didn't want to dissolve and lose itself altogether by melting into the soil. She could understand that impulse.

She also could understand the snow's desire to hang on. Her search for an elixir of life grew out of a similar need to suck at the teat of existence and not let go. Her bees seemed to have a parallel attachment to their queen. They were totally dependent on this female, just as the Pacheco household had been dependent on Ana Cristina Hernandez. Curva didn't think of herself as a queen bee exactly, but she did feel territorial and would run off anyone who threatened her status at home. She was queen of her greenhouse, of her farm.

And while Sabina may have been queen of Billie's ancestral bones, Curva was queen of his bone. She exerted a power over Billie that no other woman had, except maybe his mother, and Curva knew it. Nor did his attraction to Curva diminish over the years. Billie never failed to respond to her, the stiffening between his legs like a hypersensitive antenna whenever she came within shouting distance, though Curva's scent always preceded her. The odor reminded Billie of the musky quality some animals give off. Whenever he got a whiff of it, as he did now, his heart beat faster, the hair on his body bristling, signaling she was in the vicinity. He lifted his head and sniffed the air, dropping the chisel he'd been using; it clattered onto the cement floor. Victor, who had started helping out at the museum at Sabina's urging, and was learning how to carve wood, picked it up and handed it to Billie. He thanked the boy.

At that moment, Curva was approaching a major intersection near the town. She reined in the horse to let the cars go by before she crossed, and Dios heeled as well. While she was studying the distant Rockies, their jagged edges jutting into the blue expanse as if wanting to join with the sky, Shirley's small plane swooped down, spooking Pavel. The horse flew across the road.

Curva clung to the saddle horn as the horse leaped over a moving car, clipping his hooves on the roof, but Curva kept her seat. As they flew, she stood in the stirrups and hovered over his neck, crooning *Bésame Mucho* into his ear.

The words calmed him down, and he stopped pulling at the reins, landing in one of Henry's fields, Dios nearby.

Shirley circled the pasture, buzzing dog, horse, and rider. Curva shook her fist at him and cursed loudly in Spanish, but her anger didn't deter Shirley. Nor did the horse's discomfort. If anything, both egged him on even more.

The horse drooled, its mouth working at the bit, its eyes rolling wildly. Dios raced back and forth across the field, growling at the plane. Curva patted Pavel's neck and mane, trying to calm it down, periodically shaking her fist at the sky. She said, It's okay, boy. Pavel's sides heaved, and her mount looked on the verge of flight.

Curva felt less confident than she sounded, and Pavel seemed to sense it, flinching at the slightest movement on the road or in the field, as jittery as Curva. Relieved to see Shirley finally fly away, Curva dismounted, hoping to calm the horse and herself. She attached a rope to its bridle and led him back to her place, the visit to the Center temporarily suspended. Dios ran ahead, mouth open and tongue hanging out, feet kicking up dirt. Then Dios raced back, yapping, trying to match Curva and Pavel's pace. She leaned over and patted his head. Good boy, she said, and Dios jumped up and licked her face. Pavel rubbed its nose against her arm. *Sí, sí, mis amigos.* You want food. We'll be home *pronto.*

Around that time, Billie's physical responses to Curva's odor sputtered and died out, his erection softening. False alarm. Billie returned to the work at hand, chipping away at a replica of an outdoor fire for one of the exhibits, Curva hovering on the edges of his consciousness.

She walked along the road's shoulder. The Scotch thistles had invaded already, the spiky purple blooms almost in view, cluttering the ditch and beginning to assault the fields. She

260

had grown to love not only the thistle but also the many shades of gold and brown vegetation that filled the landscape during the dormant season, visible when the snow melted. Her boots clinked against the fine gravel and scattered it. The sound made a counterpoint with the horse's hooves, a reassuring rhythm that reminded her of some Mexican songs she knew.

Still shaken by Shirley's appearance, she thought of her beehive, her own queen bee status threatened by him. As in the bee colony, it wasn't just aspirants to her throne she had to fend off. She also needed to put Shirley in his place. It wasn't something she could settle with guns. If it were, she needn't worry. No, it would take more than guns, though she didn't know yet what that might be.

Curva finally reached the grove near her place and lingered for a moment, enjoying the smell of pine. Pavel whinnied and nudged her shoulder. In the distance, Dios barked and growled intermittently, disturbing her reverie. She started walking again down the lane through the trees to her house, thinking about the butterflies and their southern trip, trying to imagine where they were now and wishing she were with them. Having spent so much time on the road over the years, it was difficult for her to stop traveling altogether. Though she loved her home and enjoyed her new life, occasionally she also still longed to be on the move, facing new challenges and seeing new sights. But most of all she wanted to return to Mexico one day. She missed being part of the *fiestas* and rituals that mark the year— the vivid colors and songs and food, the friendly people. Weed's residents had embraced her for the most part, but she knew they would never fully adopt her, especially now that Shirley's influence had caused so many changes for the town and beyond.

At the end of the narrow road, her *casa*, greenhouse, and other outbuildings appeared, a haven in this foreign land. The fountain's burbling settled her down after the upsetting run-in with that crazy *gringo*. She planned to hang out for a while with her plants and creatures; working with them always calmed her.

That's when she saw Shirley's plane. It was parked in the same spot where he'd landed during his first visit, as if he had a claim to her place. He stood there, leaning against the fence, Stetson pushed back on his head, lighting up a cigarette. He tipped his hat and said, Welcome home, *señora*.

Pavel neighed and rose on its hind legs. Curva pulled on the rope and said, *Establezca abajo.*[8] The horse shook its head from side to side, trying to get away. *Tu caballo loca,*[9] she said, and tied it to the fence, crooning a Mexican song. Then she loosened the cinch and dragged the saddle off Pavel's back, dropping it on the ground.

Need some help with that thing, *señora?*

Curva brushed dirt off her gauchos and flicked the riding crop towards Shirley. The tip streaked out like a snake's tongue, grazing his arm, and she snarled, You could've killed me and my horse, you fool!

Shirley laughed. Relax! I was just having a little fun.

Fun for you but not for the horse and me. Get off my property!

Curva led the horse past Shirley and turned it loose in the pasture. She said, My horse only understands Spanish. He doesn't like you, *señor*. And neither do I.

Shirley shrugged. Can't please everyone, *señora*, he said,

---

8 Settle down
9 You crazy horse

262

tapping the ash off his cigarette. Then he dropped it onto the ground and crushed it under his heel, stepping a little closer and snorting, Your property? Just a minute, *señora*. I was in town checking the records and you haven't paid any taxes since you bought this land. *Comprendes?*

Don't treat me like a fool, she spat out, her cheeks flaming at his words as well as at his intense appraisal of her hips and breasts. Of course I *comprendo*. I speak *inglés* too. I also read it.

Shirley hooted: So you should know you owe the government a lot of money. I'm surprised the tax people haven't taken over the place. They can, you know. You're just lucky they're either so lax or so lame.

Curva turned away and entered the house: You can't scare me, *señor*, she said, slamming the door behind her, his laughter following her inside.

But he had frightened her. The idea that someone could take away the *poco paraíso* she'd created in this new land made her *loca*. She didn't want to admit to Shirley that she never read those boring, official-looking papers the government sent her. She also rarely went near her post office box since she received so little mail.

Curva stood at her kitchen window watching Shirley's plane take off and hurling insults in Spanish the whole time. The *híbrido!* She considered grabbing her rifle and shooting holes in his plane tires, but thought better of it. She had enough problems.

To calm herself down, she puttered in the kitchen, chopping onions and cutting up beef for *carne asada*, singing to herself, trying to blot out Shirley's visit and the threat that now hung over her.

Taxes?

Why should she pay the government for land she already owned?

What did it give her in return?

She didn't have an answer to these questions, but maybe Billie or Sabina did. That girl got smarter every day. She learned things in school that Curva never had. Curva lovingly took in every detail of the nest she'd created for herself and Sabina and wandered through the four rooms, pausing in her daughter's bedroom. Photographs papered the walls, a variety of images that included pictures of Curva herself, shooting her guns at targets. That girl knows how to shoot, too, Curva thought. She stood there for a long time, drinking in Sabina's world.

To the Rescue

Shirley's threats lingered for days afterward, unsettling Curva. During that time, she wandered every foot of her land, absorbing each element of flora and fauna, of buildings she had resurrected and of animals she cared for. The thought of him taking everything away overwhelmed her.

Inside her *casa*, she paced, cracking her knuckles and longing to wring Shirley's neck as she did her chickens. That bad *hombre* needed to be put in his place. To distract herself, she rolled down the top of her gauchos and tied the ends of her blouse under her bust, freeing her ample stomach. It jiggled and shook, along with her breasts, as she rotated her hips, clicked the finger cymbals she'd made out of bottle caps, and hummed an accompaniment. The exotic rhythms soon eclipsed the concerns she had about her property or Shirley. They also attracted Suelita and Xavier, who burst through the door.

Suelita said, *Olé!* You're getting it, Curva. Just bend your back a little more and push your pelvis out. Like this. *Mira.* Wearing purple harem pants dripping with gold fringe and a matching top that exposed her middle, Suelita slithered into the room, pulsating her belly, hands above her head and arms moving sinuously. The two women faced each other, Curva imitating Suelita's movements.

Olé! I like, Xavier said, clapping his hands and circling them. He was wearing a three-quarter length blue silk kimono over black harem pants. Where's my guitar? I'll give you some real music to dance to.

He spotted it leaning against a wall, slung the strap over his shoulder, and began to play. His fingers made the strings sing. Lively Middle Eastern songs filled the room, and the dancers gave themselves over to the tempos, smiling and swirling and swiveling their hips in that Alberta kitchen, Curva's worries about losing her land slipping away. The sound carried across the prairies, making even tone-deaf townspeople shuffle their feet and rotate their pelvises. Some men found themselves carried away as they plowed the earth, their feet and their draft horses picking up the rhythms and trying them out. So did the women, whether hanging clothes on the line or shopping at Smart's.

Xavier's music entered Curva and Suelita so deeply they couldn't stop dancing. Finally he quit playing and the two women—flushed, sweat leaving large half-moons under their armpits—flopped onto chairs, breathing hard.

I must be getting old, Curva said, fanning her face with a kitchen towel.

You, old? Xavier threw his head back and laughed. Not you, *mi hermana.* You'll never age. Like me, no? A few gray hairs maybe, but the spirit, that's still young. It's the spirit that counts.

Curva laughed: I thought you two were traveling the world. Cuba, Hong Kong?

Xavier propped the guitar against the wall and strode over to her, bending and brushing his lips across her cheek. So warm, he said. So enticing, *mi hermana*. We were traveling the world, but I picked up your *desolación*. I said to Suelita, Curva needs us, and here we are, at your service.

Gracias, but what can you do to help? Curva explained her problems with Shirley.

Suelita pointed to herself. This body still leads men astray, right, Xavier? I could keep *señor* Shirley so busy he wouldn't have time to bother you. Happily! Or I could cast a spell on him. He wouldn't wake up for a hundred years.

Xavier hooted. I could give him the kiss of death. Make him squirm a little. Every time he came by here he'd feel it. That should keep him off your property.

Curva nodded. Xavier's solution sounded like the best one.

He pointed to the scrolled map resting on one part of the tabletop: Any progress?

Not since you spilled *vino* on it. *Nada!*

Xavier opened the fridge. Nothing here either, he said. I guess you didn't expect me.

I'm making *carne asada,* your favorite.

And mine, Suelita said.

Xavier took the jug of dandelion wine from the fridge and glasses from the cupboard. Then he poured them each a tumbler full and said, *Salud.* To a long life!

Curva ignored him, opening the scroll and spreading it out on the table. She used the salt and pepper shakers along with the sugar bowl to anchor the corners. Both Xavier and Suelita leaned over the parchment, their breath animating

266

the squiggly lines, causing them to spread like a virus on the page—a combination of incomprehensible words and an outline that looked vaguely familiar to Curva.

It still looks like Greek to me, Xavier said.

Sí, Suelita said, yawning. I need a *siesta*.

Curva stared at the parchment, waiting for words and map to penetrate, hoping something would come to her if she concentrated long enough. We need Kadeem to help us, she said.

You know him, Suelita said. He could be on the moon by now. So unpredictable.

Curva said, Let's check on the seeds he gave me. Sabina's been watering and talking to them.

Xavier did a little soft shoe. Let me escort you, *señoras*.

They left Curva's *casa*, one woman on each of Xavier's arms, and swept into the greenhouse, greeted by a variety of birdcalls, lush green vegetation, a riot of color, and the endlessly gushing fountain.

Where are those seeds, *mi hermana?*

Seeds! Seeds! one of the parrots shrieked.

Curva laughed. Quiet, Manuel. It isn't feeding time. She pointed: Over there, in clay pots.

Xavier shrugged. Clay pots? I just see four *huevos grandes*.

Huevos grandes? she said.

Huevos grandes, Manuel cried.

That can't be, Curva said. Eggs?

Transformations, right? Suelita said. Kadeem's specialty.

Curva strode over to where Suelita and Xavier were standing, staring at the ground. Four ostrich-sized eggs had shattered the clay pots and were huddled together amidst the terracotta shards. The pots' remains resembled fractured eggshells themselves. A purple finch was perched on one of the big eggs, warbling and looking protective.

You think that *pájaro pequeño* laid that *huevo grande?* Suelita asked, laughing.

Suelita and I will have to roost on them if you want them to hatch, *mi hermana.*

You? There are four eggs.

We'll take turns, Suelita said.

You have other things to do, no?

No, Xavier said. Hades is going through a recession, too. Not much happening there these days. This is where the action is. Weed. Your farm. *Mucha acción.*

Even Berumba appears dead these days, Suelita said.

Ouch, Xavier said. Don't use that word around me, *mi amiga.*

Berumba?

No! Dead. I'm allergic to it. I break out in a cold sweat when I hear it. See? He held up an arm and pushed back the sleeve of his kimono. Goose bumps covered it, topped by a layer of sweat that seeped into the silk.

DEAD, Manuel cried.

Ignore Manuel, Curva said. He's a loudmouth. You'll catch your death of cold, Xavier.

He extended his arms wide as if attached to a cross. Don't remind me, he said.

You're so suggestible, *mi hermano.* You always were. I don't think I really shot you. You heard the gun blast and keeled over.

You mean I'm not really a corpse?

Curva frowned. I hate the word corpse. I hate it more than dead. The dead can live. A corpse can't.

I like your logic, Curva. So I'll be dead.

Her head nodding, Suelita had curled up on a ratty couch

Curva kept in the greenhouse for her trysts. She crawled under the throw that covered it, her eyelids flickering and then closing. A loud snore occasionally erupted from her, causing the birds to scatter and Curva and Xavier to laugh.

You never snored like that, *mi hermana*. So ladylike you were.

Me ladylike? Curva exploded in a belly laugh that rattled the glass and made the giant eggs tremble. You're mistaking me for someone else. A lady, yes. Ladylike, no.

To me you are.

You see things the way you think they should be.

And you don't?

I see things the way they are.

Xavier snorted. Nobody sees things the way they are. Words make us see what they want. You want me to be dead, not a corpse. But isn't that what you're accusing me of doing? Seeing what I want to see?

All these words make me *loca*, Xavier. They confuse me.

They're supposed to! Eeny meeny miny mo. Catch a tiger by the toe. Does that make sense? He twirled, his kimono flaring open briefly, and pivoted on one foot, doing a karate chop with his flashing hands.

Curva shook her head, as if she had just awakened. Nothing makes sense, she said. Why are we here instead of in Me-he-co?

The Old North Trail cast a spell on us. And here we are.

You mean here I am. You and Suelita are free to go wherever you want. Sabina and my *granja* depend on me now.

Did you call me? Suelita said, stretching and yawning. She threw off the cover and stood up, shaking the fringe on her harem pants. I need some *carne asada*, she said, and headed to the house.

I thought you liked it here, Xavier said, wrapping an arm around Curva's shoulders.

Sí, I do, I do, she said. Manuel cawed I do, I do.

Shush, Curva said, heading for the butterfly habitat, Xavier following. But I miss traveling sometimes, especially now with all the changes in town and on the land. Anyway, you know me. I still like adventures and visiting new places.

Curva was surprised at how wistful she sounded saying these words and tried to brush away such thoughts. She had a home now for the first time since she was a girl, and she had her own daughter to think about. She didn't want to lose what she'd created in Canada to Shirley or to the government or to anyone.

Suelita returned from the house, and Xavier expanded his arms: Join us.

Two is company, Curva said. You know the rest. Besides, I can't leave all my *bambinos*. Sabina's too young to care for everything.

She doesn't think so.

You've been spying on my daughter?

Not spying. I'm watching out for her. She's my niece!

The drone of a plane passing overhead gave Curva chills. It's that *gringo* again, she said. More trouble.

Don't worry, *mi hermana*. I'll take care of him. Leave him to me.

She ran outside and looked at the sky. Every time Shirley circled and prepared to land on her property, he ran into a gust of arctic air. Xavier's kiss of death rocked the plane, creating a kind of vortex that the *gringo* just barely pulled out of.

Returning to the greenhouse, Curva found Xavier sitting on two of the huge eggs in a meditative posture—legs crossed, eyes closed, a slight smile on his lips. Next to him Suelita perched on the other two eggs, leaning forward, her elbows on her knees, her chin resting on her hands. She had fallen asleep again, her snores rattling the windowpanes and sending the birds into flight.

Curva on the Old North Trail

Hola, mi estimado Xavier,

The weather is hot again, and I want to be naked so I can feel the heat on all of my skin. I pretend I'm back in Berumba with you, sitting under the banana trees and howling at the moon.

It was full last night and we travelled under its cool light. Everything looked milky and soft, and I had to trust the horses to find our way. So far they haven't let me down.

As I write this, it's daytime, and my saddle sits on the ground. I lean back against it and grab your guitar. Blow some smoke. Everything looks *muy bello* now. The sun licks the leaves and turns them yellow. Crickets chirr, even in daylight. Mosquitoes whine near my ear and black flies whiz by. They take turns biting me. Sometimes they attack at the same time and I bite back. Or I blow smoke at them and hope they'll inhale it and forget me. They just laugh and take a few more nips.

The sun hasn't gone down yet. It hangs in the sky like a giant red balloon. I wonder what would happen if someone poked it with a pin. Maybe gold would pour out and make everyone rich. But where would the sun be then? In everyone's pocket?

Not a good idea after all, but it makes me laugh.

The moon is friendly yet not in the same way as the sun. The moon's glow barely grazes me, but the sun pierces me

271

like a lover does.

Music also fills me. I can't stop playing the guitar and singing. I think it's because I'll be leaving the trail soon and want to store up as much of you as I can. I feel you're with me in the music. All the songs we used to sing together: Bésame Mucho. La Bamba. El Rey.

Dios and Diosa try to sing along. They let out sharp little barks and moans. I bark a little too and Dios nuzzles my arm.

Manuel and Pedro blurt out, Kiss me Kiss me. That makes me laugh too. Crazy birds.

I should be in Sweetgrass, Montana any day. I like the name Sweetgrass. I wonder if the town looks like its name. I'll spend the winter there. It's not far from Calgary and its *grande* rodeo. I hope to reach Calgary *mañana*—many *mañanas* from now. Sometime next year. In time to compete. After that I'll put down some roots for a change and stop traveling.

I've had enough. So has Dios. He's a very old dog now and can't do much walking any more. It worries me. We've been together a long time. I can't imagine what it would be like without him tagging along. My bed partner; my sidekick. He's better than Don Quixote's amigo Sancho Panza. Dios and I do everything together.

I'm not getting any younger either.

I'm worried, though, about leaving the trail for good. You know me, Xavier. I like my freedom. It will be hard to live somewhere permanently. I won't be able to take off when I get tired of it. I know, I know. I'll gain some things. But I'll lose a lot. The total freedom I have here. The wonder I feel daily about all these creatures and how they survive so many different conditions. How I've learned to survive with them. Finding places no other human has ever seen. The beauty of

272

the wilderness.

I don't mean to make it sound like everything is perfect here. There are lots of *problemas*. That's what makes life interesting. These warm days have brought us visitors. Big black flies torment the horses and me. I found a way to fool them. Sometimes we travel at night and stay covered up during the day when they're out attacking anything that moves. The dark seems to scare them away. They don't bother us then. Maybe they sleep, too.

The past few days have been really hot. I found a creek for all of us to use. After stripping off my clothes, I waded up to my knees. The flies don't like water, and these mountain streams feel good when it's this balmy. I splashed the dogs and the horses. Even Manuel and Pedro like me to spray them a little after being locked up in their cages so much. They screech and say *más, más*.

After, I sprawled on a hot rock like a lizard dozing, letting the sun and water lap at me. It felt delicious. The clouds chased each other across the blue, blue sky and changed shape. So many different animals appeared up there drifting into each other. I drifted with them.

I pretended I was floating down a river and Mexico was waiting for me when I woke up. But I never got there. The wind blew up a dark cloud that blocked the sun and let loose with a sudden summer shower. The parrots screeched. The dogs hid under some bushes.

I didn't move. I liked the patter of rain on my skin. It soon ended and the sun dried me in no time. I wanted to stay there forever, letting the sun eat me alive. I hope I return as a lizard in another life so I can find a rock like this for my home and never leave it.

Those Bones

Billie drove Sabina home after the museum closed and parked his truck next to Curva's. Dios greeted them with sharp barks, jumping up and down. Good day's work, he said, patting Sabina's arm. See you tomorrow.

Sabina pushed back the brim of her hat, leaned over, and gave him a smack on the cheek, causing him to blush. Thanks, she said.

Billie adjusted his eye patch, displaced by Sabina's buss: Say hi to your mother for me.

Sabina paused before opening the vehicle's door, her eyebrows raised: You aren't coming in?

The farmhouse door flew open, and Curva planted herself on the stoop, legs spread and arms crossed, a mock frown on her brow.

Guess I am, he said, shrugging his shoulders.

Sabina laughed and waved at Curva, skipping away to the barn and calling out, I'm off to feed the horses and take a ride before dinner.

Billie stepped out of the truck, brushed off his khaki trousers, and strode over to where Curva was standing, Dios sniffing at his heels. He said, Thought you might come by the museum today.

Sí, I planned to. Got sidetracked.

He took a pack of Players out of his breast pocket, shook out a cigarette, and lit up, inhaling deeply. Lots of visitors today, he said. Biggest crowd we've had so far.

Curva uncrossed her arms, slid her hands into the pockets of her culottes, and gazed at the distant Rockies. I don't recognize the town anymore, she said, her long hair pulled back into a ponytail, highlighting her prominent cheekbones.

274

She shook her head: New shops springing up everywhere.

Billie took another drag on his cigarette: Yeah, we're not an outpost anymore. We're in the world!

She glanced at the sky and said, Thanks to Shirley.

He looked at her, quizzically. You still bugged at him?

I guess you could say that. He gets on my nerves.

Mine too. Billie sucked on the cigarette and blew out the smoke: He does more than get on my nerves. He makes me furious! You know he keeps telling everyone he meets that you're a wetback.

A slow burn crept across Curva's face, turning it the color of the sunset. She spit out, Wetback! That's like saying I'm not human. I don't have a right to be here. What's he know?

Billie stared at the ground. Enough to cause trouble, it seems. He's telling people you give the place a bad name.

He's *loca*. He's the one who gives this place a bad name. He's a thief! He's robbing the earth and all of us. When the oil and gas is gone, poof! Then what are people left with? A lot of messed up land.

Billie took one last puff before grinding the cigarette butt beneath his heel. I agree, he said, but most folks like the money he's brought to the area and don't want to cross him.

Curva spat out the words: *Dinero*. Is that all they think about?

Staring at the ground, he said, Seems that way. I'm sorry I had to sign up with him. I know it bothers you a lot. But we never could have preserved our culture without that money. We're dependent on Shirley's oil boom.

I know, I know. I just wish there were another way. She nodded at the house, Aren't you coming inside, Bee-lee?

275

He chuckled. You haven't invited me.

She swatted his arm. Since when did you need an invite? She opened the door and both Billie and Dios followed her, the dog settling on a rug by the woodstove. I made your favorite dish, she said. Hungry?

He sniffed the air: Smells great.

Curva walked over to the stove, lifted the lid on her pot of *carne asada*, and slammed it back down. Laughing, she said, Looks like I've had some visitors with beeg appetites.

Billie looked surprised: It's gone?

She lifted her arms and dropped them. Yes, gone!

He turned towards the door. Grab a coat. I'll take you and Sabina to town for dinner. Want to try that new Chinese café?

Frowning, she said, I don't like going into town if I'm being called a wetback.

Billie stared at the worn linoleum floor: I don't like it either, but they don't pay attention to me when I protest. In their minds, I'm worse than a 'wetback'.

Curva flopped onto a chair at the table and stared at Billie, a dark cloud descending on her face. She said, Who makes these stupid laws? Could they throw me out of the country?

He looked out the window at the gathering dusk and said, Not if you marry me.

She sat up straight. What?

He shrugged. Could be a solution.

She shook her head and said, Marriage and me don't mix. Like oil and water. You know that.

He fingered the ribbing on the hem of his jacket and said, They couldn't touch you then. You'd be legal. He glanced briefly at her and away again. We don't have to live together.

She stared out the window, thinking, watching a family of cumulus clouds gather on the horizon. Curva One Eye?

Not likely. Curva Foot in her Mouth sounded better. She ran her fingers over the map Kadeem had left, as if it were coded with Braille, and said, Shirley says I owe taxes and the authorities will take my place away from me.

Billie ambled over to where Curva was sitting and rubbed her shoulders. Not if you pay them. Need money?

She shook her head: I still have some stashed away. I just don't like giving it to the government—to strangers. What right do they have to control my life? If I'm not legal, why do they want my *dinero*? Isn't the money illegal too?

Billie pulled up a chair and sat down next to her. He said, It's not worth getting upset about. Save your energy for something else. He glanced at the parchment Curva was unconsciously fingering: Hey, where'd you get that old native map?

Curva stared at him, her raised eyebrows resembling crows in flight. Native?

Yeah. The writing is Algonquin. He studied it for a few minutes and blurted out, Amazing! It's a map of this area.

You're kidding, Bee-lee! I thought it was Greek...maybe Egyptian.

He laughed. Nope. Where'd you get it?

Curva told him about Kadeem's visit. He said he found it in an Egyptian desert. It held the key to immortality.

Your friend's a good storyteller. He must've gotten lost and found the map here—on the prairies. You said he traveled the Old North Trail, too.

Sí. But this area, how can it be connected to immortality?

Billie shrugged. You've got me. He lit another cigarette, dragging the chipped glass ashtray across the tabletop. There are worse places, he said. Maybe immortality isn't something you go out and find. We're born immortal. So what's the big deal about immortality? We have a soul. It outlives us. Period.

Curva looked at Billie with renewed interest. They'd never had this conversation before. He usually didn't talk about his views on life and death. She assumed he honored a spirit world like lots of Blackfoot did and saw the earth itself as sacred—even the precious oil that was providing income for the tribe.

The map may not have originated in Egypt, but Curva's time in Weed showed the surrounding area held mysteries, too, keys to the past and the present, relics that contained secrets within secrets.

All those bones!

To Billie, a single bone held the history of a species, and he had become keeper of the bones.

Eager to learn more about her lover, she took Billie's hand in hers and turned it over so she could see the palm and what it contained. A worker's hand, the skin cracked in places, dirt etched into the crevices, fingernails jagged. The lines crisscrossed and meandered across the plain of his palm, resembling shallow river and streambeds, leading into a forest of hair on his arms.

His whole body was a map—his posture, the lines and other marks on his skin's surface. His head jutted forward, leading the rest of him, suggesting impatience and a desire to dive head first into life. But he also had a certain wariness about him, his one eye always alert to the surroundings, watching, noticing. Balanced on the balls of his feet, he appeared ready to move in any direction in a fraction of a second.

Curva realized if she looked carefully enough at one person, she not only would discover his/her story but also—at

278

some level—a chronicle of the race. Humans differed, certainly, at least on the surface, but were they really that different at their core? They all had the urge to procreate, to socialize. They all had similar fears and anxieties. They all needed to eat and work together to survive. They all sought love in some form. Once cultural disparities were stripped away, these basics didn't vary much.

Maybe that's what Kadeem was trying to communicate to her: the Canadian prairies, the Egyptian desert, and even Berumba weren't all that different. They all held treasures that illuminated the past, the human soul. They all had gone through many different ages. But the message seemed to be that life and death would keep their mysteries more or less intact, ensuring that seekers like Curva would continue to probe their boundaries. That's why the parchment Kadeem delivered was only invisible until she was ready to see what it revealed. Her forays into finding an elixir that would extend life indefinitely were childlike in their innocence.

Billie coughed and shifted in the chair. Then he crushed his cigarette into the ashtray. He asked, You find what you're looking for?

I was looking for your soul, Bee-lee, she said, her fingernails skating across his palm. Where do you keep it, *señor?*

Out of sight, he said. In my bones.

Sí, makes sense. Hidden but *esencial.*

He fingered some crumbs on the tabletop and looked thoughtful: Our old burial ground has taught me a lot. About bones. About death. About life. I swear those bones still speak.

What do they say, *señor?* Do you want this dance? I'm thirsty?

Don't make fun of me, Curva. I'm serious.

Sí, I know you are. I am too. *Muy serio!*

Billie took Curva's hand: Those petrified dinosaur bones will live forever. Some of my ancestors' bones will also. They're like fingers pointing to the past and the future.

Curva looked puzzled. What do you mean 'the future'?

They say, Hey, humans were here before you. So were animals. Lots of different grasses and shrubs and plants—all fossilized now. You too will pass and something new will take your place. You know, it's incredible! He smacked the table for emphasis. They lived on this earth and now they live inside it. We walk on their former homes every day. Those bones pulse. Throb. That's how they speak now. Through vibrations they give off.

Ah, Curva said. Music only dogs can hear.

Dios raised his head and howled.

Curva laughed, So only dogs understand them?

Billie looked at her: Or humans that hear like dogs.

An airplane buzzed overhead.

Curva shook her fist at the sound and howled herself.

Shirley

Shirley would not have admitted it to anyone, not even to himself, but Curva drove him mad. Mad. Mad. Mad.

She made him angry.

She made him feel foolish.

She made him lose control of all his previously held beliefs. And what were they?

1. No woman would ever set him on his heels.

2. Women definitely were the second sex.

3. No female could best him at his own game.

He took off that morning from his Montana home, determined to discover once and for all just what Curva was hiding at her place. Of course, he was hiding a few things too: he had a nice little woman watching over the home front as well as their two kids, a boy and a girl in their teens whom he saw now and then. He didn't mind being a father, but he also liked his freedom. His wife knew that, and she accepted his comings and goings—mostly the latter. She knew he was a restless type who needed a long rein.

She gave it to him. Otherwise, she knew he wouldn't stick around for long.

So what did he want from Curva? It wasn't just the oil he was after, though he felt she had the richest pool in that area. That woman was sitting on a lake of black gold. He was sure of it from the geological assessments he'd had done of the area.

But she also had something she was hoarding for herself, her loopy daughter, and the Indian. When he'd first arrived in the area, the locals had told him numerous stories about Curva and the greenhouse. They described giant tomatoes and avocados and other fruits and vegetables that flourished in her care, summer or winter. They claimed she could see the future in their cards and tealeaves and palms. They raved about the fountain that appeared mysteriously, surging night and day, certain the former inland sea was seeking the surface through the many layers of her land, drawn somehow to Curva herself. They also described phantom streams that occasionally appeared in her presence and vanished when she left. And many people still believed she caused the tornado that upended their lives years earlier. There also were the guns and her highly unusual skill with them.

Shirley hadn't seen many of these things for himself and pooh-poohed them, though he frequently could hear her fountain from as far away as Sweetgrass. He also had seen the greenhouse expanding and contracting, depending on the season or time of day. It never appeared the same. That puzzled him.

No question: She knew something he wanted in on. Shirley believed she might have certain knowledge that could increase his wealth and power.

He now flew low over her land, barely missing the building tops, hoping to get a glimpse inside the greenhouse. But an impenetrable, invisible wall prevented him from getting closer to it. Rather than discouraging Shirley, it made him more determined to find out what the hoopla was about.

No woman could do all the things attributed to Curva.

It wasn't possible.

After all, she was human. He'd discovered just how human when he told her she was in Canada illegally and that she owed a lot of taxes. The government could take over her land. Her body had stiffened and panic flooded her dark eyes. He'd seen that look many times in animals he'd cornered while hunting. It felt good to have her trapped. He'd heard the Canadian authorities were lax at collecting overdue taxes. If he had to report her, he would. He also would let them know she was an unlawful foreigner. When some administration toady took back the property, Shirley would pay cash for it himself. Then he'd find out her secrets and own the most fertile land in the area. But he also wanted to bed that woman and was determined to do so. Then he could have everything.

After landing on one of his own fields, Shirley tried approaching Curva's place on foot, but her damn dog ran him off. He realized he might have underestimated the woman's resourcefulness. She wasn't going to be easy to tame and she had accomplices. Some wetback that said he was Curva's brother and looked like a ghoul had visited Shirley in a dream recently. His stringy hair swung over rotting features, and he warned Shirley to leave his sister alone or he would be attacked by the shades of hell. Then he rattled some chains and passed through a wall like a knife through cake.

Shirley laughed off the dream and called it a cheap trick. He wasn't going to let some two-bit spic scare him off. Still, he knew Curva didn't suffer fools gladly, and he may have been a fool to think he could match her. From wrestling alligators as a younger man, he could see Curva had more teeth than those reptiles, though they may not have been so visible.

Curva and the Old North Trail

Hola, mi estimado Xavier,

I've left the trail for good, *mi hermano*, and am writing this last letter from the casa I bought with my winnings. I also left parts of Curva behind. And you. While on it, I could feel you nearby.

My new place reminds me of the one we grew up in. That gives me some comfort. But it's so different from the trail. Sleeping under a roof instead of the stars. Closed in by fences. A flat prairie surrounding me instead of trees.

I'll need to get used to clocks again. Time stopped when I was traveling and didn't exist except when winter approached and I had to find a town to hibernate in. The seasons helped me keep track of how long I'd been on the trail. At night the heavens opened themselves to me, and the stars and constellations gave off piercing slivers of light. I lost myself in shooting stars and all the other activity up there. That's when I felt nearest to you, Xavier. I believed you were one of those stars.

All that has changed. And so have I. The twenty years since you died have forced me to become much stronger. These letters have shown you some of what I experienced to get here. And look: I finally finished what we started!

I'm sure I saw you applauding as I rode away from the trail. Applauding us. You were with me the whole time. Prodding. Laughing me through tough moments. Cheering. I couldn't have done it without you. I'm sure of that. You gave me courage to go on.

Sometimes I backtracked and lost my way. Sometimes I didn't want to continue packing up and moving on. But the trail lured me back to it. The trail and you.

Anything seemed possible there, and I saw things I never would have if I'd married and stayed put in some town. I also learned I could meet any challenge. *Una mujer fuerte.*

The day I left that ancient route for good all of the animals—wolves and bobcats and bears and squirrels and the rest—whimpered and howled and growled. I'm sure they were as sad to see me leave as I felt in saying goodbye. I couldn't help tearing up when I looked back and saw them all on the forest's edge watching us for the last time. I almost changed my mind. But I also knew it was time to give up my years of wandering. It was time to claim my own life. I couldn't keep living for both of us.

I don't know exactly when I crossed the border into Canada. There was no trail marker. No sign that said *recepción a Canadá.*

I traveled all day along a road leading to Calgary. Puffy clouds chased each other around the heavenly blue sky's border. It was a relief to finally see tall buildings in the distance. I rode Alanzo into the city with a parrot on each shoulder

284

and paraded through the streets. Melosa was pulling the travois and the dogs trotted behind. Don Quixote, the goat, was tied to the travois.

Men, women, and kids stuck their heads out of car windows and gawked. People on the streets stopped and stared at me. Excited to be with people again, I smiled and waved and called out, *Buenas tardes*. Some of them waved back and shouted words I didn't understand. I still don't get everything in English. But I keep improving. Especially my writing. I have time now to get it right.

Calgary's a real city and we stopped traffic. The animals and I didn't pay any attention to the horns honking. I pretended they were Canadian geese and just kept moving. I've seen those birds everywhere on my travels. They're taking over the world and leaving their mark.

I asked a woman in a big white Stetson and baggy jeans for directions to the stampede. She said I was in luck because the grounds weren't far from there. She asked if I was riding with the Indians in the parade. I guess my darker skin made her think I was one of them.

I said, Could be.

She said, You need to sign up at the stampede grounds and pointed the way.

I said, *Gracias* and followed the directions.

Everyone was wearing a cowboy outfit for stampede week, and the place looked like a cow town. Bales of hay hugged the sidewalks. Chuckwagons were everywhere. A few Indians roamed the streets. I'd seen enough real western places to know this wasn't the real thing.

Relieved to finally arrive at the grounds, I told the *hombre* at the gate I was riding with the Indians in the parade and competing in the rodeo. He looked at my American money and sent me to a nearby bank to have it changed into Canadian dollars. After, he sent me to the Indian village and said I could stay there.

I didn't plan to ride in any parade. I just wanted to get the rodeo over with. It was the last time I would have to pretend I was you when I competed. The judges still won't let women do anything but barrel racing, so I was lucky no one caught on over the years to my disguise.

I pulled my long hair back and tightly tied the chinstrap on my sombrero so the brim shaded my face. The other cowboys thought I was some weird Chicano. Of course I had to bind my breasts so they didn't bob around and give me away, and as usual I pretended to be mute.

After bedding down my animals in one of the barns and pitching my tent next to the teepees, I settled in for the week. My neighbors didn't pay much attention to me, and I didn't try to get friendly with them. I just wanted to collect my money and leave town.

At the rodeo competition, I ran into a few *hombres* I'd seen at other events in the States. They weren't happy to see me and kept their distance. They knew they didn't have much chance if I were competing too.

First I entered the bareback bronc riding. As long as I get a good grip on the rigging strap and make the right connection with the horse, I can stay on forever. Or until the horse gets worn out.

I won every prize in sight.

During my last saddle bronc ride that week, I shocked everyone. I untied my hair, flung my sombrero at the crowd, and whipped off the scarf I used to bind my breasts. They flopped up and down as I rode the bucking horse and held the hack reign tightly with one hand. I never missed a beat.

The crowd roared, It's a woman for crissakes!

I sang *Besame Mucho* to the horse and he eventually stopped bucking. Then I circled the ring, whipped out a Mexican flag from beneath my shirt, and waved it at the crowd. A lot of them cheered. Some booed. I didn't care.

I rode off with most of the prize money that day.

Kadeem's Wandering Troupe

Kadeem's ragged band passed through Weed for the first time on one of their world tours, along with some Berumba adventurers. Over fifty of them paraded in the streets with their weathered, horse-drawn wagons and worn out wares. Some of the men played accordions, violins, and guitars they'd picked up on their travels, fingers unleashing unfamiliar minor-key melodies with a hint of cinnamon, cumin, and cardamom. These musicians accompanied the female singers' trilling and the belly dancers' rotating hips, the sounds streaming into the Weedites' houses and shops, drawing many into the street.

The sight of these foreign travelers traipsing through town, their animals dropping scat on the fresh asphalt, angered Nathan Smart. He had just swept the sidewalk in front of his store and swore at the strangers. Speaking to those standing nearby, Sophie mocked the strangers' tattered clothing and shouted at the visitors to leave: You're in the wrong place! This isn't the Calgary Stampede. Ian Mac-Gregor and his sister Edna nodded in agreement. They didn't want their town blemished by these ragged aliens.

Kadeem, cheeks dimpled in a perpetual smile, waved from his seat on a red wagon, loosely holding the horse's reins. He laughed frequently at his troupe's antics, his body shaking in merriment. His signature stovepipe hat, bound in the red, white, and black colors of the Trinidadian flag, flopped on his head. Inspired, he picked up a steel pan resting next to him and placed it on his lap, flipping sticks over the drum's many bumpy surfaces, the sounds so enticing that eventually the Smarts were unable to hold off and began moving their feet to the irresistible rhythms. Ian and Edna frowned at their friends' response, but then their feet began to patter, the music striking an inner chord. Even old man Hawkins found himself rapping his foot on the sidewalk and doing several intricate steps. Soon more townsfolk were in motion, each swirling and swaying to the songs. A cyclone of sound burst over the land, reaching those working on the nearby farms and ranches. Shortly, those people were also drawn to Weed and the *fiesta* happening there.

Eyes popping, jaws dropping, the townsfolk watched members of Kadeem's band perform on frayed Arabic carpets that levitated above the crowd. The acrobats juggled lit torches and created human pyramids, violating gravity, causing viewers to crane their necks and *ooh* and *aah* in amazement. Several children, wearing scarlet harem alibaba trousers, did cartwheels and somersaults at the head of the procession, making spectacular flips and spins in the air.

Eager to execute moves she'd been practicing for months, Curva joined the dancers, rotating her hips and clicking her homemade castanets. She wore Suelita's purple harem pants fringed with gold and the matching top. Clapping, Kadeem nodded at her in appreciation and shouted, *Bueno, bueno, señora,* his black cape flapping behind him like wings.

Now fully caught up in the *fiesta* spirit, the townspeople clapped, too, cheering on Curva, reminded once again of how important she had been to them. Shouting *ole*, Catherine and Inez encouraged other women to twirl their hips, trying to imitate Curva and the other belly dancers' movements. Even the men stiffly swiveled their bodies, glancing uncertainly at each other, envying the dancers' fluidity, a motion that appeared as natural as a waterfall.

A scruffy elephant followed Curva, kicking up dust in the road, carrying a dark-skinned beauty in its mouth: she appeared almost naked, wearing only a G-string with two sunflowers covering her nipples. The crowd gawked, tittering and snickering. Another curvaceous woman followed. Standing on the back of a white horse, wearing a pink tutu, she gracefully held her arms aloft and slowly pirouetted. The animal snorted and threw back its head, shaking gold tassels that hung from its bridle.

The exotic images titillated everyone, expressing a world that Weedites knew little about. Adults and children alike were agog, their eyes fixed on the spectacle passing before them. Pop-eyed, they imagined themselves living a life free of restraints and the bruising banality of the everyday, following their whims like these entertainers instead of being herded by daily tasks, whether in town or in the countryside. They stood clustered on the sidewalks until the troupe had disappeared up the road, bodies still moving to the music, unable to return just yet to their work. Some ran after the group, hoping to get a ride on the elephant, Victor leading the charge.

But soon the followers fell behind. They felt as if they were treading on a magic carpet themselves that kept slipping backwards, preventing them from gaining traction. Running in place, they couldn't catch up with the group no matter how fast they moved. Disappointed, they watched Kadeem and his band fade into the foothills. Their last image was of the elephant's tail swishing back and forth like a metronome, the beat staying with them for days afterward.

The Weedites, moving in a daze, lingered in the streets, swaying to the remembered melodies, smiles on their faces. Wondering if they had imagined the whole thing, they frequently peered into the distance, hoping for just one more glance of Kadeem and his band before returning to their usual routines. Nathan's feet continued to tap out the rhythms he'd heard, and Sophie hummed some of the songs. Ian did a little soft-shoe shuffle on his way home.

The group had offered a fresh perspective that gave everyone a boost. In days to come, the memory of Kadeem and his entertainers would arise frequently when their daily routines and the weight of existence bogged them down. But it also reminded them that Curva still lived nearby, and she had a similar effect on them.

Right after the parade, Inez Wilson and Catherine Hawkins met for lunch at a local café, both crooning the same tune. They laughed at themselves for duplicating what they'd heard and howled about Curva's sultry dancing, reminiscing over the old days at her place. Inez said, I miss Curva's dandelion wine and other goodies. You know what I mean?

Catherine nodded and said, Curva was right. We need more of that elephant's rhythms here. Not Shirley's. And they both gazed out the window at their neighbors still dancing in the streets, some of the children trying to do flips themselves, smiles on everyone's faces, laughter softening their bones.

Making Music Together

Before moving on, Kadeem and his crew camped on Curva's property, cooking over open fires that burned until all hours of the morning and continuing to play music, slower now and mellifluous, growing more melancholy and bone piercing as the night progressed. Curva joined them on Xavier's guitar, not surprised when he and Suelita showed up, as did Ana Cristina Hernandez and Ernesto Valenzuela Pacheco. Their arrival made Curva feel as if she were back in Berumba. Family surrounded her again—the Pachecos now seemed like a mother and father, Xavier and Suelita her brother and sister.

Curva glanced at everyone's faces, some familiar, some not. They all had certain characteristics in common. They gestured frequently with their bodies and hands, smiling readily and laughing with ease at the slightest provocation. Unlike the Weedites that were weighted down by new responsibilities and even debt, her visitors seemed fully alive, reflected in how lightly they moved, buoyed by the air surrounding them. Many broke out in song, playing off one another's tempos and words, spontaneously inventing new tunes. Laughing, they tossed refrains back and forth, faces lit by campfires, music just another language for them. All shared a passion for *fiesta*, for adventure, for unusual experiences. Feeling fully at home at last, Curva didn't want the evening to end.

Xavier tapped Curva on the shoulder. May I, *mi hermana*, he said, and took the guitar, embracing it like a long lost child. He stood in the center of the camp, wearing a white shirt, black pants, and purple vest, a scarlet kerchief tied loosely around his neck. Someone added wood to one of the fires, and it flared up, the flames turning Xavier's face the color of red clay. A harvest moon hung behind him in the sky, almost full—a gold pendant. A hush descended over everyone.

Xavier strummed the guitar flamenco style and ululated

291

in Spanish of lost love and human sorrow, his deep baritone voice piercing his listeners' hearts and sending shivers
through Curva. Tears ran down the faces of men and wom-
en alike, creating rivulets in the earth that eventually flowed
into the Pacific, leaving behind a trail of salt that cattle licked
off the land for months afterward. The music rippled across
the plains, following its contours, awakening residents for
miles around. It spoke of longing and loss, all emotions they
had experienced at one time or another but couldn't themselves have articulated so intensely. Xavier somehow conveyed these feelings in music's universal tongue that needed
no interpretation.

The songs even reached Shirley in Sweet Grass. The
sound knocked him off his feet. Shaken, he looked around,
wondering where the music came from. Something new had
entered his vocabulary: feelings. He didn't know what to do
with them. Nor did many of the others whom Xavier's
singing touched. The melodies reverberated in everyone's
bones and lingered long after he had stopped.

Curva felt as if she were floating on one of Kadeem's
carpets. The group's energy held her aloft, each person's face
aglow from the firelight, as if lit from within. The music
wove them together, resonating within each person's cells,
connecting everyone—the dead and the living—through the
reverberation of atoms. Xavier and his music linked them
to past, present, and future, a tone first made in primordi-
al time undulating through the centuries, uniting each new
generation.

Was this the elixir she had been searching for all these
years? Were they all originally part of something larger so
that their individual identities lived on in this way? Or was
the idea of immortality itself immortal, humans' ability to

think of immortality already suggesting timelessness?

Before going to bed that night, Curva decided to visit the greenhouse and invited Kadeem to join her. He scratched his head and yawned: At this hour?

Sí, señor.

The roosters will be crowing soon.

I think they already are, *señor.* Don't you hear them?

Sí. And the hens are cackling too—with delight, Kadeem said, ambling next to her on the path from his group's camp, wrapping himself in a cape made from Trinidad's flag. Curva shivered in her thin cotton blouse and peasant skirt, wishing she had brought a serape with her. The full moon bathed everything in a crepuscular light.

Remember the seeds you gave me, *señor?*

Ah, the *germen. Sí, sí.* What happened to them?

They turned into *huevos grandes.*

Huevos? Imposible.

Not *imposible.* It happened. I'll show you.

Kadeem followed her into the greenhouse, the two of them startling Sabina. She was sitting on a stool in front of the cage Curva had built for the butterflies, eating popcorn, wearing a pair of coveralls and her sombrero. Dios was sleeping at her feet.

Curva felt a rush of affection towards her daughter, wanting to hold her close, longing to hear Sabina call her *madre. Hola,* Curva said, touching Sabina's shoulder. You're missing all the fun. Listen!

Music and laughter drifted into the room. Sabina glanced at her mother and shook her head vigorously. She said, They're the ones who are missing out. Look! The butterflies are hatching.

293

Sabina had spent hours in the greenhouse, taking pictures of the new pupas and waiting for that incredible moment when the butterflies appeared. She had watched the caterpillars turn into chrysalides a few weeks earlier, setting up her camera so she could catch the different stages and have a record. It always stunned her to see them create this unique home out of silk that they eventually outgrew. She felt she was doing something similar with her photos, creating a kind of dwelling for herself to return to again and again.

Though she had experienced the process several times now, it never failed to amaze her when the butterflies unfolded their brilliant orange, black, and white wings, as if in a dream, slowly unfurling them, clinging to the pupa with their legs until ready to fly. Even that seemed astonishing: They instinctively knew how to glide through the air.

Kadeem bent over to see the cocoon more clearly. She's right, he said to Curva. They're almost ready to pop out.

Curva introduced the Trinidadian to Sabina. Without taking her eyes off the cage, Sabina shook his hand and said, *Hola*.

Manuel and Pedro croaked *hola* from behind the cover on their enclosure. Dios woofed once before going back to sleep.

Kadeem laughed. I'm no match for the butterflies or these parrots, he said, and walked away. Curva brushed Sabina's hair with her lips before following.

Show me these eggs, *señora*.

Curva led Kadeem to the other end of the greenhouse so he could see a different metamorphosis. She explained how she'd planted the seeds he had given her, fertilizing them with dandelion wine and crushed butterfly chrysalides, among other things.

Ah, he said, you have the magician's touch that every gardener needs. I couldn't have done better myself.

Sí, but—

But what?

The seeds turned into *huevos*. Curva spread her arms wide: *Grande!* I didn't expect that to happen.

Sí, señora, life would be dull with no surprises. How often has a plant turned up in your garden you didn't put there yourself? *Muchas* times, right?

Curva nodded her head. But eggs, she said, from seeds? Even a great sorcerer like you couldn't make that happen.

Kadeem waved one hand: Nothing is what it seems. Carpets fly. Plants give birth to animals. Characters escape from novels. All this is normal.

Brushing aside the avocado tree's leaves and drawing closer to where Curva had planted the seed, they were startled to see fragmented shells scattered on the ground where Xavier and Suelita had roosted on the eggs.

Curva blurted out, I can't believe it. They've hatched since I saw them last!

She called for Sabina to come and see, but the girl didn't answer.

Kadeem laughed: They must have been *Mariposas gigantes.* He pointed at the shells: I think they were *crysales gigantes* and not eggs. They're off to Me-he-co.

Kneeling on the ground, Curva said, Wait, *señor.* You're wrong. My special fertilizer produced something stranger than drunken *mariposas.* Look at this!

Curva clasped a book she found amidst the shattered remains and handed it reverently to Kadeem. He took it and laughed: Don Quixote's poems! That scrawny old rascal. That old fake. He's still stirring things up.

Sí. Curva said. I tried reading his poems once, but they don't make sense.

The seeds of language, of meaning? These words don't need to make sense. Kadeem skimmed through the book, muttering, Life doesn't make sense! Why should poems? But they still give birth to ideas and images—to new ways of thinking and being.

He stood there in the dim light, peering at the print. I'll need to study this, he said, and tucked it carefully into one of his pockets.

Curva said, Wait, the eggs have produced more! She reached into the rubble and withdrew a purple velvet bag, silver sequins glittering like tiny moons on its surface, the top secured by a drawstring of stars.

Kadeem took it from Curva and held it gently in his hands. Ah, he said, it's been a long time since I've seen one of these. A bag of dreams. *Muy útil. Muy importante.* What's life without dreams? You're a lucky woman to have this.

It's yours, *señor.* You gave me the seeds to plant.

No, no, *señora.* I was just the messenger. You brought them back to life.

Gracias. I have much dreaming to do then. Maybe I'll join Don Quixote.

He could use a new companion. That Sancho lacks much imagination. And the third egg?

Curva nodded and picked up a pair of shoes covered with plum-colored tapestry. Stiletto heels, she said. *Muy* sharp.

Ah, Kadeem said. Amazing what those eggs hatched! The shoe protects the sole—such an important part of the body.

They were in the other two eggs, *señor,* One in each.

I'm afraid they aren't my size, he said, smiling at his own joke. But some lucky woman will be happy with them.

With what? Sabina approached them, yawning, hands in her pockets, shoulders slumped, walking barefoot.

Curva said, What's wrong, Sabina. You look so sad.

I am sad. I can't stay awake any longer, but the butterflies look ready to leave their cocoons any time. It's not fair!

Curva enfolded the girl in her arms and said, I know it isn't fair, *mi amor*. But hold them in your dreams tonight and they'll be waiting for you in the morning. I promise. Before you go to bed, look at this, and she pointed at the workbench where she'd placed the shoes. Remember the seeds I planted? You saw them when they turned into eggs. Well, they've hatched! Here's what was inside.

Yeah, I remember, Sabina said, leaning against her *madre*, her eyelids drooping. She turned to leave.

Wait, Curva said. Take a look at these shoes before you go.

Wow! Great shoes, Sabina said. And they came from the eggs? She leaned over the workbench and studied them. Look, she said, they have butterfly wings on the back!

You're right, Kadeem said. Smart girl. Observant.

Sabina picked up one shoe and studied it. I think it's my size, she said.

Try it on, Kadeem urged.

The greenhouse door blew open, and Suelito rushed in, startling everyone. Wait, she said, those are my shoes!

Curva frowned: How did they get into the eggs?

Laughing, Suelito said, They weren't in the eggs. I was wearing them when Xavier and I became like hens and roosted. I took them off at some point. You thought they came from the eggs?

Too bad, Sabina said. I like them. She started yawning again. *Buenas noches*, she said, heading off to the house and

297

to her bed.

Buenas noches, the others called after her.

Curva handed Suelita the shoes and said, You must have seen the hatched eggs before we did. What was in the other two?

Suelita laughed: We hatched them. We deserve half of the contents.

And your half? Curva asked, tapping one foot impatiently.

Suelita turned around and flapped two gorgeous wings attached to her shoulder blades. Vivid oranges and yellows dominated, framed and threaded with intense black that circled white dots of various sizes. They looked totally natural on her.

Wings! both Kadeem and Curva shouted together.

Sí, wings, Suelita said. Xavier has the other pair. We're *ángels*.

Curva hooted: You, an *ángel! Absurdo. Imposible.*

Why *imposible?* Xavier asked, joining them, his eyes shining with a new clarity, levitating a little when he fluttered his wings. He did a modified split mid-air before landing.

Bravo, Kadeem said. I would like wings too. I need some of those seeds. He dug deep into his trouser pockets and felt around for more. *Nada*, he said. I must go hunting again.

Xavier planted himself in front of Curva, his hands on his hips: You don't believe in *ángels?*

Curva tossed her head: I don't believe in you two being *ángels*.

Xavier spread his arms and waved them. We have wings, he said. Doesn't that make us *ángels?*

Curva imitated his arm movements. You have wings, she said. Doesn't that make you birds?

Xavier chirped a few times and then threw up his hands, causing his wings to shudder. I can sing like an *ángel*. I can't sing like a bird. So I must be an *ángel. Correcto?*

I can ride and shoot like a man. That must make me a man. *Correcto?*

You a man? *Absurdo.*

You an *ángel? Absurdo.*

Kadeem plucked a tomato from a nearby plant and popped it into his mouth. *Delicioso*, he said. Not *absurdo.*

Curva said, You are wrong, *señor*, it is *absurdo.* You don't know Xavier. You don't know Suelita. *Ángels?* Never. They're too much of this earth.

Ah, but I do know them. They've asked me to marry them. I've given them my blessing. Waving goodbye, he said: I'll see you in Mexico for the wedding.

Curva felt puzzled. Xavier marrying Suelita? That was even more *absurdo* than the two of them being angels. Suelita, who had introduced Curva to walking marriages? Suelita, who consumed men the way Xavier now consumed food? Why would she marry?

She realized Xavier and Suelita were waiting for her to say something. Married? Curva said, squeaking out the word. I've never heard of *ángels* marrying. She busied herself at the workbench, rearranging flowerpots and stakes and trowels, suddenly feeling terribly alone. More alone than when she was on the trail. More alone than she'd ever felt in her life.

For all these years, she and Xavier had been inseparable in spite of him being dead. Even because of it. The letters she wrote to him while on the trail had kept him close by. Now just this one word, marriage, while it joined Suelita and Xavier, severed that intimate connection and created a barrier between them. She glanced at Suelita, who was clinging to Xavier's arm and gazing at him adoringly. Xavier returned the look, stroking Suelita's face. The obvious intimacy confirmed the relationship, and Curva had to accept that Suelita was supplanting her.

Curva couldn't shoot her way out of this situation, but she could accept that Xavier finally had a chance at happiness and wish the two lovers well.

Brother and sister looked at one another. Xavier spoke first. Sorry, *mi hermana*. I planned to tell you myself. The cat got out of the bag.

Curva attempted a rueful laugh, but it came out sounding like a sob. She said, I think you mean the wings got out of the eggs, and the two of you flew off together into the blue. It would make a good "B" movie. When's the beeg day?

Tomorrow night in Tiquicheo, Mexico. We want to be married under the full moon and the stars. Heavenly, don't you think?

Curva was relieved the ceremony would be where she and Xavier were born. She turned back to her workbench and dipped her fingers into some potting soil, wanting to lose herself in the rich black earth and to bury there the strong emotion she was feeling. Shoulders shaking, her tears fell, irrigating the seeds she had placed in the dirt. Green shoots shot up, flower buds already straining to open while doors seemed to be closing all around her. The government and ultimately Shirley could take over her farm. In Canada illegally, Curva could be deported at any time.

Though she had preferred walking marriages to static ones, she liked feeling planted in one place after all her travels. And whether she admitted it or not, Billie had become important to her as well. When he had suggested she marry

300

him so she wouldn't be expelled, he hadn't pushed for an answer. But now she was ready to give it, and it wasn't just out of necessity.

Curva also needn't just cling to the Berumba of her fantasies. She now had her own bag of dreams that offered a different kind of future trail for her to follow. She could borrow an Arabian carpet from Kadeem and fly anywhere in an instant. Already she could feel the wind in her face and the sensation of soaring above the ground, closer to the clouds. She could take Sabina and Billie with her, introducing them to a larger world. But they would always have this one to return to.

Billie and Curva

The music from Curva's place had carried over the prairies to the rez, its plaintiveness awakening Billie. Xavier's ardent singing and guitar playing had turned Billie's heart upside down and inside out, filling him with longing and melancholy. His first thoughts were of Curva and Sabina, how important they were to him. He also was reminded of Sighing Turtle and the songs she had sung to him and his sisters when they were children.

Recently, he had dreamed she was trying to reach him. In the dream, she was old, hair ratted and gray; she didn't resemble the mother of his memories, but he recognized her anyway. Her blue eyes and the sound of her voice gave her away immediately. The dream wasn't more than a sliver from a long night's sleep. Still, it haunted him for many days.

He had mentioned the dream to Curva, and she had frozen when he described the woman in the dream. Oh *Dios mio*, she said, shocked, her hand covering her mouth. I met her on the trail, years ago. She said her name was Ann, not Sighing Turtle.

Billie's eyes had widened. He said, Ann was her non-Blackfoot name. She wouldn't have called herself Sighing Turtle then.

She said something about trying to find the Blackfoot reserve and her *niños*. I thought she was *loca* wandering around like that—so frail. Near death. She must have died looking for you and your sisters.

Billie had asked for details of the meeting, and Curva told him everything she could remember. It consoled him to think his mother might have tried to reclaim her kids and had received some comfort from Curva before she died. He realized she must have thought of Billie and his sisters often, holding them close that way. No wonder he felt such a bond with her.

That's when he told Curva that Sabina looked a lot like Sighing Turtle. The resemblance is weird, Billie said. The hair color. The facial expressions. The eyes. I swear she's related to me.

Maybe, Curva said, a Mona Lisa smile playing across her lips. Stranger things have happened.

Unable to sleep, Billie wasn't surprised when Curva appeared a little while later, as if carried there by the music. His antenna had picked up on her proximity, stiffening, tingling, alerting him to her arrival. She strode into his main room, wearing her gauchos, knee-high leather riding boots, and a blue wool serape. He had never seen her look so stricken—or more beautiful, her face a road map to what she was feeling inside. Her eyes looked haunted, sunk into her face, dark circles like half-moons beneath them.

You look like you've seen a ghost, he said. Is Sabina okay?

Sí, sí, she's fine. Sleeping. I have seen a ghost, Bee-lee, she rasped. Xavier.

Billie looked puzzled. But hasn't he been visiting you regularly?

He's an angel now. So is Suelita. They have wings and are getting married.

Aren't both things something to celebrate?

Sí. But now that he's an angel, I don't know when I'll see him again.

Billie walked over and encircled Curva, nuzzling her neck. She didn't resist, letting him embrace her, smelling cigarette and wood smoke in his hair. It felt good to let him hold her. His hard body reminded her of a sturdy tree trunk whose roots go deep into the earth. She needed something solid to hold on to. She felt her whole world had tilted, and she didn't know how to right it again. He rocked her back and forth, the rhythm restoring her equilibrium. It wasn't necessary to speak with Billie. He somehow absorbed anything she was feeling and left her renewed.

They stayed like that for a long time. Finally, he helped her undress, slowly, gently, almost like a parent. He took off his clothes too. He even removed the patch covering his blinded eye. Curva touched where the patch had been. He flinched.

It's okay, she said. It's not so bad. Do you still want to marry me, Bee-lee?

Of course. I meant what I said! But I thought you only liked walking marriages. If we marry, I won't want to share you with other men any longer.

Curva laughed: We can just pretend we have a walking

303

marriage, but we'll only walk back and forth between our places.

They climbed to the lookout tower and lay on the mattress under a quilt his grandmother had made. Turning onto one side, she folded her body into his and they spooned. Slowly his *polla* stiffened, probing between her thighs. He stroked her breasts and nibbled at her neck and ran his hands over her whole body. Pretending she was a cat, she purred. *Sí*, she said, *es bueno. Tan bueno.*

Curva turned to him: You're the only other man who has really touched my heart, Bee-lee. Have I touched yours too?

Sí, he said, hovering over her, licking her breasts, her stomach, lowering himself till he could probe her bush with his tongue, exploring her button first until it had doubled in size. Then he dipped his tongue in and out of her *coño*.

Ah, she said. *Más! Más!*

Gasping, she arched her back, pressing herself against his tongue, her body calling for more. Shaking, he entered her and slowly moved back and forth. Then he withdrew and circled her opening with the tip of his *polla*, drawing moans of pleasure from Curva. Their eyes locked. And then both exploded, their cries piercing the skylight and reaching the heavens, awakening the gods, the goddesses, and all their ancestors.

Later, they lay in each other's arms. On such a clear night, they could easily see the constellations. Looking at the stars and holding Billie's hand, Curva said, Tell me about them again, Bee-lee. She snuggled into his body and listened to him tell about the sun, the creator of the world, one of the *spomi-tapi-ksi.*[10]

---

10 sky beings

He said, *Kokomi-kisomm* the moon turned against her husband *Natosi* the sun and the children they had—seven stars of the Big Dipper. Now she constantly chases them across *Spomi,* the sky. Furious, *Natosi* cut off one of her legs, so she has to take frequent rests. She disappears periodically to recover from the wild chase. But she never can quite reach him and the kids again, and the chase never ends. That's why *Kokomi-kisomm* constantly changes shape and only appears at certain times.

Sí, a familiar story. Women still try to catch *los hombres.* We get so caught up in the chase, we forget who we are and where we belong.

Where do you belong?

In Weed. I've put down roots with all of my plants and my friends and my *hija.* And you. But I have to warn you, I can't stop being like the moon in your story. Disappearing now and then. Waxing and waning.

I know. It's what I like most about you. You're never the same. It keeps me on my toes!

She laughed and said, I've never thought of you as a ballet dancer, Bee-lee. Picturing him in a tutu made her laugh even louder, sending them both into hysterics. The sound bounced off the walls, escaping into the night, embracing anything it came into contact with. Their mirth tumbled over the prairies, causing any bone it touched to tremble and twitch, and inducing the sky to change color, turning it from a deep indigo to a pale cornflower blue. A rosy tinge hovered around the edges.

Bone Song

The earth can't hold
us now. We've turned
it inside
out, our voices
freed to speak
again.

Coda

This isn't the end of the story, of course. Curva and Billie could have many years ahead of them, and she'll likely continue her search for immortality, not realizing that she and the others will live on not only in this book but also in your imagination.

What about Sabina and Victor? Their lives have just begun. We don't know if they'll end up together as Curva and Billie did any more than we know what our own future will bring. Victor might join Kadeem's group. Sabina could become a strong advocate for the Blackfoot and others that have been disenfranchised. Or perhaps some other fate awaits them.

As for the other Weedites, though they'll resist at first, eventually they'll adjust to the many changes life and the weather will bring them and their community. Catherine Hawkins will run into the young man Curva had forecasted and enjoy an illicit summer of lust, meeting him in the fields and the barn after her husband and kids are safely asleep. Life continues afterward with a bittersweet flavor. She's tasted the forbidden, and she likes it.

Edna, in an attempt to tap down her impulses, becomes a faithful Baptist, attending prayer meetings every night and on Sunday, beseeching God for deliverance. So far she's been successful, but it's a daily struggle. Her brother Ian surprised the townspeople when he visited Ni-tsi-ta-pi-ksi Cultural Center and told Billie what a fine addition it was to the community. He volunteered to help Sabina catalogue and photograph the various fossils.

Sophie Smart returned to gardening in her birthday suit in spite of mosquito and black fly attacks, still trying to emulate Curva's ease with nudity.

And if you're wondering about Shirley, the feelings Xavier's music had awakened in him so pierced his heart with sorrow when Curva married Billie that he ended up wrestling alligators again for sport, finding them more malleable than Curva.

Suelita and Xavier? They have earned their wings, grasping an opportunity and taking it. Whether they are angels or not remains to be seen, though the next time you hear a swishing sound nearby, it could be them, hovering, keeping watch over the living. And the dead.

The bones? They'll continue to sing their disjointed songs of longing, commenting on life from their underground home. Rattling. Trying to get our attention. They'll never make the hit parade. Some people will hear them. More won't.

Acknowledgments

Writing a novel is primarily a solitary task, though each day I'm constantly surrounded by the characters I've created. I want to thank them and my muse for being so faithful.

But once the initial narrative is completed, expert readers are indispensible, and I have several to thank. I submitted some sections of *Curva Peligrosa* early in the process to the members of my online writing group, and they gave me helpful recommendations. Nina Schuyler, who was then part of that group, also read an early draft and gave me valuable feedback. So did fellow Canadian novelist Hugh Cook, as well as editor Steven Bauer. I also must mention New York agent Stephen Fraser, who believed in the novel, although I was then a "debut author."

Regal House Publishing also recognized *Curva Peligrosa*'s merit and has been a superb advocate for the book. The Regal House editorial team's detailed feedback on the manuscript has strengthened the narrative and been indispensable; any errors that remain, after their diligent efforts, are entirely my own.

My research for *Curva Peligrosa* came from too many sources to mention here, though Walter McClintock's *The Old North Trail: Life, Legends & Religion of the Blackfeet Indians* was essential. In 1886, Chief Mad Dog, "The high Priest of the Sun Dance," adopted McClintock, a member of a U.S. Forest Service expedition, and he spent four years living on the Blackfoot reservation. His personal account of this period gave me valuable knowledge of the Blackfoot legends and religious rituals.

I also want to thank my husband Michael for his unfailing support of my many writing projects. And I would be remiss if I didn't mention my son Leo's constant backing.

Discussion questions

1. Curva's letters from the trail have a unique function in the novel. How does your understanding of Curva evolve based on these letters? What role do Curva's letters have in the narrative? How does the Old North Trail educate Curva? What difference is there in the first and third person perspectives?

2. Poems ("Bone Songs") appear between major sections of the narrative. What is their purpose? What dimension do they add to the work?

3. Sabina appears mysteriously as Curva's daughter. How does their relationship shift over time? How would you describe their relationship? How are mother and daughter similar and different? Who is Sabina's father?

4. The Weedites collectively play an important role in *Curva Peligrosa*. How would you describe what they contribute? Who are your favorite Weedites and why?

5. Billie One Eye figures significantly in the novel. In what ways is he an important character and why? How does he complement Curva?

6. When Billie goes on his vision quest, he hopes to have the sight restored to his one eye. It isn't, so he believes the quest was a failure. Is he correct? Why or why not?

7. Not only is *Curva Peligrosa* a fiction, but there also are additional fictional worlds within this novel, such as Berumba, created by the imagined novelist Luis Cardona. How do Berumba and its characters interact with *Curva Peligrosa*'s narrative? How is the novel about storytelling and the ways people get succor and enlightenment from it?

8. Bones of various kinds turn up in Weed. In what ways do they complicate the story?

9. The novel starts out with a tornado, and Curva's arrival in Weed two years earlier was almost a tornado in itself. What

did she introduce to the town? Is she a positive or negative influence there?

10. Curva's twin brother Xavier is more than a ghostly figure in the narrative. How do you understand his part in the book and his relationship with Curva?

11. What are the parallels between Curva and Don Quixote? Is Curva mad? Is Cervantes' Don Quixote mad? Do Curva and the knight share the same goals? Does Curva have her own Sancho Panza?

12. Curva makes it clear from her first meeting with Shirley that he's a danger to her and what she believes in. How do you understand his presence in the narrative and the nature of Curva's attraction to him?

13. Does the natural world function as a character in Curva? If so, how would you describe its part in the narrative?

14. From the beginning, Curva makes known her desire to discover the elixir of life. Has she fulfilled her quest for immortality?

15. *Curva Peligrosa* fits into the magical realism genre, though realism also plays its part. Describe the magical elements in the narrative and how they interact with the more realistic ones? What qualities give *Curva Peligrosa* a mythic/fairy tale tone?

16. Several different worlds intersect in *Curva Peligrosa*: Berumba, the Blackfoot reservation, Weed before and after Curva's arrival, the American oil scene, etc. How do you understand the ways in which they relate to each other?

17. Curva, who grew up in Mexico, resists living out the kind of traditional female role prevalent then, in Mexico and elsewhere. Is she successful?